ONE HUSTLE

A Novel

Cortney Gee

BROWN GIRLS BOOKS

Houston, Texas * Washington, D.C. * Raleigh/Durham, NC

One Hustle © 2017 by Cortney Gee

Brown Girls Publishing, LLC

www.BrownGirlsBooks.com

ISBN: 978-1-944359-56-0 (Digital)
       978-1-944359-57-7 (Paperback)

First Brown Girls Publishing LLC trade printing

Manufactured and Printed in the United States of America

What people are saying...

"Cortney Gee has crafted a witty story that will have you up all night turning pages. An awesome debut novel from one of the funniest guys in the game."
-**Travis Hunter**
National Bestselling Author and Film maker

"Cortney's wit is undeniable. Sometimes, it's fall-on-the-floor funny and sometimes the comedy is cold and savage. Whichever the case, you can always, and I do mean, always, count on him to be authentic. Maybe it's the Cleveland in Cortney. Maybe it's the gift and curse of his talent, but never does he mail it in. Cortney will open up a vein on stage if he has to, because comedy is life for better or worse. This book is the spurts of blood pumping from his heart."
-**Kevin (M.C. Chill) Heard**
Call & Post Newspaper

ACKNOWLEDGEMENTS

First and foremost, I would like to thank The Creator for the gift of life and laughter. I know I don't always do what I'm supposed to do with this talent you have blessed me with but HEAVENLY FATHER you know my heart and that my intentions sometimes supersede my attention.

Secondly, I have to thank my beautiful wife Charlene McLemore-Gilmore for enduring sleepless nights and championing my efforts as a burgeoning author even if it kept me from coming to bed when she told my grown ass it was time to go night night. Her backing my endeavors helped me to finish this literary journey even when I didn't believe I could complete the task.

To my sons, Marcus, Miles and Cortney Jr. I thank you for the inspiration to be a better person. I owe a great amount of thanks to my sister, Aimee Exum, whom served as one of my readers when this book was going through its' infancy and kept it real with her criticism of its' development.

To my Facebook family that pushed me to finish what I started.

I appreciate all that encouraged me to stop talking about how I was going to write a book and just fucking do it.

To Vincent Cook, I owe a ton of thanks to for lacing my shoestrings to LA's underbelly, man was I green when I first landed in The City of Lost Angels. Good looking out, bruh!

Shout out to Shawn Belk, Sista Sandy Miller, Arrette Renee Harvey, Shelley Fleming, Tiffeni Fontno, Sherry Sanford, MC Chill, M. Raye Turner, old school hoop buddy Poncho and my brother Griffy 2 Trillion for being the keep it close to vest crew that read the first rough draft that was so Ruff so Tuff to probably dredge through and gave me notes to better my final product. Much love also to my keep-it-close crew, James Aranda, Jackie Brown and Chandra Singleton.

I have a group of authors that I consider real friends that inspired me to challenge myself to join their ranks that I want to give credit to Travis Hunter, Lolita Files, Eric Jerome Dickey, Victoria Christopher Murray and ReShonda Tate Billingsley, I thank you. I hope this book does you proud.

Big ups to Apple Products and Dragon Dictate for without them I would still just have a bunch of paper with my illegible handwriting scribbled across them.

Above all I would like to dedicate this book to the memory of my mother, Ernestine Ross, who left this earth before she could see her son show the world that being educated is cool like she always told me. Never a day goes by that I don't feel her guiding my actions.

CHAPTER 1

It was Wednesday night in the valley. The sun had receded and given way to the cool night that surprised folks who came to Southern California thinking jackets weren't necessary. I was sitting up in the bed wrecking my mind about how to escape the grasp of the financial depression that held me by the throat. Food was scarce.

I would have to forsake eating just so my live-in girlfriend and our twin sons could eat.

Karen was a week from her payday and I didn't know where my next dollar was coming from. I looked at her in her chocolate loveliness, as she laid next to me, oblivious to my worrying, replenishing her energy so she could work another day at the VA Hospital in Santa Monica. My sons, Malcolm and Martin were in the living room of our Van Nuys one-bedroom apartment, either sleeping on the pullout bed or doing a great job of fooling me into believing that they were.

The stillness of the place gave me the opportunity to think of how, just a few months ago, I was riding high after my appearance on Russell Simmons' *Def Comedy Jam*. Promoters from all over the country were ringing my manager's phone offering me work.

Tony felt that this was a good opportunity for me to raise my appearance fee and I wasn't going to argue with him about obtaining more money for the both of us.

We were working the wave of good fortune. Then I made a bone-headed mistake and got on his wife's bad side, causing us to part ways. I wasn't even mad with dude. If I had to make the same choice, I would have parted ways with me, too. Our business separation had my career sailing rudderless and my fortunes were shipwrecked at the present. At the age of 29 and after making three television appearances, I couldn't bring myself to the point of getting a job at Mickey Dee's or any other minimum wage-paying establishment.

My pride was still greater than my hunger pains.

My mother, Irene, used to always say, "Pride cometh before the fall."

Now I could hear her loud and clear as my situation was plummeting.

The only thing I could think of to do that would get me some instant legal tender was to wake-up early and stand in front of Home Depot and hope there were not enough Mexicans to pick oranges.

I should have been ashamed. I mean, really, after spending four years at Grambling State, picking fucking produce should be something I would never consider. But considering I had to feed my family, I had catapulted my vanity.

I turned off the TV and was about to call it a night so I could rise to work in a citrus field when I received a call from my man and fellow comedian, Lance Brooks. He was one of the smoothest brothers in the game.

So smooth and good at stand-up, he actually changed his name to Lance, the Great, Brooks.

I always thought the nigga's name sounded more like a magician than a comic, but I respected the brother's style so I never gave him the business about it.

"What's up, Lance?" I asked quietly into the receiver as to not disturb Karen. She could be an evil so-and-so when she was rustled from a slumber.

"Nothing, my brother. I was on my way to the Comedy Store, but I got a call from this young thang in the Valley so I'm headed over there. I just passed your apartment building and I told myself to check in on ya. What you doing?" he said.

"Not a damn thing since your manager ain't our manager no more, shit been in slow motion," I explained.

"Yeah, I heard about you having some choice words with Wanda."

"So that's what they call cursing a chick out in California, huh? Anyway, shit has been tighter than a boxer's fist around here."

"So you don't have any gigs lined up?" he asked me, already knowing the answer.

I was sure Tony had told him and the rest of the camp that he had cancelled all the bookings I had.

I was sure they were dividing up the spoils.

"Nope. Nada. Nothing! It's fucked up, too, seeing that Karen doesn't get her check until next week and we are down to just enough milk for the twins to eat cereal in the morning."

"So what's your plan, young blood?"

"Shit, I'm going to get up in the morning and see if I can get on somebody's truck and make some loot. Ya dig?"

Lance couldn't hide his amusement.

He laughed as he said, "Nigga, there ain't no way I can even imagine your big black ass snatching oranges from no trees. Man, you crazy!"

"I'm serious, Lance. Shit has hit the fan, brother."

Lance was still laughing. He was close to conjuring up my dark side until he said, "CB, I'm turning around on Sepulveda right now. Meet me downstairs. I'm going to holla at you about something."

"All right, but don't come over here teasing me and shit; I'm not in the mood to be mocked," I told him, making sure he knew the deal.

"Ain't nobody came to clown you, bruh. I got something I wanna holla at you about and before you ask what, I ain't saying shit over the phone."

I agreed to meet him downstairs and hung up the phone.

Rummaging in the room that was dark except the 100-watt bulb in the adjourning bathroom didn't make it easy to find some jeans and a sweatshirt without waking Karen.

I thought I had accomplished the task until I heard Karen ask, "Where are you going, baby?"

"Oh, Lance is downstairs. He wanted to get at me about something. I shouldn't be long," I explained, assuring her I wasn't making a creep move.

I slid on a Brooklyn Dodger's hat and some Nikes and dipped out to the elevator so I could catch up with Lance. When I reached the front door, he had already pulled up in his gun metal 944 Porsche.

Lance rolled down his window and invited me to join him in the car, which was still running.

"My man, Cameron Bernard, don't look so glum. Your uncle Lance brought you an early Christmas present," he said, turning down his sound system that was cranked up and banging Chuck Brown's "We Need Money."

Lance was decked out in all black with his silk shirt, pants, Mauri crocodile shoes and matching belt.

Lance didn't tour the road or have a television show but from his condo, whip and gear you couldn't tell it. He looked like money, hell he even smelled like it.

The Washington D.C. native had taken me under his wing. He constantly told me the reason he laced my shoes was because I was more east coast than west and since I was from Cleveland we needed to stick together.

"So what's up, Lance? What was so important you couldn't holla at me over the phone about it?" I anxiously asked him.

"Damn man, you act like you really trying to go to sleep and go pick oranges or something. You are one funny man, Cameron."

My face was twisted as I thought to myself that I had just told this motherfucker I was in no mood to be ridiculed.

"Really, Lance? Man, I can't believe you would rather be here clowning me instead of being up in some chick," I spat.

The worst thing about having comedians as friends was sometimes they didn't know when to turn it down or off.

"I was just fucking with you, my brother. Calm down; like I said before, I come bearing gifts." He pulled a wad of cash from his pocket.

I was at a loss for words as he handed it to me, which is saying a lot for someone in my profession. We were paid for always having a snappy comeback. I thumbed through the cash and counted twenty crisp one hundred dollar bills.

"Man, Lance, I don't know what to say."

"Nigga, I think 'thank you' is the proper response," he snapped.

"Of course, thank you, but I can't accept this kind of loan. The way my cash is now, I don't know when I would be able to return it." I tried to hand him back the cash.

"I know when you are going to give it back," he said as I looked at him inquisitively. "Think of it as a cash advance or better yet a signing bonus."

"For what job?" I asked.

"You have a bank account?" he questioned.

"Of course I do, but ain't shit in the savings or the checking."

"That's cool, long as it isn't overdrawn, we good."

I still couldn't believe my man had just given me two grand 'cause I had a bank account. It did feel good to have some cheese though, and long as I didn't have to walk into Bank of America and hold them up, I was cool. Lance looked at his watch and noticed he was behind schedule for his hook-up with whatever hot valley girl he had sweet-talked into giving up her goods.

"Man, I ain't got time for you being all emotional 'cause I helped you and your family out. I'll holla at you tomorrow. Be up and ready to bounce around ten," Lance said dismissively.

I got out of the car, thanked him again, and watched him pull off on Victory and make a left on Sepulveda Blvd.

I looked up to the sky and thanked God for the salvation. Even as I gave the Creator thanks, I had a feeling I had just signed a deal with the Devil.

I was anxious to go back upstairs and tell Karen of our good fortune, but I decided to head to the twenty-four hour Ralph's on Ventura and pick up some things for the barren fridge. I climbed into my Datsun 240z. There was only so much you could fit in the car, but it was better than being on foot, or a bus.

When I arrived at Ralph's, I took full advantage of the loot Lance had prepaid me with. All the while I was putting things in the shopping cart, my mind couldn't help but wonder what part I would play in whatever Lance was into. Now, assured my family wasn't going to be hungry, I decided to stop tripping and enjoy the moment.

"That will be five hundred and sixty-five dollars," the cute Mexican cashier said as she motioned for my preference of paper or plastic bags.

I didn't realize I had burned up more than a third of my loan in one swoop. I paid the cashier and vamped out to the parking lot. The tiny sports car was filled to capacity. It looked as though I had an entire family of plastic as passengers.

Luckily, I was only minutes from my spot, and the police had real crime to fight in Van Nuys versus harassing motorists who didn't own enough car to haul their cargo.

It took me three trips up and down the elevator to get all the groceries into the apartment. After I put everything away, I slipped two hundred dollars inside Karen's purse and laid down. I was content, even if it was through the aid of another. I held onto my responsibility of taking care of my family.

CHAPTER 2

I was awakened the way every man could get used to. Karen had her soft lips wrapped around my manhood. With my eyes half open and half shut I watched her weave her magic on my wand until I shook from an orgasm.

"Well, good morning, Ms. Richardson," I said, fully awake but ready to fall into a cum induced coma.

"Yes, it is a good morning and it would be good mornings like this all the time if you made me Mrs. Bernard," she said, wiping her mouth and offering future naughtiness if I wifed her. Then, she ran to the bathroom to rinse and gargle.

I sat up in the bed and looked at the clock. It was too early to have her on that 'when you gonna marry me' shit.

"I told you, I'm waiting to get myself established in the comedy world before commitment. My female fans might turn against me, might stop coming out and supporting if the fantasy of having me is taken from them," I yelled out to her, trying my best to appease her with logic.

"Whatever, nigga, you should have thought about that before dropping twins in me. You better be glad I have good genes and snapped back." She entered the room from the bathroom, putting on her scrubs preparing for work.

I had to admit my Georgia peach of a baby's mamma was fine. Karen stood 5'9" and her 160 pounds were distributed in all the right places. It made me mad she had to go to work as she pulled the scrubs over her thick sculpted ass. I wanted to put in work.

I lifted my 250-pound, 6'4" body from the bed and stood behind her as she finished dressing and touching up her make-up.

"Cameron, don't start anything you know you can't finish," she said as she felt me hardening against her round behind.

"I can finish any and everything I start. You're the one trying to beat traffic," I replied, already aware that the 405 freeway was by now, fast becoming the world's largest parking lot. What should have taken Karen 15 minutes to get to work would be a 45-minute odyssey if she was delayed anymore.

I conceded and abandoned my attempt to get a shot of that bomb she owned.

"Look, I see you're running late, so don't worry about the boys. I'll drop them off at Lulu's before I have to make a run with Lance," I told her, knowing that with her being behind schedule, she had intentions of asking me to do so anyway.

"Thanks, Cameron, that's very sweet of you and what possessed you to go shopping at the wee hours of the morning?"

"You know I could see we were short on cereal and milk, so I went after Lance gave me a deposit on a show."

"Oh, okay. That's why you got the royal awakening. Sometimes you are so thoughtful." She kissed me on the cheek.

I followed her into the living room where the boys were still asleep. Karen walked over to them and leaned over to kiss them goodbye.

"Uh, uh, unn you better not put those lips on my sons," I teased, but was kinda serious when I said it.

"Boy fuck you, these is my babies," she said before planting kisses on the twins.

"I love your crazy ass." Karen walked by me and headed out the door.

I couldn't wait for her shift at work to end. I figured if some groceries had earned me some morning head, when she found that two hundred dollars, it was going to be on and cracking when she returned home.

If I had learned anything from dealing with Lance it was punctuality. So, I made sure to get the twins over to the babysitters with enough time left over to beat him to my crib.

When I pulled up with seven minutes to spare, I was shocked, my boy was already parked out front.

"Damn, Lance, when you said ten you weren't bullshitting," I said, trying to lighten his mood in case my arrival after him had Lance irritated.

"Time is money, my brother and if you want to get real bread, being on time ain't good enough," he scolded as he pointed at his Rolex.

In an effort to not press the situation, I took my lumps like a man and inquired if he wanted me to follow him in my car or roll with him in the Porsche.

Lance's arrogant ass looked at my Datsun and said, "We're about to meet up with some folks. Ride with me."

"I know you aren't clowning my Japanese Classic," I said, defending my well-preserved automobile.

"Man, I'm not cracking on your whip. I'm just saying an upgrade wouldn't be a bad thing."

Just because he had loaned me two grand, it didn't give him the right to clown my circumstances.

Instead of firing off on him, I agreed with him; if and when I hit a lick, I would purchase an automobile that spoke of my finances the way my 1973 240z screamed I was broke.

We pulled off and headed south on Sepulveda and veered onto the 405 S while the sounds of Trouble Funk played over the speakers.

"Do you ever listen to any other music besides Go-Go?" I asked the D.C. native, knowing it would push a button. *Fuck it*, I thought. It served him right that he got a taste of his own medicine.

"Nope. Not if I can help it."

"But it all sounds the same. I mean, there are different words, but the bongos, cymbals, and drums are identical in every song."

Lance was livid.

"Cameron, you come from a place where there is no indigenous sound. I mean there's the Motown sound, the Philly sound, hell even Memphis has Stax. What would be the Cleveland sound?"

I could have let him win the debate, but just for argument sake I pushed on.

"We have soul on lock, The O'Jays, Bobby Womack, Levert, The Rude Boys. The only Go-Go performer in that class is Chuck Brown."

"You keep disrespecting my music and I'm going to make you get out," he joked as he turned the music down. Then, he said, "Look blood, when I introduce you to my people, just listen. Chill out, ya dig?"

I agreed to be quiet and follow his lead.

"This is your show, my brother, I'm not trying to be ringmaster, I'm just part of the circus," I said, assuring him I would stay in line.

We exited the 405 at La Cienega and made our way to Denny's by the airport. Lance parked next to a black 740il with tinted windows. He instructed me to give him a minute as he exited the Porsche and walked over to the driver's side of the BMW. The window came down just enough for me to see the driver was a woman wearing sunglasses.

Lance and the woman seemed to exchange pleasantries, then I witnessed the lady pass Lance an envelope, roll up her window and vamp out.

Lance waved for me to join him as he headed into Denny's, making sure he locked the doors by remote once he was sure I had exited the vehicle.

We headed toward the rear of the restaurant and sat in a booth occupied by a mature gentleman I suspected was in his late 40's. He had a light brown complexion with freshly cut hair and a hairline that showed evidence of recession. If this wasn't enough to believe my estimation was correct, the salt and pepper sprinkled in his goatee confirmed it. He stood up and Lance introduced us.

"Moe, this is Cameron, Cameron this is Moe."

The first thing I noticed was this cat had what my father said every good businessman owned, a firm handshake.

"Greetings, Cameron, pleased to meet you," he said to me.

I told him it was my pleasure. Then he slid his 5'8" portly body back into the booth. Lance sat down and slid by the window offering me to sit next to him. I suppose he did that so Moe could look at both of us straight in our eyes.

Looking into Moe's eyes was quite a frightening task. I had never witnessed any human with such lifeless orbs, it was as if he owned no soul at all.

He looked at me in a predatory manner, not in judgment of me, but more like I had been served up as the Last Supper.

I reminded myself that Lance didn't want me to say much, but to observe the deal.

"So did you get the package?" Moe asked Lance.

"Yes, Sarafina came through as she always does." Lance handed Moe the envelope to inspect.

Moe nodded.

Our waitress came over and asked us if we would be ordering as she freshened up Moe's cup of coffee.

Lance ordered a vegetarian omelet, toast and orange juice. I ordered a grand slam and a coffee.

Moe told her that he wasn't hungry and she whisked off to the kitchen.

"So, you trust your man will play ball fairly?" Moe asked Lance.

"Oh this young brother's solid," Lance replied, patting me on the back. "Cameron understands not to bite the hand that feeds him."

I was becoming wary of them talking about me like I wasn't there instead of talking to me.

I was glad to see the waitress return with water and coffee and Lance's orange juice. It gave me something to do, seeing I wasn't invited in on the conversation the two had going.

I put two Sweet and Lows in my coffee and began to stir when Moe looked at me and said, "You know that kills laboratory rats."

I smiled. "I read a report that the laboratory workers aren't keeling over from putting it in their coffee so until that happens, I'll keep enjoying it."

There was a pause at the table for minute. I thought that my smart mouth just fucked up whatever deal Lance and Moe had in mind for me. Then Moe erupted into laughter.

"You're right about this youngster. He's quick on his feet and doesn't mind being an asshole toward authority."

I was relieved that my loose lips hadn't offended him.

"So Cameron, is it agreed that we share equally in this transaction?" Moe questioned me.

Without even knowing what was in store, my thirsty ass agreed and shook his hand again.

His handshake was as firm as it was when we first were introduced. He pulled out a fifty- dollar bill and excused himself from the table.

"It was good doing business with you, see you on Monday," Moe said before leaving.

Lance and I bid him farewell and he dipped. I was intrigued to see what kind of car Moe would be getting into. From the window I watched him climb inside a candy apple red Mercedes 500 SEL and told myself it was indeed time for me to step up my whip game.

Our food arrived and Lance clowned me about eating pork.

"Man, you half Muslim motherfuckers kill me hating on the pig. You do know it's the other white meat," I told him.

"It's a filthy animal and the Bible and Koran states that it is not to be consumed," Lance replied.

"So right now you're eating what would have grown into a chicken?" I asked.

"Yeah and what genius enlightenment do you have to share about my breakfast?" Lance questioned as he put another portion of the omelet in his mouth.

"I'm just saying. Obviously, you've never been on a farm because a chicken is about one of the nastiest animals on the yard, flat out."

"Cameron, you're trying to convince me that the chicken is nastier than a pig? I'm not buying it."

"What I'm trying to say is I think pigs just have bad public relations, plus this bacon tastes too good to be bad."

That was just how Lance and I got down.

We challenged each other over some of the dumbest shit just to see what lunacy the other would spout out of his mouth. It was like we were exercising our quick wit at the other's expense.

Once we finished our breakfast, Lance finally gave me a hint about what was in the envelope. It was just in time too, because curiosity was gnawing at me.

He pulled out a contract that was addressed to my DBA BDatzFunny Entertainment and me.

It stated that a Christopher Swenson had funded a comedy tour featuring comedians of my choice and myself with an investment amount of ninety-two thousand dollars.

"Ninety-two stacks of cheese? We need to start getting our lineup together, lock down some venues and coordinate travel schedules!"

Lance sat there with a look so unfazed on his face like our careers hadn't just been boosted.

"Man, we ain't going on no fucking tour," he said, confusing the shit outta me.

"But you just showed me the contract."

"And I'm showing you this." He pulled a check out making sure not to put his fingerprints on it, handling the check with his knuckles.

I found that to be strange.

"If you act right, like I know you will, this is the first of many," he continued.

Receiving almost-hundred grand checks was more than enough incentive to be on my best behavior.

"So what's next?" I questioned.

Lance informed me that we were going to just deposit the check into my account and on Monday I was going to write a check to Chris Swenson, divide up the take, and get ready to do it all over again.

It sounded simple enough.

My Cleveland instinct told me that getting $92,000 had to come with a catch and I should pull out, but I was already two stacks indebted to him.

Our waitress, Anna, came back to the table to see if we needed anything else. I said some sly shit to amuse her even though I knew I was flirting with disaster. If Karen had any knowledge of me sampling this hot tamale, all bets would be off. She gave us a check and I slipped her the $50 bill Moe had left and told her to keep the change. She was more than pleased with the $30 tip. So thankful, she wrote down her number and told me to buzz her.

Lance and I left Denny's with the future fortune in the form of a promissory note.

We hit the 405 northbound, focused on putting the check in my account at the Van Nuys branch of Bank of America.

I had a lot of questions but Lance was short on answers.

He told me the less I knew, the better off I was if anything went wrong.

"Make sure you keep this contract with you at all times. Make a copy and leave it in your car. Do you feel me?"

"I got you, Lance. Like I said, it's your game. I'm going to play this like you guide me, brother," I said, again assuring him that I understood.

We arrived at the bank, I deposited a check, and that was it.

No alarms went off, nobody asked me any questions and I wasn't detained. The challenge for me was that the check wouldn't clear until Monday.

Now I understood why Moe was looking to see me on Monday, that was to be our payday.

"Yo Lance, who is Saban Entertainment?" I asked when we got back in the car because when I saw that name on the check I thought it sounded familiar.

"Do your boys watch the Power Rangers?"

"Of course they do. They were pissed they both couldn't be the red Ranger for Halloween."

"Well, that's the company that the check was issued from," Lance said as he continued to inform me that the woman in the BMW was the comptroller of the financial department and that we would be issued payments from a vendor account that she had been instructed to purge so they didn't have to pay taxes on.

"It's amazing how quickly leftover change can turn into millions of dollars, my brother."

Lance pulled in front of my apartment and dropped me off.

"Remember don't do anything with your account, be cool and don't draw any attention to it."

"I got it, coach. Hey let me use your horn real quick. I need to call Speedy for a spot. You going to The Comedy Act Theatre tonight?"

"Yeah, I'm going to be a little or a lot late. It's all depending on how my valley girl is acting. You know you really need to get your own phone, bruh." He scolded me before letting me use it.

After securing the both of us slots on the show, I gave Lance his phone back and he jetted off to be with his new boo.

After a full day of hanging out and hustling with Lance, I headed upstairs to the apartment. Before entering, I made sure to toss the piece of paper containing Anna's number. Karen had a second sense that was borderline supernatural when it came to finding incriminating evidence against me concerning other women.

Luckily, she wasn't as tech savvy as me. My electronic Rolodex was safe. I would program female information as male names and Anna had become Dan Nee.

That sounded like an Asian guy, but my memory served me well enough to keep track of my lies.

When I opened up the door to my apartment, I was greeted by the joyful sounds of my twins playing in front of the television and the soulful aroma of macaroni and cheese, collard greens, and fried chicken that Karen was laboring over in the kitchen. It was moments like these when I felt shameful for my extracurricular activities.

When things were good between Karen and me, they were good. Unfortunately, when it was bad, I was looking to one up her.

I mean sure, Karen was fine and she was southernly schooled in domestication. But we were in LA. La La Land was a place littered with the baddest broads from every city all over the world and someone had convinced them they should all be in pictures. It was too easy for a man like myself, blessed with a silver tongue, to down one of those would-be starlets. I couldn't help but sample the offerings from time to time.

Karen was still in her work outfit as she prepared our meal. Normally that would have pissed me off. I mean really, you work at a hospital with people sick from God knows what and just because you wash your hands, you think it's cool to be over my food? Like disease is allergic to clothing material.

But today I was satisfied with the possibilities of bettering our lives and decided not to start an argument.

"Hey baby, it sure smells good up here," I told her as I walked toward her.

"Cameron, if I knew you put that money in my purse, I would've let you get a taste this morning," she said in a hushed tone so the twins didn't hear what a freak their mama was.

"There's always tonight. You can show me how much you appreciate a brother." I nibbled at her ear.

Malcolm and Martin ran over to us; I don't know if they were just happy to see me or if they were cock blocking. As they came between the two of us, I concluded it was probably a mixture of both.

Our kitchen wasn't big enough for an entire family gathering, so Karen ushered us all out of there so she could finish cooking.

My sons dragged me to join them in the living room; now without a shadow of doubt, I knew they had been cock blocking. They were jumping on and off of the couch doing high kicks, imitating the characters on the TV show. I asked the boys what had them so excited.

"Power Rangers!" they exclaimed, still jumping and doing karate moves.

"Oh, so you like the Power Rangers, huh?"

"No, we *love* the Power Rangers!"

I thought about the twenty-three thousand I had coming on Monday and I joined in their delight.

"Daddy loves the Power Rangers, too!"

CHAPTER 3

The weekend breezed by. Karen and I had a blast as we dined at Gladstone's. The lobster dinner had her even more thankful than the two hundred bucks I had laid on her. Thank God for Lulu, who kept the twins overnight so that we could attend to some grown folks' business. Over the weekend, I even had a chance to see Anna again, but this time it wasn't her serving me breakfast at Denny's. It was an early dinner at her place Sunday before I headed over to the Laugh Factory.

Lance and I were meeting there. He wasn't performing, but I had a nine o'clock slot and it was an opportune rendezvous spot.

Afterward, we cruised over to Jerry's Deli and hung out there with him laying down his instructions that I would be following tomorrow morning.

***

It was 10 AM and I was suited and booted, more than ready for Lance's prompt ass. I had been told to look business casual for the day's work. I put on a single-breasted navy blue suit with wide leg trousers, a crisp white French cuffed shirt and some blue David Eden alligator loafers.

If there were a business I was representing by my attire, it would have been pimping.

I figured if I was about to take down twenty-three racks, I should look like the thousandnaire I was about to become.

Lance was already downstairs waiting when I walked toward the door. I thought to myself that he must set his watch ten minutes fast or something.

When I got into the car, I wasn't about to be berated.

"Fuck you, I was on time and I look good," I said to shut down any bullshit he might gripe about.

"And good morning to you too, motherfucker. You ready to get it in?"

"Whose car is this?" I asked him as I stepped into the Burgundy 300 Mercedes-Benz.

"Oh this is my valley girl, Gwen's whip. She took my Porsche today so that we could have some extra room."

"Hell yeah, I'm ready. I'm dressed for success and excess, brother, let's go."

We pulled off and instead of turning left for my bank, we turned right and headed toward Sherman Oaks.

"Yo, the bank is the other way," I instructed him.

"I know; we have to pick up the most important piece in today's play."

"And that would be?"

"Not what, but whom. A white guy to get the money! Did you actually think Bank of America was going to give ninety-two thousand to some niggas? I don't care how well dressed and articulate we are; we would have to give a fecal specimen to withdraw five hundred dollars."

It was a sad indictment on the racism that still existed where folk's trusted white people to fleece them but wouldn't trust a brother.

We pulled into an apartment complex that was an obvious black eye on the affluent area. Where the surrounding properties were well maintained and manicured, the apartment was in desperate need of a paint job and its shrubbery was overgrown.

Lance grabbed a pair of shoes and a garment bag and I followed him upstairs.

"Why are you carrying a change of clothes? You look more than dressed for the task at hand?" I asked.

"I'm going to prove to you that you can clean a white boy up and watch the world open up before him."

Lance knocked on apartment 206 and an unkempt young white chick answered.

"Hey, Lance," she said, scratching her arm like she was in need of a fix.

"What's happening, Amanda, this is Cameron. Cameron this is Amanda. She's Chris's better half." I lied, telling her that the pleasure was all mine. I couldn't help but think how fucked up Chris must be if this bitch was his better half.

"Amanda, if I didn't know better I would think Chris was black; he's always on colored people's time," Lance said loud enough for Chris to hear.

It worked because Chris came out of the bedroom.

He was blonde, about 5'7, medium build and clean-shaven, but there was a frailty about him I couldn't put my finger on.

Lance was right: the raggedy blue jeans and a polo shirt with a hole in it made Amanda look almost pleasant.

"You have everything together?" Chris asked like it was important that Lance hadn't forgotten anything.

"Yep, everything is there. Now please handle your business so that we can handle mine," Lance pleaded.

Now I understood why Lance had brought his girl, Gwen's car; Chris was rolling with us.

By the time we left with Chris, it was close to 11 AM and the smog had burned away in the Valley. The heat index was climbing into the mid-nineties already.

Lance had the air-conditioning turned on high as we drove to the bank. Chris complained about being cold and had a bad cough to prove he wasn't bullshitting.

"Have you been taking meds like the doctor told you to?" Lance questioned.

"Yeah, but the AZT is hella-expensive," Chris replied.

"Man, you're getting paid today. I'm taking you to the pharmacy myself, don't play with your condition."

Now I was no dummy and I knew that not one doctor had ever prescribed AZT to fight the flu. I was pissed off and frightened when I realized that Lance had me in a car, with rolled up windows, with a motherfucker with the skinnies.

I quickly let my window down and chanted the Buddhist Nom Yo Re Keyo.

Chris couldn't exit the car quick enough so I could confront Lance's stupid ass. We pulled into the parking lot and Lance gave Chris some last-minute instructions.

"You know the drill, Chris, take the briefcase. There's a check written out to you. Get the loot, be cool and meet us back here," he said.

It was obvious Chris had worked with Lance numerous times before.

Chris nodded his head and exited the car.

As soon as I saw Chris walk into the bank, I let Lance have it. "Are you fucking kidding me? You got me in a car with an AIDS riddled motherfucker, coughing and shit with the windows rolled up?" I asked angrily.

"Unless you plan on fucking or tongue kissing Chris, I don't think you have shit to worry about!"

He sounded like Karen when I tripped about her work clothes. My fear was probably based on ignorance, but that didn't make me happy.

My dark mood was brightened though with the sight of Chris walking back to the car with a smile spread across his face.

"We good to go?" Lance asked Chris.

He confirmed all was well and we took off.

Instinctively, I looked in the rearview mirror to see if we were being followed. My heart felt like it was going to jump out of my chest, which was in total contrast to the other occupants of the Mercedes. It was just another day at the office for Lance and Chris.

"Are you guys hungry? I'm starving. My treat," Lance said, breaking the silence in the car.

Chris and I both agreed that a meal provided by the man who made the most money today was right on time. He suggested we dine at PF Chang's at the Sherman Oaks Galleria.

Chris and I agreed with his choice of Chinese. I had been meaning to try what I had been told was some high-end Asian dining, but my money had been funny.

Lance parked the car, took the briefcase from Chris, then we entered the restaurant.

"Will you gentlemen be needing a booth or table?" asked the attractive tanned brunette who served as the hostess.

Lance took the lead since he was treating and let her know we would need a booth.

"We'll take that one if you don't mind," he said, pointing to a booth that was situated away from the other patrons.

"Oh, I'm sorry, sir, that section is closed."

Lance pulled out a crisp one-hundred-dollar bill and asked her if that would be enough to reopen the section.

Her eyes widened and a bright smile stretched across her face.

"I'm sure we can accommodate you gentlemen. By all means please take a seat. Your waitress, Cindy will be right over."

We sat down at our well-paid for private office.

Lance sat across from Chris and me.

As we were promised, Cindy, a young blonde who had no sexual appeal but owned a great personality, came by. She gave us menus and took our drink order.

Once she left us alone, Lance asked, "So gentlemen, would you like to settle up now or would you rather do business on a full stomach?"

I found no reason to delay getting my cheese, but if Chris had decided to wait I wasn't going to be the one who looked thirsty.

"I believe my meal would be even more pleasant with my share in my pocket," Chris said.

I agreed with him and told Lance to break bread.

He put the briefcase on the table and counted out five stacks, placed it in the envelope and handed it to Chris.

"Yep, it's all there; thanks, Lance," Chris said after concluding that Lance had done right by him.

I was thrown off by the small amount that Chris had been paid. But if he counted it and it had been no problems, I had no right to make mention of it.

Per Lance's instructions, I brought along my briefcase, an envelope wouldn't have accommodated the amount of money that I was to receive.

"Cameron, my good man, if you would please open up your briefcase I believe I might be able to make a deposit," Lance said, counting twenty-one stacks of cash out.

I frowned. "If I'm not mistaken, I was owed twenty-three, playa."

"Man, you obviously forgot the little advance I gave," he said with a cool tone, but sternly enough to let me know that before I accused him of messing over me I better have my thoughts together.

"Damn, brother, I didn't mean to. Forgive me, my bad," I apologized, making a mental note to really make sure he realized I had a brain fart and meant no harm.

I set my briefcase on the floor and took a sip of my water. I had to admit I was feeling a certain kind of way about Lance clearing sixty-six thousand bucks and I had twenty-one with me being the person whose name was on the bank account.

Cindy returned with all of our drinks and we ordered our food. Lance had MISO CHICKEN, savory miso-tamarind sauce wok-tossed with sliced chicken breast, baby carrots, Asian mushrooms, bok choy, candied walnuts and corn, topped with fresh cilantro. Chris ordered SHRIMP WITH LOBSTER SAUCE, garlic white wine sauce with Chinese black beans, mushrooms, scallions and egg. And I had the MOO GOO GAI PAN, sliced chicken breast and tender shrimp served with mushrooms and sliced vegetables in a mild sauce. The food was delicious and I had to admit, I had plans on returning with Karen in tow. The way they served it, we were able to share each other's entrées.

After we finished, Lance paid the tab and gave Cindy a generous tip.

She responded by slipping him her number.

"Honestly, Lance, if you were going to pursue anyone after tipping them, it should have been that hostess, she was fine," I told him as he exited the restaurant.

"You think that way because you're engaged in a relationship and you have to cheat vertically. You have to literally fuck up. I, on the other hand, am single. I don't care if I fuck up or down. I have the room to fuck around, so to speak," Lance replied, educating me to his train of thought.

Chris was howling at Lance's soliloquy.

"I don't know what you're laughing for, our next stop is Rite Aid. You're going to get all your prescriptions and not waste five gee's self-medicating, ya dig?" Lance scolded Chris as if he were a child.

Chris stopped laughing and got in the back seat of the Mercedes, upset that Lance had fronted him about his addiction.

In an effort to keep things light, I inquired about when we might be able to work another check.

"After I drop off Sarafina's and Moe's loot. I'm sure we'll be back in business again this week," he replied.

We left PF Chang's and went to the Rite Aid in North Hollywood then, dropped off Chris at his apartment. Whatever it cost him to purchase the medicine must have put a dent in his take. He was upset that Lance had forced him to buy medicine instead of shooting the cash into Amanda's and his arms.

It was at this time that I realized why there was no cure for the diseases that plagued our society like cancer, AIDS and diabetes. It was way too much money to be made in the medicating and not enough to be made in eradicating the disease.

Chris mumbled, "Thanks," and said he would see us soon, then headed upstairs to what I was sure was an anxious girlfriend.

"So what you have planned for the rest of the day, Cam?" Lance asked me.

"Well, I can tell you what I won't be doing."

"And what might that be?"

"I won't be putting this back in the bank, that's for damn sure," I quipped.

"I know that's right!"

"I figured I'd do a couple nice things for the family, like find a spot where the boys can have their own room. I'm going to buy Karen a new wardrobe and put away some of it so that I can upgrade my wheels. Fucking with Moe, Sarafina and you has convinced me that that's in order."

"What do you have in mind as far as whips are concerned?" he asked me.

"Did you play that's my car when you were younger?"

"Of course I did. Every kid from the hood played that growing up."

"And what car was your car?"

"The one I own, a Porsche, but not the 944 -- the 911 Carrera. I didn't get exactly my car, but I got pretty damn close."

"I feel you; my car was the convertible Jaguar. There was a Cleveland Cavalier who spoke at my school when I was a junior. When he pulled up in that automobile it was my fantasy from then on."

"Oh, so it's British luxury you prefer. I never figured you as a secret agent double oh seven type. With your Midwest upbringing I guess I envisioned you going out and splurging on a caddy, but everybody has a right to like what they like."

I realized right then and there that I hadn't shared that much about my true nature with my comedic friend and now partner in crime.

James Bond, John Shaft and James T. Kirk raised me. They were the same cat just in different circumstances. They had nice rides, were smooth as hell and got all the women. Hell, Kirk even fucked the green bitches.

"I mean, I don't need a new one but I'm definitely going to be on the lookout for a well-maintained, pre-owned one."

"Say no more, my brother, I got you. Tomorrow have about seven geez with you. I want to turn you onto something real slick."

"Shit, we don't have to wait until tomorrow, I'm down to do that right now."

"I know that money is burning a hole in your pocket, but right now I need to take care of people so they continue to bless us with the work, you feel me?"

I knew Lance was right. But him telling me I was so near to getting my car had me happier than a sissy with a bag of dicks.

Lance drove me to my crib and before letting me out, he reminded me to keep a copy of the contract in my automobile and home. Plus, he suggested I buy a safe, one that was fireproof.

I jumped into my Z car for what might have been the last time and headed out to handle the task I had already planned, and the ones my criminal mentor had suggested.

CHAPTER 4

Every day was a day for some small lesson to be learned from my cool sensei. It was instilled in me by now that when Lance said 10 o'clock in the morning, I had to be out of my house and downstairs by 9:45 AM.

"Well, good morning, Mr. Bernard," Lance said as I jumped in his car. "It's nice to see you're ready to do business, my brother."

"'Sup Lance? Just so I know, what's with you and 10 AM? I mean every time we link up, it's at that exact time."

Lance explained to me how by 10 o'clock the highways of traffic that locked Los Angeles were normally smooth sailing. By 11:30 AM, 12 o'clock they became jammed with people either rushing to work from lunch or heading out to eat. His explanation made perfect sense to me, especially when you owned a sports car. It seemed like such a waste to own a car that went from 0 to 60 in less than a minute when you were bumper to bumper, taking forty minutes to go three miles.

We were heading east from my apartment on Victory Boulevard. From what Lance had told me yesterday, I believed we were headed to a car dealership.

"Just out of curiosity, Cameron, what did you do first with your cash?"

"I already told you, I wasn't entrusting it to any bank."

"True dat. That's smart of you because if they suspected anything, they would have frozen your account."

"I bought a safe, then gave Karen two thousand for a new apartment and another two thousand to get her and the boys whatever they needed."

"That's good, elevating your game, blessing the folks you love and making sure that your take was secure. Yo, did you tell Karen how you came about that kind of cash?"

"First of all, I didn't tell her how much money I had. She's under the impression it was a deposit from a show that I marked on the comedy calendar. I figured that would help if I needed to get with my little enchilada for a few days."

"So you and Anna are hitting skins, huh?"

"Yes sir; she's been letting me come over late at night after I do a set at The Comedy Act Theatre. With my passing dough to Karen, she hasn't been grilling me about my whereabouts."

Lance was happy I was having fun with my Mexican acquaintance and encouraged me to bring her into the fold.

"I've seen you work verbal magic on women. That could be a great asset to our organization."

I could see where Lance was coming from, but I was no pickup artist. I just happened to be highly adapted to opening up myself to be chosen. Rarely did I go after a woman that I was attracted to. I waited to see who wanted me and if she was attractive, I didn't get in the way of her pursuit.

"So you brought the seven racks I told you about yesterday, right?" he asked as we pulled into what looked more like a wrecking yard than a car dealership.

"Yeah I have it. What are we doing here?" I looked around at cars smashed, parted out, and piled to the sky.

"Cameron, I swear sometimes I forget just how green your Cleveland ass is. This is Statewide Autos, where you can ball on a budget."

I clearly was ignorant because I didn't know what the fuck he was talking about. "What do you mean ball on a budget?"

"LA is all about fronting. Before you get a movie or TV deal, folks cop salvage title whips from my man, Albert. It helps to keep people guessing about your social and economic status."

I was still confused. "Albert? Salvage titles?"

He then proceeded to school me about the salvage game. Folks would have accidents and the insurance company would declare the cars to be totaled.

Albert would then thoroughly fix them up and sell them at a reasonable price. If you didn't have all the cash up front, Albert would work with you, too. All you had to do was write him dated checks to cover the payments.

As we parked, I saw that Statewide Auto was loaded with a plethora of high-end foreign cars on its lot. Range Rovers, Mercedes, BMW's, Audi's, Lexus's, Bentley's, Rolls-Royces and Jaguars were scattered all over the place. Though I was impressed with the varied inventory, my heart was set on a Jaguar with the brains blown out.

We got out of Lance's Porsche and checked out the Jaguars. Of the six Albert had available, there were only two coupes and only one of them was convertible. A 1990 powder blue one with a navy blue top and cream guts.

As we were looking around, a man in his late 30's came out to greet us. Immediately, he recognized Lance.

"Lance, my friend, I see you're still driving the 944. You know we have a nice all-black 911 that just came in," said the Armenian man, who looked more like an Ahmad than an Albert.

"Let me see how my next week turns out; I might just holla at you about that. What are you asking for it?"

"Well, if you bring back the 944, I'm willing to take six thousand. But if you decide to keep your car, I'm willing to take ten thousand for it. Either way I'm practically giving away the car. I can get sixteen thousand for it right now, but you bring me so much business I'm forced to do good deal for you."

Again Lance told Albert he would think about it. Which really meant he wanted to hit another lick. This revelation was good news for me because if Lance was going to be making moves, I would be clocking more dollars as well.

"Albert, this is my man, Cameron and he fancies that convertible Jaguar." He pointed to the powder blue convertible. "Can you do better than nine thousand?" Lance asked, hoping his discount would be extended to me.

"So you like?" Albert asked me as I admired the V12 sports luxury automobile.

I loved the car but I wasn't feeling the high price tag. I had only brought eight grand with me just in case I had to splurge, but nine stacks was out of my range.

"She's beautiful, can I hear her purr?" I inquired.

"Give me your license and you can do better than that; you can test drive the car and see if she's a fit."

I quickly pulled out my license and Albert instructed his office worker to bring me the key. The worker must have been a close relative because the resemblance was remarkable. I took the keys and waited for Albert to accompany me.

"You are coming with, right?" I asked him.

Albert told me to take Lance along with me. He was expecting another customer and didn't want his younger brother handling his business.

I opened the door to the automobile and was impressed by the well maintained interior. She had no tears in her seats and was without cracks in the wood panels. The four-year-old luxury coupe was in pristine shape. I turned the ignition and she cranked up on the first try. As the engine ran, I felt it growl without putting my foot on the pedal. Satisfied that the kitty purred perfectly, I slid in Jayo Felony's cd and pumped "Whatcha Gonna Do" over the Bose speakers. I let the roof down, then Lance and I took the sexy cat for a ride on the Five freeway.

There was nothing not to like about the automobile -- except for the price.

We were ten minutes into the drive when I said, "Lance just keeping it real. I brought eight thousand with me but I refuse to part with more than seventy-five hundred of it," I said in a raised voice to be heard over the music and rushing air.

"Albert is a fair dude, I'm sure he'll work it out for you and if not, I'll swing you the rest. That is, of course, if you'll turn down this racket for the rest of this test drive."

He didn't have to say that twice. Shit for fifteen hundred, I almost ejected the cd and threw it out of the speeding car.

After driving around for a while, checking out ladies in other cars and having them checking us out, I drove the car back onto the lot where Albert was standing there waiting for us.

How do you like? You like, no?" Albert asked, convinced that he had a sale from the joy plastered on my face.

I made a mental note to work on my bluffing better the next time I found myself in a situation such as this.

"Oh no doubt; it handles well, accelerates smoothly, and ladies dig it. Hell, even Lance picked up a number on the passenger side," I said with excitement in my voice. Being so close to owning my dream car made it impossible to try to front.

"Albert, I know the sticker says nine thousand, but if you can help my man out some on the price I would appreciate it," Lance said, cashing in a favor on my behalf.

Albert didn't want to budge. He was standing firm on his price because the car had low mileage. Lance argued the point that most Jaguars that had low mileage was either because they stayed at the mechanic's or were constantly stored in a garage.

Albert paused before speaking. "Okay for you, I will take eight thousand cash, but if anyone asks you it was ten thousand," he told me in an effort to keep his reputation as a salesman who couldn't be Jewed down.

"Make it seventy-five hundred dollars and I'll tell people I paid $12,000 to make you happy," I said.

"Oh my goodness, you guys are killing me." He made exaggerated gestures like he was being stabbed.

We went inside the office and had the paperwork drawn up. He gave me the title and we bounced.

Our next stop was in Santa Monica. I followed Lance as we darted through traffic. His Porsche was quicker, but the bottom end of my sophisticated V12 equaled his speed.

We exited the 405 South unto Santa Monica Blvd. I parked behind him in front of the cellular store, which sat three blocks from the exit heading West. We walked into the store and again we were in the midst of a bunch of Armenian men. I had no idea there were so many Armenian folks in LA.

As soon as we entered, a tall dark-haired man greeted Lance.

"Lance, my friend, how are you doing, family?"

"Every day above six feet is a great day, Alan. What's up with you? Are you performing magic today?" Lance replied.

Now it was even more than clear that I was green, but there was no way Alan, who did look more like an Aladdin than an Alan, was the next David Copperfield.

"Of course, my friend, is your horn not working?" asked Alan.

"Oh, I'm straight. My man Cameron needs to purchase his own personal horn and see the magic show."

"Do you understand that it is two hundred dollars for the horn and fifty dollars each time you want to see the magic show?" he asked me.

Honestly, I had no idea what he was talking about. I figured I just needed to slide Allen two hundred bucks. I nodded and handed him the loot. He took the cash and headed to the back of the store behind a closed door, and miraculously he reappeared with a Motorola StarTac phone. Now, I was in business. I had long grown tired of asking Lance for the usage of his cell phone and my stomach cringed at the thought of using one of those nasty ass pay phones.

"This should last you for about sixty days. You have problem, you come back and I do the magic for free."

Damn unlimited calling for fifty bucks a month? I was sprung.

I called Lance so that he could lock in my number. I was now armed to do business.

"So what else you got planned for the day?" Lance questioned as we walked to our cars.

"I'm going to take Karen and the boys for ride and something to eat. Tonight, I'm going over to The Comedy Store."

"Oh, you have a spot on The Phat Tuesday show?"

"Hell nah, I have an unlimited cell phone and a new whip with the brains blown out. I feel like a boss and I'm going to floss tonight!"

Lance shook his head, tickled by my statement. He had created a monster, but unlike Dr. Frankenstein, he liked his creation.

***

Karen brought the boys into the apartment with her.

"What's for dinner?" I asked.

She gave me a look like we were going to be eating cornflakes if she was needed to prepare it. "Ah baby, I'm so tired; can we order a pizza or something?" she asked.

"No, but I tell you what. How about you change out of those work clothes and we go grab something."

She reluctantly agreed to go, went into the bedroom and changed. Karen came back to the room looking hella sexy in her formfitting DKNY white T-shirt and blue jeans. The responsibility of cooking for three males being nullified had given her a boost of energy.

"I'm ready, let's go," she harped.

We all left out and headed to the parking area. Karen and the boys stopped short, stunned when I walked over to the new convertible and started it up.

"Cameron, what are you doing?"

"I'm taking my family to dinner unless, of course, you all don't like our new car." I made sure to emphasize that we mutually owned it, even if it was the furthest thing from what I actually felt.

The boys ran over to the car screaming, "Dad this is so cool!"

I knew they were twins, but it would always trip me out whenever they said things in unison.

Karen sashayed her fine ass over to the car admiring our newest material possession.

"This is so nice, Cameron, and it's convertible. I'm going to have to let my hair grow out or buy myself a weave so the wind can blow through it," she teased as she ran her fingers through her short well-kept coif.

"I'm glad you agree with the purchase." I flashed my pearly whites.

We backed up and headed out of the parking lot. In the CD changer was Prince's Greatest Hits CD. "Raspberry Beret" piped through the Bose speakers.

"Cameron, I don't know what you and Lance got going, but you bet not stop until get you me a Land Cruiser," she said.

CHAPTER 5

Cameron, you have to upgrade your fits, young blood. Here we are bringing down Fed Time Funds, and you are still buying your gear at Men's Warehouse," stated Lance as he drove toward Beverly Hills. It had been two months of good business and I thought I had done good job with my wardrobe.

I looked at my slacks and loafers and saw nothing wrong with what I wore.

"I paid good money for this stuff. Don't knock the Men's Warehouse. They have fine men's ware at an affordable price."

"You are over there sounding like a paid spokesman for that bearded white man. The way you're talking, you should be supplied with free clothing."

"So what do you suggest I do? Go to the Fox Hills Mall and get gaudy gear from there?" I questioned with irritation in my voice.

"Hell nah! You wouldn't catch me dead in that cheap shit. I'm taking you to my man, Dion Scott's spot."

"Dion Scott? Who the fuck is that?"

"Who is Dion Scott?" he asked as if he couldn't believe my question. "Cameron, I swear your green ass kills me."

"All right, you've made your point. I'm a country Buckeye. But you haven't answered the question of who is Dion Scott?"

"He's the clothier to all the black stars of Hollywood and when we get out of this car, you'll be able to say he's your personal stylist as well," he told me, parking the Porsche in front of a posh Beverly Hills boutique.

"I don't have but a few hundred in my pocket," I said as I exited the sports car.

He sighed. "Do I have to teach you everything? Lesson number one, always have at least five thousand on your person. We are doing Alphabet Crew Crime. You never know what could happen."

"Alphabet Crew Crime? What the fuck is that?"

"You know. The FBI, IRS, ATF, DEA, and CIA. If being state property is all you aspire to be, I don't want you on my team, ya dig?"

"I feel you, but about the bread, again I wasn't prepared to do any major shopping," I said as we walked toward the door.

"It's cool. You can charge it to my account today and hit me off when you get home." Lance opened the door and gestured for me to enter.

When we entered the establishment, we were greeted by a well-groomed, tailored dressed, brown-skinned brother wearing glasses. I supposed he was Dion Scott. I was wrong. The man who welcomed us was Dion's trusted apprentice, Reginald Jenkins.

The boutique was filled with suits that were either being constructed or completed. The walls were lined with shirts on one side and reptilian footwear on the other. Dion Scott's reeked of big money to be earned and spent.

"My man, Lance the Great. So you finally brought in Black Comedy's latest meteorite," said a tan light-skinned brother in a double breasted forest green suit and cream shirt. "Cameron B., it is my pleasure to have you here. I've been watching your television appearances and kept saying to myself the day that brother lets me dress him...watch out world."

I couldn't be mad at his appraisal of my wardrobe after looking around his store. I realized just how lacking my attire was. The two men took my measurements and showed me swatches of fabric. After deciding on my suits and a couple of sport jackets, Reggie helped me pick out some shirts to be made.

While I was being attended to, Lance sipped herbal tea and read the latest issue of GQ magazine.

"Make sure he gets some shoes as well, Reggie. Those Florsheim's and Hush Puppies just won't do with his new gear," Lance teased.

After Reggie finished getting me together, I found myself before Dion at the cash register to total the damage. He rang up five custom made suits, six tailored shirts, three sport coats, five wide legged cuffed trousers and four crocodilian and alligator shoes with matching belts.

"That will be ten thousand four hundred dollars," he told me carelessly, like he had said one hundred. "We take cash, American Express, Visa, Master Card, and Discover."

Over my shoulder, Lance said, "Dion, put it on my account. Young blood didn't know he was getting suited and booted today."

"That's fine. You know your line of credit with me is good, Lance. You'll see that I discounted many of the items with a First Time Buyer Incentive Discount."

I was still stuck on Dion's telling me I had just paid more for my clothes than I had for my car.

"If you like you can take your shoes and belts now or we can have them all ready for pick up next week," Reggie chimed in.

"Oh, I can wait until next week. There's no use in me wearing them with my inferior wardrobe," I cracked.

Lance signed for the clothes and we said our goodbyes to the two tailors.

As soon as we were outside, I said, "Damn. I just spent ten racks and some change on some shit and I don't even have a bag to show for it. Tell me how was that a discount?"

"Believe me, brother, that's the best price you are going to ever get walking out of Dion's. He hooked you up. After you put on your gear, you'll be addicted."

"You make it sound like I'm going to be a dope fiend for clothes or something," I said, getting into the car.

"Everyone has something they are addicted to, Cameron, never forget that," Lance replied as he turned the ignition and drove off.

CHAPTER 6

Lance and his folks were happy with my proficiency. So happy with it that within the last three weeks Sarafina had deposited checks worth one hundred twenty, one hundred eighty, and two hundred thousand into my account. Chris was as efficient as always going into the bank and grabbing our take.

Lance kept our crew together, constantly schooling me in the ways of fraud.

He was jovial and in a free spending mood. I figured his share that totaled one hundred forty-three dollars was the reason behind his disposition. That, along with the 911 Cabriolet that Albert had hooked him up with.

Nothing excites a man like money, some new pussy, and a fly car and Lance was drowning in the depths of all three. I only guessed this was the reason because I found myself in those very same waters. I was so busy juggling my life as a hustler, father, live-in lover to Karen, and hush-hush boyfriend to Anna that I had been neglecting my standup career.

Of course I had been frequenting the comedy spots around town, but not to perform on stage. I was preoccupied with sitting outside on my Jaguar, clowning starving artists who weren't blessed to be befriended by Lance, like I was.

My hunger to be the next big thing in comedy had been sated by my ill-gotten gains.

"Cameron, are you trying to go up tonight?" asked Speedy the host and MC of the Comedy Act Theater as he walked past me. I was leaning on my car, parked in the lot of the theatre.

"How long do I have to wait?"

"Nigga, you wait until I call you; ain't shit changed because you just got a new ride," he spat back.

I told him I would think about it. But I said it in a manner not to diss him. He was my peoples, plus he and Jamie Foxx were real tight. I knew it wouldn't be smart burning a bridge with Jamie by dogging his right-hand man.

Honestly, it wasn't that I was tripping, I was waiting on Anna to meet me. She and her friend, Donna, were behind schedule and I was only waiting to escort them inside. I didn't like the idea of being out with the both of them. I needed a wing man and Lance was busy in Diamond Bar with this new chick he had met at The Century Club.

Speedy came back out to harass me about acting like a prima donna right when the girls pulled up.

Anna approached me affectionately. She was looking gorgeous in a blue sundress and heels. "Hey baby, I am sorry we were late; can we still get in on the guest list?" she asked, flashing a puppy dog face, begging me to forgive her.

As yummy as she looked, even if I had been mad it wouldn't have lasted long.

"Hey, Cameron, don't be upset with Anna, it's all my fault. I had to find a cute and comfortable shirt to put the girls in," Donna said, adjusting her breasts to exaggerate her point.

Donna was an attractive lady from Philly, high yellow, long hair, a juicy rack and wide hips. She was a little large for my taste. But if it hadn't been for that, tonight could've turned into something special.

Before I could tell the ladies all was good, Speedy jumped into the conversation.

"Hey, Cameron, you didn't tell me you had *two* beautiful women coming tonight. Let's not make them miss any more of the show; I'll get them in," he said, motioning for them to follow him inside.

The owner's sister, Sharon, comp'd my companions and had her son, Omar, who doubled as doorman and DJ, take them to their seats. I had to give it to Michael Williams, the owner. He knew how to keep the money in the family.

I hung back by the bar to tell Keisha, the waitress, to get the ladies whatever they wanted on me.

"Well, look at you, Mr. Bernard. What? Black women aren't good enough for you anymore?" she asked, obviously not approving of my doting over my Mexican acquaintance.

I didn't blame her smart ass mouth and the fact that she was prejudiced. But it wasn't just that; she was probably mad because she had given me some pussy before and I acted like it never happened.

I mean really, why would I? She didn't suck dick or like taking it from behind. As far as I was concerned, she was a waste tress and not a waitress.

"Those are my friends, they're good people. I'm just looking out," I explained even though this frigid bitch didn't deserve an explanation.

She went off to see what they wanted and left me alone. I was happy to watch her walk away. Keisha's firm round ass was quite a vision but even more reason for me to loathe her.

The packed house was in for treat tonight. All of the comics from the hit *Fridays* movie series were in the building. Angela Means was on stage doing her thing, much to the delight of the crowd of two hundred and twenty people. She had been given a flashing light and was wrapping up her set when Speedy rolled up on me.

"So your girl's buddy needs to be occupied tonight, huh? I play an excellent second-in-command. Hook me up," he said.

"For real? You don't think she's a little overweight?" I asked, surprised he would be interested in Donna.

"Fuck yeah, big girls pay what they weigh. Make it happen and I'll put you up right after Chris Tucker and Faizon Love," he said, dapping me up before running up to the stage to introduce the next performer.

Speedy's words were true; if I had been stuck with both of them it was going to be a frustrating night. Trying to out wait a girlfriend is only second to dealing with the baby whose mama you're trying to fuck. And it wasn't like I had all night to mess around.

Karen realized that a lot of Hollywood business was conducted after hours, but she was serious about me having my ass home by four am.

I walked over to Anna and Donna's table just as Speedy was introducing Chris Tucker. The crowd went wild as the southerner from Decatur, Georgia stalked the stage with his manic style and ultra-high pitched voice.

"Hey boo, is everything all right?" I asked.

"Yes, oh my God, I can't believe that we're here seeing Chris Tucker for free!"

I told her of Speedy's interest in Donna.

Funny thing was that Donna had just asked Anna about the possibility of hooking her up with him. I laughed to myself because now Speedy was in my debt for a cush spot on stage for something he had coming to him anyway.

I noticed that there were still no drinks in front of them.

"What's up, didn't you order your drinks?" I inquired.

"Yes, we did. The waitress is just taking her sweet time about bringing them back. What the hell is her problem?" she asked, then thought about it. "Ooh Cameron, you put it in all the way, didn't you?"

I was cold called out and had no reply, which was all that Anna needed to verify her deduction. She was cool like that; Anna kept it real.

I didn't have to lie to her about my live-in girlfriend or my twin sons. All she required of me was that when we were together, I treated her with respect. That was easy for me. Real folks get real respect.

After Chris Tucker finished his set, Speedy did a few minutes of time in order to get the crowd's mind off of the young movie star and also to flex his own comedic muscles.

The MC position of the Comedy Act Theatre was a coveted job.

The likes of Robin Harris, Joe Torry, DL Hughley, and Martin Lawrence had held the position before going on to fame and fortune. Now that Speedy had the mantle, he had every intention of keeping with the tradition.

After blazing a patron about his too-small outfit, Speedy brought up Faizon Love, and once again the crowd erupted as soon as they saw the San Diego native hit the stage. His character, Big Worm, had been a hit with black people across the nation. It was so popular that he said people refused to call him by his real name. His set was dedicated to his frustration with newfound fame and the crowd was eating it up.

While he was performing, Speedy slid up to me and asked, "So did you hook me up with your girl's buddy yet?" like the possibility him getting his dick wet was equal exchange for prime stage time.

I realized that it was.

For a comedian, prime stage time is just like sex. You either boom or bomb. If you ripped, it's just like if you handled your business in bed -- you receive instant gratification and a call back. On the other hand, if you bombed on stage or your sex was whack, you couldn't exit the stage or a bedroom quick enough and you could completely forget about any talks of a sequel.

"Yeah, Donna is all in and she thinks you're handsome. I tried to convince her that you were just all right but she wouldn't hear of it," I replied.

"Fuck you, Cameron. You just get ready because I'm bringing you straight up," he told me.

"Cool, make the intro hot, pimp!"

"Gotcha."

I went over to the DJ booth and asked Omar to play Frankie Beverly and Maze "Before I Let Go." Faizon finished his set and as promised, Speedy went straight into my introduction.

"All right y'all, coming to the stages is a brother from Cleveland. You've seen him on *Showtime at the Apollo* ... ripped it, BET's *ComicView*, handled his business, and just had a standing ovation performance on Russell Simmons' *Def Comedy Jam*. Give it up for the Ohio player, Mr. Cameron B."

Omar dropped the cued music and I headed onstage, clapping my hands to the beat, gesturing to the audience to join in with me as I arrived before the microphone. I had been out of practice, but my ego wasn't about to allow the *Friday* movie special guests to show me up. I knew that I wasn't about to out-funny Chris Tucker or Faizon, but I knew I could out-entertain them. Frankie Beverly began singing and so did I, much to delight of the female portion of the audience.

"You make me happy, this you can bet. You stood right beside me, and I won't forget. And I really love you, you should know...I wanna make sure I'm right, before I let go."

I gave the DJ the cut music signal and had to wait a few seconds before going into my act because the crowd was still singing and clapping. When they finally settled down, I went straight into my signature drunk bit.

"Let me apologize to the brothers in the room for my singing, you know how it is when you get fucked up and you sing your song. I don't care if you don't know all the words, you will sing the words you do know and hum the rest of those motherfuckers you don't." The crowd laughed as Keisha handed me my double Jack neat that I'd ordered for affect.

"As you all can see, I'm already high as giraffe's pussy and the kind folks at the bar have given me another drink. So here's a toast. Drink up, this shit is a lot more funnier when you drunk."

The crowd was eating up my acting like I was inebriated and they were enjoying my observations from a drunk's perspective. For 15 minutes, I had them feasting from the table of good humor I offered, then I thanked them for the good time, and said good night.

Speedy gave me dap as I exited the stage. "You ripped that shit, boy. There are few folks I want you to meet so don't dip off."

I assured him that I wasn't going anywhere and our deal was still solid -- he was rolling with me and the girls. I walked away and stopped by the table where Anna and Donna were sitting.

"Ooh Cameron, if I didn't have to be on the under about us, I would kiss you in the mouth. You were fabulous," Anna told me.

"Well, I don't want to kiss you and shit, but you did rock the stage," Donna said.

I thanked her for the compliment right before she asked me about Speedy. "So is your boy really interested? Because he can definitely get it."

"Oh yeah, we are definitely going to go get something to eat afterward," I replied.

"Tell Speedy I got something for him to eat all right, let him know I'm sitting on it, keeping it warm for him."

While Anna laughed like she was used to that kind of talk from her friend, Donna's comment shocked me. I would have been standing there with my mouth wide open for not the fear of what she would have stuffed it with.

Before we left the club, Speedy introduced me to Grace Wu and Lisa Noonan, two women who stood out in this crowd like a brother at a Klan meeting. They were a vision of extreme difference, Grace was a diminutive woman of Asian ancestry. (Of which variation, I wasn't sure, but since I dug the Wu-Tang Clan I figured it would be of Chinese origin.) Lisa, on the other hand, was an amazon of Caucasian ancestry dwarfing her companion, standing 6'1" with closely cropped brunette hair. Grace was the first to introduce herself.

"Cameron, I found your performance to be quite entertaining. I'm Grace Wu." She paused to give me her business card. "I work for NBC's diversity casting division and what I saw in you tonight makes me believe you might be just the kind of talent that we've been searching for."

I was wowed by the compliment and opportunity she presented.

"Thank you, Ms. Wu. I really appreciate you noticing me." I shook her petite hand.

"And this Cameron, is my friend, Lisa Noonan from Three-Story Entertainment."

Lisa extended her hand with a business card as well and introduced herself. "It's a pleasure to meet you. I was wondering if you had management to help guide your career?" she asked.

"The pleasure's all mine and to answer your question, at the present time, I'm without management or an agent," I replied, not disclosing that my "management" had booted me because of my chauvinistic attitude toward his wife.

"Well then, I would like to do lunch next week; is Monday good for you?" Lisa asked.

Upward movement in the comedy game was welcoming, but Lance and I had developed a rhythm over the past few months that couldn't be disturbed. I had standing meetings with Lance until Wednesday so the lunch couldn't take place until after I had clocked that haul.

"Of course! I would be more than interested in meeting with you and discussing the direction of my career. But can we do it Thursday afternoon? I have prior commitments that I need to attend to," I explained.

"Sure that would be fine. I look forward to seeing you this Thursday, let's say twelve-thirty at the Wilshire Hotel?"

Grace informed me that she would be in touch after talking to some of her colleagues about me. We exchanged goodbyes and they left out.

"Man, they must really be looking for the next big thing to be in the heart of the Crenshaw district looking for it," I told Speedy.

"They know that if they want to find blacks who connect to the pulse of the black population, they're not going to find him in Hollywood at The Store or the Laugh Factory. They got to come the Hollyhood!" exclaimed Speedy, making perfect sense to me.

We stayed at the club until about midnight when it closed, leaving more than enough time to have something to eat, kick it with the ladies, and get my ass back in the Valley before Karen started blowing up my phone wondering where the hell I was.

The girls were hungry; they wanted to feed the alcohol they consumed. Speedy suggested we go to Jerry's Deli in Beverly Hills, but that was driving toward the Valley and away from Anna's apartment near the airport. I suggested that we head over to Johnny's Pastrami on Adams, leaving us more time to hang out.

Everyone agreed and we headed over to the best sandwich shop in the hood. After getting four sandwiches and pickle spears, we dipped over to Anna's. Her one-bedroom apartment was nice. I had given her a few dollars to purchase an oversized couch and a love-seat so that I could be comfortable when I spent time there as well as a California King size bed.

We all sat in the living room eating our food while listening to my homeboy, Gerald Levert's "Groove On" CD. Though it had only been out a few weeks, R&B fans were already taunting the compact disc as a soul classic.

After finishing our meal, Anna and I excused ourselves to her bedroom. We were eager to get our freak on, plus Donna and Speedy could use the privacy to handle their business.

As soon as I closed the bedroom door behind us, Anna lifted her sundress over her head and laid on the bed to remove her underwear, pleading with me to come join her. Though I knew I didn't have a lot of time to spend with her, I removed my clothes in a slow, methodical fashion, taking the time to fold each article and neatly place them on the dresser.

"Don't make me wait; bring me my chocolate fix, Papa," Anna cooed.

"You sure you just want some chocolate?" I teasingly asked her as I crept closer to the bed with a hard-on that begged for attention.

"And I want the cream filling, too," she stated seductively as she pulled me down between her gaping legs, inviting me to a carnal fiesta.

We attacked each other's bodies in sensual warfare until the clock on her nightstand read two forty-five in the morning.

"Baby, I have to get going," I told her, wishing I could split myself in two, giving her one-half and sharing my other half with my family.

"Papa, I understand. I appreciate all the good you do for and to me. I knew what it was when we started," she replied, before she kissed me deeply with her tongue probing my mouth.

It took all the strength I had not to just lay it back down and enjoy myself, but I couldn't allow her promises of more pleasure to get in the way of my need to be home.

I lifted myself out of bed and went into Anna's bathroom to shower with soap (that matched the brand I used at home) and splashed on some Egyptian musk.

"Papa, you smell fresh enough to ravage all over again," Anna said the moment I came out of the shower, reminding me why I liked being around her so much. She knew how to make a man feel appreciated.

"I'll call you tomorrow and see you soon." I promised her as I left the room.

I was quiet, trying to respect Speedy and Donna, thinking they might've been asleep. Much to my surprise, Speedy was banging away at Donna who was bent over the couch. Her face being forced by each stroke into the cushions muffled her moans of ecstasy. Speedy, with his retarded ass, shot me the thumbs up, then delivered a thunderous slap across Donna's wide ass.

I opened the door and exited, lighting a Punch Robusto cigar, allowing the large plume of smoke to surround me so as to change my fresh-out-of-the-shower scent into a I've-been-hanging-in-a-smoke-filled-club aroma.

I walked downstairs to my car, put on Method Man/Redman's hip hop hit "How High" and pointed my kitty northbound on the 405 freeway.

CHAPTER 7

I had been so busy doing business with Lance and hanging with my new manager, Lisa, that I hadn't had time to look for a house so that we could move out of my cramped apartment.

Sarafina had upped the ante by dropping a check on me worth three hundred and twenty-five thousand dollars.

Lance said this was my last tango with my account. The fact that we had moved $917,000 and not had a snag made Lance speculate that either everything he knew about law enforcement was wrong or they were building a case against me and were waiting for the right opportunity to spring the trap on me.

Again, he implored me to keep the contracts he had given me with these transactions on my person and/or in my vehicle.

I wasn't the type who needed to be constantly reminded to protect myself. Self-preservation was engraved in my being.

Lisa had me working on a spec script to submit to Grace Wu so she could place me on the writing staff of a new show starring a nationally known comedian. Grace had also encouraged me to write a spec script about a show I pitched to her. The sitcom revolved around a struggling comic. It was called *Barely Standing,* starring me as the lead, along with a diversified cast of multiracial comedic characters.

I was in a very creative space, using the Final Draft program on my PowerBook laptop, working on the assignments and writing new material, that is when Lance, Chris and I weren't sticking up banks.

Karen was hyped that I was busy writing, which kept me home more and with all the money we had pouring in, the level of stress in our house was virtually erased.

I should have known that things going so smoothly was just the quiet before the storm. Instinct should have had me concerned about when the roof was going to fall in. But I was just enjoying this good space in my life.

The beginning of the end started the day when Lance and I went to pick up Chris and he was so sick he couldn't show his white face like he had shown it so many times before. I prayed that he got better, but Lance wasn't optimistic at all.

"Cameron, I know you're going to think that this is fucked up of me, but it would be to our advantage if Mr. Swenson doesn't pull through," he told me, being morbidly honest.

"You're right, I do think it's fucked up. Chris has helped us bring down almost one million bucks. You could at least join in prayer that our friend gets better," I snapped.

"The first and only lesson you need to know and better learn is that there ain't no friends when you're hustling."

After Lance said that I tuned his ass out, realizing that the same shoes were on my feet. He would rather chuck dirt into my grave than throw me a lifeline.

Mentally, I thanked Lance for unknowingly teaching me the greatest lesson he could have ever taught me. In the game it was truly no shook hands in Crooklyn.

CHAPTER 8

Cameron, baby, I'm running late. Do you mind taking the boys to Lulu's for me?" Karen asked as she walked past me.

I was sitting at my computer hutch, busy typing away with two fingers trying to complete the task of meeting a deadline.

"Yeah, that's cool, let me just finish this script. Lisa is expecting it. I'll drop them off when I'm done."

"Ah, look at my man trying to be all busy," she said, giving me a hug from behind. "I'm so proud of you."

Of course, Karen had no idea that I was being deceitful in our relationship and I had been lying about our finances. What she *did* know was that things were better; she just had no clue how good shit really was.

If Karen had any clue that our loot was stacked like it was, she would have told the folks at the VA to kiss her ass. She was content with the couple of thousand dollars that I had given her for a new place as soon as our lease ran out. But if she had known the combination to the safe in the closet, I was sure that quarter of a million dollars I had stashed would've told her that all the bullshit I'd been telling her was nothing but a cover for something illegal.

I finished the script and printed it out, then went into the kitchen with the twins and fed them some hot cereal while they watched early morning television.

"Are you fellas ready to go see LuLu?" I asked them.

"Yes, but can we stay with you today?" they asked, freaking me out with the unison twin shit they did.

"Next time, I promise. Today I have some important meetings to attend to." I felt bad letting them down.

"Ah, man. You said that the last time."

"Yeah, but when I came to pick you guys up, I got both of you pizza and ice cream, right?"

"Yes!"

"Then today after I'm done, I'll come pick you up and whatever you guys want I'll get for you." I flashed a wad of loot to make sure they knew I had it. Maybe it wasn't right for me to be bribing my boys like this, but after so many slim times it felt good to splurge now that the opportunity presented itself.

I got their things together and we went to the Jaguar parked in our apartment garage.

The boys both got in the back, even though I asked which one of them wanted to join me in front. They both refused, choosing to sit next to each other. Again I shrugged it off as some more of that crazy twin behavior. Lulu's was around the corner from us so however they wanted to ride for six minutes, I wasn't about to argue about it.

It was a pleasant August day in Van Nuys but that was only because the sun had just awakened and hadn't yet gotten into the full swing of torturing the folks of San Fernando Valley. I blew the roof off the coupe and played some feel-good Michael Franks, "Popsicle Toes."

I tried not to play rap music around the twins. They were at an impressionable age and I didn't want to be the reason why they knew the words to "Fuck The Police" before they could spell their names well.

As we arrived at Lulu's the song was fading down. I parked the car, grabbed their bags, and took the children inside.

"Hey, Cameron," Lulu said, greeting me at the door.

"Wassup, Lulu? What's good?" I replied.

"You bringing over the twins and me making this money," she quipped.

"I know that's right. The twins have already eaten, so don't let them worry you like they haven't and they're starving. It'll all be game."

"Don't worry, Cameron, they can eat all they want. Lulu don't have no problem feeding these babies."

We said our goodbyes and I headed back my car. I entered the Jaguar, put the key in the ignition and before I could take off, two men (one black, one white) approached me with guns drawn. The first thing that came to mind was I was about to be the first nigga to get jacked at a babysitter's house. *Fuck, now I had to give up my dream car to spare my life. Damn!*

Then, I heard one of the men say, "Cameron Bernard, put your hands up."

CHAPTER 9

Sweat was gathering on my forehead and pooling in my arm pits. I would have blamed it on the August temperature if I wasn't staring down steel. My whole world slowed down. In my mind, I played out how I was about to lose my whip and the five thousand I had in my pocket.

Then, it dawned on me that these men had to be the police. I had seen every hood and gangster movie there was and I had never known a carjacker to say a motherfucker's whole government name.

That realization brought about a whole 'nother kind of dread. Fuck losing a lil bit of change and a used vehicle, these two men could take away something much more valuable - my freedom.

The Rodney King beating was still fresh in the consciousness of all Americans and I wasn't but thirty minutes from Simi Valley. These policemen didn't have to worry about me not complying with their demands.

I raised my hands as I was told to do.

"Excuse me, gentlemen, what seems to be the problem?" I asked as I could hear my heart racing.

"Slowly step out of the car," the white officer told me, sounding like he was hoping I moved quickly so he had a reason to give me a beat down, or worse, just shoot me.

Again, I did as instructed as the white officer and his black partner moved from behind my car to face me with guns still drawn.

"Cameron B? Cameron B from Def Comedy Jam?" the black officer questioned.

I nodded my head, confirming his thoughts.

"He's cool, Gus." The black officer motioned to his partner to put his gun down. Then, he said to me, "I'm Detective Sanderson, Van Nuys fraud division. This is my partner, Gus Coles. We want to talk to you about suspicious activity that has come to our attention through Bank of America. Do you know a Chris Swenson?"

Without hesitation, I explained to them that I did know Chris and that I had contracts stating we were doing business on a failed comedy tour.

"I ended up having to give him back the monies after we failed to secure venues and talent." My tone was meant to assure him that I had no knowledge of anything fraudulent.

"Would you mind if I looked over the contract?" Detective Sanderson inquired.

"Of course, it's in the glove box." I gave him permission to get it.

After perusing over the documents, the detectives concluded that I was no more than a pawn in a laundering scheme.

"Have a good day; sorry for disturbing you," Detective Coles told me.

Detective Sanderson laughed. "Man we didn't disturb this brother, we probably just gave him some new material."

"I promise nothing is funny about having guns being drawn on you. But you're probably right; when my blood pressure lowers to normal, I'll reflect on this comically," I said getting back into my car, happy that I wasn't riding in the back of theirs.

"We followed you here, but my partner saw you had your kids with you, so we decided to wait and see if you dropped them off," Cole said. I knew that was just his way of letting me know if they needed me, they knew where to find me.

The two officers returned to their unmarked Crown Victoria and darted off.

I was relieved to watch them disappear. I made up my mind right there and then that we were moving out of that apartment as soon as possible, fuck that lease.

I knew I was going to have to explain myself to Karen. I was sure that LuLu saw what had happened and was going to tell her about the police accosting me. No lame excuse was going to do.

Though I was still shaken from my morning encounter with Van Nuys finest, I still had to make my way to drop off my scripts at Lisa's office on Wilshire Boulevard. So, I hopped on the 101, and hoped that I would not find myself jammed in traffic. Much to my delight, the flow of the vehicles was smooth. I knew I was going to be ahead of our scheduled meeting time, so I called Lisa to see if she needed anything.

"I'm getting off the Hollywood exit right now, would you like me to get you anything?" I asked Lisa.

"Good morning, Cameron, how thoughtful of you. If you don't mind, I could stand a Starbucks Red Eye and one of those delicious double fudge brownies," she told me.

"You must have already sold my sitcom idea," I told her.

She laughed. "No not yet, why would you say that?"

"Because a brother would have to had struck the lotto to afford Starbucks if you haven't sold it yet."

"You are too much. Anyone who dresses as impeccably as you do and drives a car that would make most executives blush, shouldn't be complaining about money."

We both shared a laugh and I got off the phone. When I pulled up to the Starbucks, I was amazed. I didn't do drugs so I was no expert, but I would swear Starbucks must have been putting coke in their coffee.

People were standing in line, bent around the corner to get their caffeine fix. While I waited, I amused myself with thoughts of patrons trying to sell TVs and offering oral tricks so they could cop a venti Caramel Macchiato. When I finally made it to the front of the line, a young kid who reminded me of Sean Penn's character in *Fast Times at Ridgemont High* attempted to take my order.

"Welcome to Starbucks; what can I help you with today, dude?" he asked me, sealing the deal of my impression of him.

"I would like two large Red Eyes and two double fudge brownies, please."

"Okay, so you want two Grande Red Eyes and brownies?"

"No, I would like two large Red Eyes."

He looked at me like I was a damn fool and repeated his question again like I was a remedial student. This went back and forth a few times until I finally grabbed the sized-cup I wanted and told him, "Put the shit in this fucking size."

"Dude, you don't have to go all postal. I'm just asking what my manager insists I say."

I kinda felt bad for going at him so hard, but ain't nobody working for minimum wage going to check me. I paid for the coffee and carefully took it to my car in a cup holder. It was a good thing that I had about ten minutes of driving to Lisa's office because the coffee was hotter than molten lava. I found that out when I arrived at Lisa's office and spilled a little on my hand, causing me to blaspheme and use The Lord's name in vain.

After taking the elevator up six flights, I arrived at Two-Story Entertainment, which made no sense to me seeing it was on the sixth floor. Lisa was the sole soul who worked in the office.

"Well, good morning, Mr. Bernard. Why the long face today?" she asked.

I informed her of my crazy re-education with buying coffee that was overpriced and the probability of at least a second degree burn on my hand.

Lisa was amused.

"Please tell me you have written this down or you talked it into a digital recorder, capturing it in its raw humor."

"No, I'm just telling you what happened."

"Cameron, you have to record all of the zany things you observe. You do have a digital recorder, don't you?"

I didn't have any idea what she was talking about.

"I would have to say that I don't."

She rummaged through her desk drawer and retrieved what looked like an itty-bitty cassette player.

"Here, you can use this one." She showed me how to use it.

"Thanks, how much do I owe you for it?"

"Put it this way, think of it as me investing in our professional future. I'm sure something you record on it is going to make us a lot of money."

The optimistic attitude Lisa had toward my success made me want to do better so that I could live up to her expectations. I had reason to believe her opinion of me. Not only did she handle my career, but she managed Margaret Smith, who had just been awarded The Comedienne of the Year award from Comedy Central.

In the month since Lisa had been my manager, I'd been afforded some opportunities in mainstream clubs because of the success she'd had with Margaret. My partnership with Lisa had become quite fruitful.

"So do you have the scripts ready?"

I reached into my computer bag and handed Lisa the printed copies. "I tried my best with the Cheers script, it's cool but my original sitcom is by far my best."

Lisa looked over both scripts as I waited patiently, drinking my now-able-to-be-tolerated cooled coffee. From time to time I would hear her emit a chuckle or giggle. Finally, she had finished reading both of my creations.

"Cameron, your original script is fabulous. If NBC passes on it, they would be absolute fools. I mean they would have a charismatic handsome lead in you, and your vivid description and development of the supporting characters should make it easy to cast." She paused long enough for me to thank her for digging my script and seeing my vision.

"I appreciate it, Lisa, I really worked hard on a project," I told her.

"I can see you put all of your energies toward *Barely Standing* and not very much effort into writing the *Cheers* script."

I felt let down after hearing her opinion of the *Cheers* script that I had labored over. "What was so wrong about it?"

She held the script in her hand. "For one, it's filled with tired clichés, which shows me either boredom or laziness."

"Well, it's not that I was being lazy. To be frank, there were no black characters to bring out my brand of humor."

"Cameron, I disagree. Black humor and white humor are the same. I know you aren't telling me because you couldn't write a few motherfucker's and bitches into the dialogue, that means it wasn't black, it wasn't your kind of humor?" she questioned, trying to drive her point home.

"No, I'm just saying if this was a *Hanging with Mr. Cooper* script instead of *Cheers* I would have had a better grasp of the material."

I sensed that Lisa understood where I was coming from, but it was her job to make me realize the serious opportunity I could be squandering.

"You could be living a plush life as a staff writer. I'm talking about one hundred fifty thousand a year to sit in a room with a bunch of nerds, writing funny things for talentless people to make come alive."

It took everything in me not to tell her I was sitting on almost double that amount for six weeks of scheming. But the reality that she was steering me to wouldn't have me being tailed by the fuzz nor find me staring down the barrel of a gun. That fact kept my arrogance at bay.

"So what do you suggest I do, Lisa? Manage me," I said with a huge smile that pleaded for a cease-fire.

"Well, now that I have you refocused, take this *Cheers* script and bring it to life with your own brand of comedy. You know the show, now make it yours. I'll stall Grace for a few days and while you're working, I'll put this *Barely Standing* script into as many producers and show runners' hands as I can."

I agreed with Lisa and promised to give a better effort at the task before me.

Her phone rang and when she started talking, I figured whomever was on the other line was important and our meeting had ended.

I gathered my things and blew Lisa a friendly kiss goodbye.

When I returned to my car I decided it would be in my best interest to give Lance a heads up about my police encounter earlier in the morning. I know I should have called him earlier but I needed to deal with Lisa in order to decompress.

He picked up on the first ring. "This is Lance, The Great, how may I help you?" He answered the phone like he was expecting a call from Caesar's Palace to fill in for a magician spot.

"We need to meet. I'm sure you wouldn't appreciate this conversation over an unsecured line." I was being cautious. I figured if the cops were tailing me, they might be listening in as well.

"Oh, okay, I feel you. Where are you right now?"

"I'm on Wilshire headed toward Hollywood. Meet me at the Hunan Café for lunch," I told him.

Lance informed me that he needed thirty minutes and he would meet me there. I turned left onto La Brea, then made another left onto Sunset and arrived at the restaurant. I dug this spot, not only did they have great food, but you could rub elbows with stars and starlets while you dined. I would be lying if I didn't admit that my television appearances and new tax bracket made me feel like I belonged in the mix with them.

I was sitting out on the patio drinking iced tea, taking in the sights of Rolls-Royce limousines, Lamborghinis and Ferraris cruising down the Sunset Strip.

Cynically, I wondered how many of those drivers had copped their cars like I had at Statewide Auto.

As I tickled myself with that thought, Lance pulled up in his jet black-on-black Cabriolet 911. When he exited the vehicle, I saw that he was in his normal swag mode, not one hair was out of place. Lance was wearing a beige linen short-sleeved shirt with matching pleated linen pants. His burnt orange Mauri alligator shoes and belt finished off his outfit. As he got closer, I could see his thick black mustache was trimmed perfectly, and of course he was bumping DC go-go music when he pulled up.

"Wassup, Cam?" he asked while removing his sunglasses and sitting down at the table.

I looked around making sure no one was paying us attention before I spoke. "Yo, the boys accosted me today when I dropped the twins off at the babysitters." I kept my voice low.

Lance just sat there with a blank expression. I assumed that he might have been mulling over thoughts of me cooperating with them.

"So you obviously had the contract with you?"

I nodded. "Of course I did and I'm glad the one detective recognized me from HBO, otherwise I wouldn't be here, believe me."

"If you're wearing a wire, you could be here," he replied dryly.

"Nigga, first off, I'm no rat. If I go down, I go down alone," I spat, insulted that he would ever suggest I would fold.

His shoulders relaxed just a little. "No need to be upset, young blood, I meant no harm. I was just saying."

"You were just saying I wouldn't stand up. I'm from Cleveland and even though I'm not from the streets, I do live by the code of the streets."

Lance wasn't trying to be confrontational publicly. So, he apologized. I wasn't so far gone in my anger that I couldn't accept the white flag he was waving.

"So what has you in Hollywood today?"

I explained to him that I had a meeting with my manager about the two scripts I'd been working on. "So we're out of business I guess, huh?" I asked him, thinking that it was a good thing that I had prospects for making a legitimate living.

"Not necessarily; you just need to find somebody who's in a tight position with a bank account that is not in the negative," Lance told me.

He didn't give me any names, but I knew that he was referring to Anna. I had been doing my best to keep her from the clutches of the hustle, but she was in need of a come-up. Busting her ass at Denny's wasn't making her enough money to keep creditors from hounding her. I reluctantly told Lance I would mention it to her.

"Great because a closed mouth won't get fed. Speaking of closed mouths," Lance said as he got the attention of our waitress.

After ordering our meals, I asked about Chris. "So have you heard how Chris is doing?"

"Yeah, Amanda told me that he's been admitted to the hospital. He's been ignoring his condition and now it's turning for the worse."

I shook my head. "Man, that is so fucked up. I hope the doctors can do something for him."

"Excuse me, Cameron, but didn't you just tell me that the police came to see you?"

"Yeah." I frowned. "But what does that have to do with Chris?"

"You need to look at Chris's demise as a blessing. If he goes, the case gets buried along with him."

Wow! I couldn't believe he said that. "You are one cold piece of work, Lance."

"These things I'm saying about Chris has nothing to do with how I feel about you. We used him to separate you from the account. You're my folks."

Just then, the waitress came over with our orders and I wasn't about to let my good food get cold just to argue a point. Lance had already instilled in me what he really felt -- we weren't friends, we were hustlers.

During lunch, he had continued to convince me that I should reach out to Anna and see if she would be interested in joining us in our criminal endeavors. I told him that the small amount he was giving to Chris wasn't going to cut it for Anna. She wasn't strung out on dope or facing a death sentence, so it wouldn't be cool to come at her like she was desperate.

"I feel you, Cameron. I see that you have developed feelings for the young lady. I'll figure out a way to get her a bigger share, I promise."

"That's cool. I'm not saying I've caught feelings or nothing. I just don't want to be in the direct line of fire if shit goes wrong. Proper pay gives birth to loyalty."

Lance and I finished our meals and hung out star gazing until around two pm, then we wrapped up our meeting and left the Hunan Café. Lance told me that he would see Sarafina as soon as I got back with him about Anna.

Feeling the pressure, I drove toward her apartment to gauge her interest in the proposal that Lance offered. I was in tight with her, but out of respect I called to make sure she wasn't busy.

"What's up, Papa," she said when she answered the phone. "You finally missing me enough to pull your face out of that script and holla at yo girl?"

"I'm sorry, sweetie for neglecting you. Believe me when I tell you I've been working diligently on these projects. I wasn't lying. Of course, I missed you. I've missed you so much I'm headed over your way if you'll allow me to."

"Stop playing. You know whenever you want to come see me you have an open invitation. *Mi Casa Su Casa.*"

I told Anna I needed about twenty-five minutes to reach her seeing that I was going to take the streets instead of the freeway. At this time of day, there would be nothing free about the 101 or 405.

I drove down La Brea and headed toward the airport, trying to figure out how I was going to drop the idea of putting a large check into her account. When I arrived at her crib, Anna was wearing nothing but an oriental robe, which hugged her Latin curves. She smelled as if she had just showered in rose petals; her scent was intoxicating and her long black hair cascaded down her back. I figured she must have just finished blow drying it.

"Hey, Papa!" Anna exclaimed as she hugged me, pressing her perfect 36C breasts against me. "I've missed you so much," she said, gazing deeply into my eyes.

"I've missed you too, baby," I responded just before she kissed me fully in the mouth.

Anna offered me entrance into her home and before I closed the door behind me, she had untied her robe and presented her naked self to me.

"Why don't you show me how much you missed me?" She directed me, walking into the bedroom and laying across the California King sized bed.

I kneeled before her and wrapped her legs around my shoulders. I was taking my time, admiring her well-shaven twat when she pleaded that I stop teasing her and get to it. As directed, I buried my face into her sweet femininity. Anna bucked as I darted my tongue in and out of her moist hole.

"Ooh, baby, it's been too long, don't make Mamma wait like this again."

I kept applying pleasurable pressure as I sucked and licked her center until she came in violent waves. Quivering and trying to catch her breath, Anna rolled over and curled into the fetal position.

In my normal, slow deliberate fashion, I took care to fold my pants and hang them and my shirt over the chair that stood before her makeup mirror. Anna patiently watched me go about my ritual, knowing that once I finished I would be pouncing on her like a tiger upon its prey.

I walked over to the bed and stood before her, trying to decide which method of attack I would deploy upon her. Anna had tired of waiting on my decision, and made my mind up for me by placing my engorged rod into her wanting mouth. She was masterful with her oral skills and loved taking me in fully, then releasing my member so that I could marvel at her sloppy wet work.

Anna stroked and jerked my dick as she moved her head up and down my shaft like a piston in a 357-short block. I was nearing orgasm and so not to blow my load, I thought of an impossible math equation to block out the release that Anna was so eagerly trying to suck out of me.

I gently directed her onto her back and placed myself between her parted legs. I guided my tool into her and Anna arched her back and raised her legs giving me full access.

"Get it, Papa, it's your pussy," she squealed as I pummeled her womanhood. I would like to say that it was a sexual marathon and I had been a world class distance fucker, but that would be lying to myself and disrespecting the wonderful chemistry Anna and I shared.

"I'm cumming!" I grunted as I released my seed deep into her.

Anna wrapped her legs around me tightly as my hot offerings jolted inside her.

It took Anna a few seconds to catch her breath. "Wow Daddy, you really did miss me, huh?"

I lay there motionless, still inside her until my failing erection made it where I could no longer hold residence within her sugar walls.

"Wow!" was all I could muster to say.

"You still haven't told me how much you missed me," she said playfully.

"I would like to think my silence and loud actions would have spoken volumes to you about how much you've been missed," I said, kissing her on her forehead. Rolling off of her, I asked, "What are you doing home today anyway?"

"My punk ass manager Randy has been cutting my hours. He's been giving them to another girl because she's willing to fuck his crab ass and I refuse to," she told me.

"So what are you going to do about finances?" I asked, seeing the perfect opportunity to share my scheme to include her in on the hustle.

"I don't know, Papa. I was hoping that you would be a sweetie and help me out."

It was then when I realized that Anna was gaming me just as much as I had been planning to game her. I didn't get mad at her for asking for a loan because Anna was giving the wares to me that could've bought her favor with her manager.

I got out of the bed and reached into my pants pocket and removing what was left of the five-thousand-dollar bankroll I always kept on me. I peeled her off fifteen hundred dollar bills and gave them to her.

"Oh my God, Cameron. I don't know what to say."

"Thank you will suffice," I replied, coolly sounding like Lance on the day when he turned me out.

"Of course, thank you, baby. Thank you and thank Jesus for your generosity."

"It's nothing, really." I paused as if I was giving something a little thought. "You know I can make it where Randy giving you a hard time wouldn't trouble you at all."

"Oh Cameron, I couldn't keep taking money from you. I don't even know when I'll be able to return this to you."

I shrugged. "Don't think of it as a loan, but as a cash advance on a business venture we're about to embark on."

I asked her the same questions Lance had asked me initially about her account's standing at the bank. She assured me that she wasn't overdrawn and she didn't have any checks out that would cause a problem.

While we talked, I could feel a change happening inside of me.

I was moving up the food chain.

No longer was I the hunted, but the hunter.

As this feeling surged through me, I forgave Lance. There was no way the deer could be mad at the bear that kills it. The bear was only doing what bears do.

Anna was aroused by my generosity and the possibility of future riches. She climbed on top, straddled me and ground herself into my groin until she stimulated me enough for penetration. We continued to make love until after 6 pm when I hoped the traffic would have broken down and I could easily maneuver my way back home.

CHAPTER 10

I walked into my apartment with Karen asking too many questions at one time for me to answer.

"Why did the police stop you? Why did they have guns out? Is that the kind of thing you want our sons to see?" And then before I could answer, she switched up. "Where have you been? Did you get the scripts to Lisa? Does she like them?"

"Are you going to give me a chance to speak or you going to keep bumping your gums?" I asked her even though I knew it was ignorant as fuck to answer a question with a question.

But seeing that Karen had belted me with about seven in a row, I was sure I wouldn't be judged for my question.

Finally, she calmed down enough to let me talk.

I put down my computer bag, gave the twins a high-five, and requested that she follow me into our room. I removed a bunch of clothes and a shoebox that I had in front of my safe, dialed the combination, and revealed its contents.

Karen's eyes got wide. "Oh my, God, Cameron, where did all this money come from?"

"Lance and I haven't been preparing for any tour, that's for sure," I replied smugly.

I explained to her the dirty dealings that I had been party to. Of course, she was concerned; she loved me and I respected the fact that she didn't want to be co-parenting with me from

San Quentin.

"Look," I began. "I think our place has gotten hot. Five-oh can come here whenever they feel the need."

I had brought a newspaper home with me, gave it to Karen, and instructed her to look for a house with an option to buy.

I had two hundred thousand dollars in cash but there was no way I could drop that kind of cash and not raise eyebrows.

"We'll piece off the loot in increments," I told Karen as she still looked at me in bewilderment.

I tried to console her the best I could. I was sure my desire to bust a quick move didn't help in comforting her, but I was hoping the knowledge that we weren't living hand-to-mouth might calm her anxiety.

"So you weren't going to tell me? Well, not until the police pulled you over?"

"I kept trying to find a proper way so that you wouldn't worry about me and you wouldn't become paranoid. Believe me I've been wanting to," I told her, wanting to give her a good reason for my negligence.

Karen thought about what I said and finally agreed that she would have been a nervous wreck and that would have made it virtually impossible for me to hustle with her in my ear.

"I tell you what...how about you call in sick tomorrow, we narrow down some homes, and we'll see what we can agree on." I hoped that the chance at a day off and me playing family man would ease her mind.

"Okay, that sounds good. I could use a day away from that hospital. Cameron, you're lucky I didn't know about all this money or else, I would've been quit."

I pretty much had already figured that out. Basically, that was why I hadn't shown her the money. We needed a legitimate check coming into the house in case we were ever questioned.

Malcolm and Martin were outside our bedroom door making a mess of noise. "We're hungry, what's for dinner?" they asked.

I knew I was still on the hook for the promised pizza and ice cream, and as far as they were concerned, if I wasn't in jail I needed to pay up.

"So you guys still open to pizza?" I asked them as I opened the door.

To my surprise, neither one of them wanted pizza anymore, but they were trying to decide between Carl's Jr. or Jack-in-the-Box. I tried to explain that essentially both were the same. I made the choice of Carl's Jr. because of the proximity to the apartment. I assured them that they could order whatever fancied them on the menu.

"So we don't have to order from the kid's menu?"

"Not unless you want to. I figure you two have outgrown the kid's menu," I told them, giving credit to my four-year-old boys for being taller than anyone their age. With me and Karen as their parents, I figured they would be well over six feet tall by the time they made it into junior high.

We all piled into Karen's forest green Toyota Land Cruiser that I had got for a steal at Statewide, and we headed out to get six million dollar burgers.

CHAPTER 11

Lance had changed the game up a bit once we enlisted Anna onto the team. No longer were we dealing with anyone walking into banks. Anna wasn't comfortable with walking into financial institutions, and I, for one, couldn't blame her. She didn't have the entertainment angle to use as a ruse like Lance and I did. With Chris out of action and possibly down for the count, Lance concocted a scheme that would take us to Las Vegas for a weekend, pulling down the money by taking cash advances against her debit card and gambling at the crap tables.

With Karen and the twins tucked away at a new place in a Canoga Park cul de sac, everything was all good.

Karen was busy, preoccupied with furnishing the house and turning it into a home, so she didn't have time to harass me about my whereabouts. It didn't hurt that I had given her the combination to the safe as a show of good faith. She was secure in knowing that if I did run into trouble, she and the twins would be more than provided for.

I was glad that Lance decided on Las Vegas as our new job location. I was in need of a vacation because Lisa had me toiling over the *Cheers* script. I had been writing and rewriting per Lisa's input and after three weeks of labor, I had a polished script that she and I agreed was ready to turn over to Grace Wu.

Lisa was a visionary and she finally had me seeing my potential as a staff writer. I had bought into her vision so much that I approached the task as if I was getting a paycheck.

Still, I was happy when Lance purchased roundtrip tickets on Southwest Airlines for our party of four. Lance decided that he would bring along his Valley girl, Gwen. At first I was opposed to taking Gwen with us. Lance convinced me it was copacetic, saying she was on the team serving the same duties as Anna, but instead of just getting paid off my Mexican companion, I would also get coin off Lance's light-skinned beauty.

I had to admit Gwen was fine as frog's hair. She stood 5'2 and she was that kinda thick that made men do double takes to convince themselves her juicy round ass was real.

For all of Gwen's magnificence below her waist, she was only fairly blessed in the breast department. I found it fun to chide Lance about making babies with this one. Not only did Gwen's body look like one baby could ruin everything, but the fact that both Gwen and Lance were light bright and almost white, their offspring could possibly come out transparent.

When I picked up Anna from her apartment, she was decked out in a yellow sundress with deep red roses splashed all over it. Her pouty mouth was adorned with ruby red lipstick that matched the leather clutch she held and the high heels she wore.

"Papa, I'm so happy to be able to get away with you. As much as I'm cool with our situation, it tugs at my heart for you to leave me after making love to you." She placed a kiss on me while I put her luggage in my trunk.

"Yeah I know, sweetie, and don't think for one minute I like bouncing either," I assured her as I opened the passenger door so she could slide her sexy ass into the XJS.

From her words, I knew what we had was running on borrowed time, but I expected nothing but a good time while in Vegas seeing that she would have me all to herself *and* she stood to clear ten thousand dollars for her part in our casino scheme.

Anna's residence was mere minutes from the airport so we arrived there in an instant. I dropped her off with the luggage and parked the car. By the time I returned, she was at the front of the line. The cheerful skycap took our bags after checking our IDs and we headed to security. To my delight, the line was light and we breezed through.

I was looking for Lance and Gwen as we made our way to the departure gate. I had already informed Anna of Gwen's icy treatment toward me. I passed it off as her not agreeing with me having a family and a Mexican mistress.

"She probably harbors feelings for you and instead of expressing them, she acts them out negatively."

"Well that doesn't make good sense; Lance is quite the ladies man."

"And so are you. Trust me, Cameron, I know women. I'm one, I know how we think."

I was pondering the things Anna had told me when I saw Lance and Gwen approaching us.

"Mr. Bernard, are you and your friend ready to get this easy money?" Lance asked.

"Does a hog love slop? Does a cat chase a mouse? Fuck yeah, we ready!" I replied.

Lance laughed and then introduced the ladies. "Gwen, this is Anna, Anna, this is Gwen."

Gwen lifted her sunglasses from her eyes and placed them on top of her head. "Hey Anna, I'm pleased to meet you," she said so pleasantly I almost lost my balance. I was shocked that Gwen was so friendly. I chalked it up to Lance telling her to dead the fucked-up attitude for the sake of good business.

I laughed to myself with the thought of how money could change anyone's attitude. Seeing that Gwen was cool with a cease -fire, I wasn't about to continue with a war.

"Hey Gwen, good to see you; you look marvelous today," I said, not lying one bit.

She was clad in a jogging suit that hugged every curve she owned and like I said before, Gwen owned curves that would make a winding highway envious.

She thanked me for the compliment and we all went back and forth admiring each other as we waited to board the plane. Lance had grown tired of the faux love fest and gave the girls the rundown on how to handle our business again.

"For the next three days, you ladies are going to keep going to the cashier's cage and getting two-thousand-dollar cash advances. You'll gamble a small amount on the table and slots, so you won't draw attention to yourselves."

"But won't they have a limit for how much we can draw out?" Anna asked.

"The beauty of Vegas is its greed. You can bleed yourself dry there and no one cares. As a matter of fact, Vegas is the type of city that banks on you leaving it all there," he assured them.

"From what I understand, you and I just have to look pretty and get paid, sweetie, and we already have pretty down pat," Gwen told Anna giving her another compliment.

Finally, we boarded the plane, and before I could order my second Jack Daniels and more peanuts, we landed at

McLaren Airport. As soon as we departed the aircraft, Lance walked over to one of the slot machines in the concourse, dropped in some money, and pulled the handle. All the lights on the machine illuminated and the chimes whistled as it vomited out a shitload of coins.

We were ecstatic, though the person who had just given up on the machine threw dagger-like looks at us as we celebrated.

"Cameron, this is going to be one boss of a weekend, my man," Lance exclaimed as he gathered his winnings and put another dollar into the machine that yielded no return.

I looked at him puzzled. "Why the fuck did you do that?"

"Everyone's good luck in this city starts from another's misfortune. I just gave back to be a blessing to the next man."

We went to baggage claim and retrieved our luggage. After obtaining all of our things, we exited the airport to hail a cab.

Oh my goodness! The heat was on hell! It seized my throat in a chokehold, making it hard to breathe.

"Damn, it's hot enough for shade to look for shade," Lance said as he looked at the display which showed that the temperature was well above 100 degrees.

The girls were too excited to allow the heat to affect their spirit.

We found a cabbie who was more than happy to put us in his air-conditioned van and take us to our destination, The Stratosphere Casino and Hotel.

It wasn't directly on the strip nor was it as gaudy as The Mirage or Caesar's Palace, but what it did offer was a crap-less dice game that Lance and I couldn't wait to try.

If there was one thing that Lance had schooled me to more than style and fraudulent savvy, it was how to masterfully toss and control dice. Lance didn't teach me to shake them up and sling them or have some cutie blow on them, but how to specifically toss and control the revolution of the die as the pair left the grasp of your fingers and thumb.

Lance was so absorbed in the game that he had a room in his condo dedicated to craps. He had an actual casino-sized table. Sometimes when we had time to kill between hustles or comedy spots, I would meet him at his North Hollywood residence and soak up as much knowledge as he was willing to share. Lance was an ocean to my sponge, not only did he teach me how to dominate the dice, he preached to me how not to fall victim to the casino's parlor tricks like free drinks.

"Alcohol dulls the senses and gambling inebriated is like handing over your hard-earned money." Everything was a distraction with purpose, he continuously told me. From the half-nude waitresses, to the music being played, and the chiming of the slot machines...all these things gave the house the advantage.

His sermon of how you can't beat the house, but you could shake the foundation on which it was built rang from his North Hollywood home to the High Heavens. I was his dice disciple and now all of my tutoring was done. After all my practicing, I was about to pit my knowledge against the odds and show just how good a student I actually was.

We checked into our rooms and caught the elevator to the 10th floor. When Anna and I entered our room, we were both disappointed with the Spartan accommodations. Anna was still looking around the room in disbelief when I called Lance. "Hey, our room is plain as fuck, is yours too?"

"Yep, but don't worry. After we mash them on that table tonight, we'll be upgraded," he replied confidently.

Lance directed us to hurry so that we could begin the first phase of our take-down of the three hundred and twenty thousand dollars that rested in the girl's accounts.

When Anna and I met Lance and Gwen in their room, Gwen wasn't ready to go.

"Lance baby, I'm burning up. Can't we go swimming first and lounge by the pool?" Gwen pleaded.

"Fuck a pool and lounging, bitch, we're here to work," he spat with no sound of love in his voice.

It was then that I realized how serious Lance was about getting cheddar. I mean, it was one thing to be black-hearted about a drug addicted AIDs riddled white dude he barely knew, but snapping on a super fine broad he was banging made me realize Lance wasn't black-hearted at all -- he was heartless.

Anna dared not say a word. I sensed she feared the same harsh treatment.

I respected Lance's gangsta, I knew that if our trip was going to be a success, we needed fierce leadership and he was our leader. I was quiet while we headed down ten stories, not out of fear, but to make sure the girls knew exactly who was running shit.

We exited the elevator and walked in the direction of the cashier's cage. Lance made sure the girls understood what they were to do and told him to meet us at the crap table. While we walked toward the gaming area, Lance must've really been feeling himself.

"Look, just do what I say and we will make out like fat cats, ya' mean?"

"Lance, I'm not one of those bitches; you don't have to drill me, I got this." I told him that just in case he forgot I was good with my hands and didn't take kindly to being barked at.

Lance felt the sting in my reply. "You cool, you want a drink?"

"Not while I'm working, brother, I told you I'm ready," I said, feeling like I had grasped the pebble from my master's palm.

"Yes sir, you are ready. I'm just glad Vegas isn't ready for us."

We went to the table that was already filled with cheering attendees. Lance and I put small wages on the point, which was six and we played the hard way. I watched the burly white man in the ten-gallon cowboy hat hold the dice in the complete opposite position of how I'd been taught -- a sure sign of an amateur.

"Do you see how he's playing on pure luck and is being controlled by the dice and not vice versa?" Lance asked me in a hushed tone.

"Yeah, that's why I'm not going all ziggity boo on my bets."

No sooner than we spoke the words, the cowboy rolled a seven and the house raked in all the cash, including Lance's and mine.

We had one person before our turn to roll. Lance offered the young lady named Terri one hundred dollars to buy the dice from her.

"Just follow me on the bets," he told the both of us.

On the come-out roll, Lance threw six sevens in a row. Lance was dominating the table so well, our initial bet of one hundred dollars had already become thirty-two hundred dollars. Finally, Lance threw the number five.

"Cameron, I'm feeling it, put sixteen hundred on Little Joe," he said instructing me to place a large bet on double two.

Lance was in that special place referred to as the zone. Everyone, no matter what their trade, had experienced the euphoria of everything they touched was golden.

Like when Tiger hit three eagles in a row and pumped his fist or when Michael Jordan shrugged his shoulders after every shot going in, no matter the difficulty.

Lance gently tossed the crimson bones across the sea of casino chips and the green felt that covered the table. The dice glided through the air without rotation, banged against the table's wall, and landed.

"Come on, Little Joe from Kokomo!" Lance demanded of the dice.

The table went wild when the numbers came as commanded. Terri, the young lady whom Lance bought the dice from was so overwhelmed with her winnings of fourteen thousand dollars, that she kissed him flush on the mouth. I was excited for my fourteen thousand, too, but wasn't moved to swap spit with my boy.

Luckily for him, the kiss came before our girls found us. I was sure Gwen would have whipped some serious ass had she witnessed it.

"Cameron, I bet you won't put that fourteen thousand on the boxcar with me," Lance challenged.

"Fuck if I won't, this money ain't mine. We playing with the house's loot." I moved my all my black chips to the double six one time bet.

The dealer took his time getting Lance the dice, much like an opposing coach calls for a timeout to put a free throw shooter on ice.

Lance told me, "Match my hundred and let's place a bet for the dealer." He coolly let the casino employee know he wasn't fazed.

I put up the black chip and waited to see if Lance was the crap expert he proclaimed to be, or if I was about to lose what we had skillfully stripped from the house.

Lance set the dice to the two and the three and picked them up. The table was quiet enough to hear a rat pissing on cotton as the other players trusted Lance's hot hand and waged generous bets following our lead.

The dice glided smoothly without spinning, then hit the wall and on two rolls of the crimson bones, one dice landed on six and the other followed suit.

It was pure pandemonium at the table as the ballsy play was paid out. I didn't know what the house had lost, but Lance, Terri, and I raked in four hundred thirty-four thousand dollars each. The patrons who had rode the ride with Lance, tipped him from their earnings and the dealer even gave us dap as he won sixty-two hundred dollars.

The pit boss was furious and ordered new dice. After clearing off our winnings, Lance, just for shits and giggles, wanted to see if he could hit the point.

The girls and I followed his lead and we each placed one thousand dollars on the boxcar bet. Can you believe this motherfucker shot a double six again?

After collecting another thirty-one thousand dollars and more chilling stares from the pit boss, Lance signaled to me that it was time to split. I wasn't even mad that I hadn't been afforded the opportunity to try my hand at shooting. I was up almost a half a million dollars due to the good courtesy of my hot-handed partner.

We said our goodbyes to the table and were on our way to the cashier's cage to turn in our winning chips, when the evil-eyed pit boss offered us a security detail and asked for our room numbers. Just as Lance had told us earlier, the Stratosphere was upgrading our rooms, offering us complimentary dinner and giving us show tickets. Boxcar Lance had rolled us from obscurity into VIP status.

After cashing in our chips and filling out forms, we were escorted to our new rooms. When Anna and I walked into ours, it was like going from a pauper to a prince.

The living room alone was double the size of our previous accommodations. The bathroom was no mere bathroom -- it was a monument to cleanliness, boasting a sunken Jacuzzi the size of a small pool. And our bedroom had a bed that could have made Shaq feel like a midget.

This was living large in Vegas and this was what the fuck I was talking about. After marveling at our digs, I put our earnings inside the safe the hotel provided.

"If I wasn't so hungry I would tell you to come and get it," Anna told me lying on the bed, hiking up her skirt and flashing her fleshy mound to me.

"I tell you what. You keep that thought until after the free surf and turf dinner and I'll have that for dessert."

Excited by the promise of sexual joy and great food, immediately Anna hopped out of the bed, straightened her dress and followed me to join Lance and Gwen whom I hoped had finished putting their money away.

When we opened the door to leave, Lance and Gwen were already outside. I didn't know why it surprised me since Lance's track record about being ready ahead of time was legendary.

"So Cameron, how do you like your new lodging that my skills have afforded you?" he gloated.

"I have to admit, you were on a hot streak. Why didn't we parlay the boxcar bet? Man, we could have shut the table down for $1 million."

"I believe in leaving the game on top. You're from Cleveland so you should know this... I call it the Jim Brown."

"And what exactly would that be?" I asked shrugging my shoulders.

"Retire in your prime, and then, even years later people will talk about what else you could have done, instead of how you fell apart."

We entered the elevator and went downstairs so that we could cross from the lodging portion of the Stratosphere to The Top of The World restaurant. Gamblers applauded Lance and I as we walked through the casino.

Anna and Gwen were getting along like old buddies. I chalked it up to the money they earned hustling and betting at the crap table along with us; that was their bonding agent. I still couldn't believe it. I never thought that Gwen had it in her to be so sociable. It almost made me feel bad that I had told Anna how rotten of a bitch she was. Now I knew for sure that I would let the past be the past between us and embrace the new and improved Gwen.

"This whole VIP treatment has a girl sprung. Lance, I could get used to this," Gwen said before tasting her glass of Pinot Grigio.

"Don't be fooled by all this, like it's a kind gesture, it's all game," Lance replied glumly.

"What you mean by that?" asked Anna who was on the same page as Gwen; I knew she was thinking that she could get used to this life, too

"What I mean is these people are holding us hostage, trying to get their money back."

"Holding us hostage?" I questioned after tasting my succulent porterhouse steak cooked medium rare to perfection.

"They give you a bomb room, great food and the best in entertainment for free. One would be a fool to leave and take their money to another casino. These casino folks are smart. They know once you hit them you feel invincible; hell they are banking on it."

"So are you saying that we are through gambling?" I asked.

"I'm saying that we aren't giving that money back. Tomorrow we play the same two hundred we played today and if you shoot like I know you will, we'll make money. If we lose, we only lose the two hundred dollars that has almost made us millionaires."

"So can we get in on you guys playing, too? Anna and I could use some new Gucci shit," Gwen said slapping high-five with my Mexican beauty.

"That's right, girl. I could stand a day of shopping my damn self!"

Lance and I agreed to let them make some money but only if they followed the same two-hundred-dollar limit. The girls were elated about their inclusion.

Anna proposed a toast.

Lance, being a non-drinker joined us with his iced tea.

"Cameron, baby do you mind ordering another round? I have to go to the little ladies' room," Anna said excusing herself from the table.

Gwen followed her as well.

It always tickled me how women found the need to go to the bathroom together. I couldn't imagine me having to piss and inviting Lance to come with.

Lance was happy the girls had left; he wanted to have a conversation without them being audience to it.

"Peep this, Cameron, I'm going to need you to keep Gwen busy for me. I need a few hours to handle some business," he told me.

"Why, what's up?"

"Because the white girl that we won all the money with invited me to celebrate with her," he answered.

"Oh yeah, I can handle that." I said, offering the pound.

"Good 'cause I'm going to go over to Circus Circus Casino and let the monkey out on her ass."

I thought Lance was mad for ditching Gwen's double stacked ass for the moderately attractive Terri. Obviously, the chance of getting a shot of strange was too tempting to walk away from.

I said, "Well at least go over to the Motown Revue with us. Use some lame excuse to dip and I'll handle it from there."

The girls returned from the toilet, giggling. I had to admit I was pleased they were hitting it off. If we were going to be working together, they might as well be chummy.

We all finished our delicious meals. The girls were in a festive mood and couldn't wait to enjoy their first Vegas show. Because both Lance and I had both played Vegas before, we weren't equally moved.

Right now, what I really wanted to do was go upstairs and ravage Anna but I realized that my friend needed me to play wingman, so I played along like I was enthused to watch the performance. My sense of loyalty overruled my own desires.

After leaving a generous tip, we exited The Top of the World and headed to The Stratosphere Theatre. A long line awaited us when we arrived, but our VIP tickets afforded us quick entry and a front row table.

Lance sat with us while we enjoyed The Miracles minus Smokey Robinson. Though the person in Smokey's stead owned a fantastic falsetto, it couldn't substitute for the green-eyed musical genius of Motown.

After the performance Lance excused himself to handle a real estate venture he had in place. Gwen was feeling too good from her third Pinot to put up a fight for him to stay.

"I don't think I'll be out all night, but here's five hundred dollars; y'all have some fun on me." He pulled off five crisp one hundred dollar bills from the knot of cash he had in his pocket.

I was no longer guessing what Lance had in mind. After dropping off the loot on me, I knew he intended for me to babysit Gwen until he drained all the fluids from his body into Terri. We wished him well on his endeavors and he peeled out.

When Lance left, the ladies ordered more wine and we watched the rest of the show headlined by Dennis Edwards and his incarnation of The Temptations.

After the performance, I escorted the ladies to The Level 107 Lounge. House music blared through the state of the art sound system. Gwen and Anna let the music take control of their bodies as they took turns dancing with me sensually and with each other as I tired.

While they danced, I bought a bottle of Moet, which awaited them when they returned from the dance floor. We drank champagne, smoked cigars, and boogied for two hours. The girls were tiring and told me that they were ready to go upstairs. On cue, I escorted the two beauties from the club to our tower.

"You two go ahead, I have to make a quick phone call." I hoped Anna wouldn't be upset that I had to check in at home.

"Okay, Papa, but don't keep me waiting long. You know I need my chocolate fix," she exclaimed through drunken lips as they entered the elevator.

I stood by the gift shop; for some strange reason it was where I had the best reception and I called Karen.

"Hello?" Karen answered the phone like I had disturbed her slumber.

"Hey, Darkness, sorry to wake you, baby, but I wanted to let you know how I was doing."

"It's okay, Cameron, I just fell asleep watching TV, well more like the TV was watching me. Is everything okay? Are you enjoying Vegas?"

"I'm doing great, so great that we're going to need to buy a bigger safe."

"Oh my goodness how much did you win?" she asked fully awake now.

"Lance was on a hot streak and we both won over four hundred thousand dollars apiece."

"Shit, four hundred thousand dollars! Cameron, that's insane. Congratulations."

"Thanks and because when I win you win, baby, take fifty thousand from the safe and have a shopping spree on me." I was trying to be right toward her even though I was headed upstairs to do her so wrong.

"Really? You don't have to do that."

"You're right, what am I thinking? Take fifty for you and fifty for the boys and go burn the mall down."

"Thanks baby, when you get home it's going to be so on. So don't have too much fun in Vegas. Because when you get home Sin City is going to be what you call our bedroom."

Had I not been brown skinned I would have blushed after that statement. When Karen wanted to be sassy she sure was sassy.

We talked for a few more minutes and even though I had just given her two years' salary in two minutes, her yawns signaled she was truly tuckered out.

We said our goodbyes and I headed upstairs to the guilty pleasure that had just cost me a hundred grand.

When I entered my hotel room, I was surprised to see not only Anna's dress and hat thrown to the floor, but Gwen's dress as well. Maybe it was all the champagne I had that didn't make what I saw, then heard in my bedroom register.

Anna was laying on her back with her legs splayed while Gwen was in front of her on all fours, lapping away. In between coos and moans, Anna realized I was in the room.

"Well, it's about time you joined us, Papa. We waited as long as we could, but you took so long we started without you," Anna said between gasps.

Gwen lifted her face from Anna's nether region.

"I have this part handled, feel free to get in where you fit in," she told me with a girlish giggle, then offered her firm round ass for me to do whatever I desired.

Even though I was disrobing and about to join in on the fray, I couldn't help but to feel a tinge of guilt.

"This is so fucked up, Lance is my friend," I managed to say as I guided my heat-seeking missile into her moistened silo.

Gwen grunted as the helmet of my manhood spread her to accommodate my girth. "Don't worry, ain't no friends when you are hustling."

Her words made me realize that Lance's creed had been his undoing as Gwen had fully accepted his dog-eat-dog mentality. I chalked it up to the game and lost myself in the flesh of my two companions.

When we were done, Gwen freshened up in our oversized bathroom. She gathered up and put on her clothes. She returned to our bedroom and kneeled over the bed where Anna and I were still wrapped in an embrace. She kissed us on our foreheads and put her finger to her lips.

"Remember what happens in Vegas stays in Vegas," she told us and then departed.

CHAPTER 12

Things had been running smoothly over the last two months. The Vegas trip had been a success. Lance's hot streak had cooled, but we still came out of The Stratosphere on top. I didn't know if my conscience had gotten the best of me, but I had only meager success throwing the dice. My winnings from my own handling of the bones were only $32-thousand. That amount would have made anyone else proud, but with all the training Lance had put me through, my earnings were a failure. Especially when Lance had fucked around and made us both millionaires when he threw those back-to-back boxcars.

The girls had done their duties well enough to entice Sarafina to issue them both larger checks to take down. Instead of heading back to Las Vegas, we travelled to Reno and then, hit the riverboat casinos in the Southern states of our great nation.

Karen was beginning to grumble about the constant traveling, but my sharing of my wealth quieted her. With all the things I had going good, my comedy career was suffering. I now understood how Lance, though always looking like a million bucks, could be so disillusioned about getting the big break. Fuck, we were already living the sitcom star lifestyle. Lisa noticed my stagnation since I hadn't done any shows and pleaded with me to get my mind back on the comedy grind. I agreed that I would put forth a better effort and would be ready for the industry showcase she developed in order for executives to see the act that inspired the sitcom I had written.

I was sitting in The Big Easy smoke shop enjoying a Cuban Series D Maduro cigar when my cellphone rang.

"Cameron, where you at? We need to talk ASAP," Lance said.

My first thought was that Gwen had hipped him to the ménage a trios, so I was hesitant to reply.

"Cameron, did you hear me, bruh? This shit is important."

I collected my thoughts and manned up. "I'm at the smoke shop on Ventura," I told him, knowing he wouldn't dare come to such an establishment. Lance was too health conscious for that. He refused swine, liquor, and above all, tobacco products.

"Meet me at Jerry's Deli across the street in fifteen minutes," he barked, hanging up before I could reply.

With all of the money I had and all the luxuries I had purchased, the one thing I didn't have in my possession was a gun. Maybe it was my ego coupled with the fact that I stand 6'4 and weighed 260 lbs.

Maybe it was my fear of being too powerful with such an instrument in my possession. Maybe that was why I never thought to purchase one.

What I did know was that Lance was armed. I also knew that I had done something to him that might warrant him to squeeze off a shot at me. I was ignorant of his knowledge of what had transpired in that Las Vegas hotel room between Anna, Gwen and me.

I pulled a long drag from my stogie, said goodbyes to the fellow patrons and owner, then left to meet Lance at Jerry's.

Five minutes later, I drove into Jerry's parking lot.

"What's up, Lance?" I said as I pulled up next to his Porsche. "What was so important that we just had to meet with each other?"

One of the benefits of living in Southern California was the weather. On this late October day, we were both afforded the ability to have our tops down. Tone Toni Tony had painted an inaccurate picture when they sang "It Never Rained in Southern California" because for the most part, LA was paradise.

"I have some good news and some bad news, it depends upon how you wanna look at it. Which one you want first?" he asked, speaking to me from his car.

From his demeanor I could tell he was in high spirits, definitely not the kind of mood one would have when confronting a man about fucking his significant other.

Satisfied and relieved there wasn't about to be any gunplay that I was ill-equipped to participate in, I answered, "Give me the good news first."

"Well, the good news is you are completely in the clear with that Bank of America investigation," he said.

I knew by that he meant that Chris was no longer among the living. I didn't know dude enough to be shaken up, but I felt sorrowful enough to ask Lance about the arrangements and if there was anything we could do.

He was merciless in his response. "Ain't no fucking arrangements and what the fuck? You know good and damn well if we give Amanda any cash, she's going to bury it into her arm," he scolded me.

"I know you're right, man. I'm just saying when a teammate sacrifices on the field, you don't leave him hanging."

"Cameron, don't get me wrong, but even if there was a funeral and we could go, don't you think those detectives from Van Nuys would be there waiting for us to show our faces?" he asked me, already knowing the answer.

I didn't reply; I just let what he said sink in.

"So you wanna know the better news or what?" he asked, breaking the silence between us.

Of course I wanted the better news. After hearing of Chris's doom, anything would do.

"Yeah, give it to me," I told him, igniting my cigar with my torch lighter.

"Well, we don't have to travel anymore using the girls. You and I are back on the frontline, and peep this, Sarafina cut Moe out of the equation so now, it's three way split."

"Damn, what did Moe do to piss her off?"

"From what I've been told he brought some unwilling parties to the table and they froze her out. Fuck it, like I said before, one man's misery is another man's joy."

Now on this bit of news I couldn't have agreed with Lance more. Moe getting a cut of the hard work I had put in was a constant thorn in my side. I didn't make a stink about it because Lance constantly reminded me that Moe okayed me into the game and it was merely paying my taxes.

"So if Chris is gone, how are we going to take down the cash? I can't fuck with that Bank of America account anymore."

"Don't worry, we have a smooth plan. Sarafina has a sweet hook-up at Merrill Lynch. It's a mutual money account. She has an inside man and we are going to kill 'em."

That sounded cool to me. Our inside lady had an inside man.

"She's going to cut the checks this week, no more sharing. I get one hundred and fifty thousand and so do you."

I was happy to be getting a full share with the money I had pulled in gambling and hustling, but now, I was more than nigga rich. I hadn't talked to Lance about it yet, but I had been thinking of retiring from fraud. Yep, I was going to go out like Jim Brown.

We finished our conversation with him running down how we would meet and begin dealing with Sarafina's guy, Richard, at Merrill Lynch. Right before leaving Lance dropped a bomb on me.

"Yo Cameron, what you think about this?" He proudly displayed a three-karat diamond ring.

"I love it, but I'm sorry I have to decline, Lance, I'm already spoken for."

"Motherfucker, I know that with your silly ass. I'm going to propose to Gwen tonight," he boasted.

"Lance, really marriage? You've only known Gwen since June, bruh. I mean she is a nice girl, but you are already a divorcé, ya mean?"

"Man, I don't need to wait. It just feels so right between us. You just don't know how special she is."

I thought about how special Gwen was as I drew on my cigar. Like how she had complete control of her vaginal walls. She made me feel like I was getting a hand job while getting some pussy, or how she didn't have a gag reflex and swallowed my seed without spilling a drop, or better yet, how Gwen was an Ol' Faithful kind of squirter. Of course I thought these lucid thoughts to myself.

"Well, best of luck to you, man. Congrats. I'm sure that you two will be happy," I told him.

"I'll call you later and tell you how it goes," he said before pulling off.

My friend was elated and I was feeling like shit. Until this moment, I had pushed the memory of that night with Gwen to the back burner of my mind. Now, I felt compelled to say something so my partner didn't get caught slipping. I was compelled but didn't move on my need to come clean. Instead, I thought of Lance's mantra: "Ain't no friends when you are hustling."

I turned on the car and drove to my residence in Canoga Park.

The next day, Lance phoned telling me that we were on for a Wednesday meeting with Richard and that Gwen had accepted his proposal. I told him that I would be ready to meet and asked him if he was thinking of having a big wedding.

"Nah, we're going to do a small private thing in Vegas, ya dig? I have a hook-up on a house there so afterward we gonna camp there."

"So you and Gwen are going to leave LA behind, huh? So what are you going to do for a living? You know the Power Rangers aren't going to last forever."

"Believe me, Cameron, I know that. With all this money I've made, I'll go to Vegas and bump around until I get one of the casinos to give me a show; call it Lance and his Great Friends."

I told him I dug the plan. It was an obtainable and profitable idea.

"So what's your plans, brother?"

I thought of several different options, but none of them amounted to me leaving Los Angeles. Shit, where else could you spend Christmas day in shorts and sandals? My immediate plan was to obtain a writing position or push my pilot ideas on the networks that were gobbling up ethnic sitcoms. Money wasn't a worry, so I was in no rush to make a decision. Christmas was just around the corner and I figured I would take the family to Cleveland so my mother, Irene, could see her grandsons and I could spoil her with my ill-gotten gains. It was the least I could do.

"Man, I think I'm just going to play my hand with this writing, my comedy and see where it lands me," I told him.

"What are you doing tonight? Wanna go to The Laugh Factory? You know Chocolate Sundays is going to be off the chain."

I told Lance I was going to spend time with family and I would see him Wednesday. We hung up and I watched a couple of Disney movies with the twins and when they went to sleep, Karen and I watched a real gangster story called *The Professional.*

"You ready to go to bed, baby?" I questioned Karen who was fighting sleep next to me on the couch.

"Only if you're going to join me," she replied.

When she was not mad with me or suspicious of my comings and goings, we had a great connection. I slowed my roll with Anna considerably, not because she did anything wrong, but for the fact I was doing all this dirt and it would be to my advantage to draw the line on some of the bad karma I was accumulating. I didn't think she minded the distance because of all the bread she was getting from our fraudulent activities. She was too preoccupied to even make mention of it.

"Of course I'll join you, now do you want to fall asleep or be put to sleep is the real question?"

"Shit, you know I want to be put to sleep, Deddy," she said, curling into me.

I loved it when she referred to me as Deddy. Do you know how good your sex game has to be for an educated sister to misspell and pronounce the word Daddy?

Even if she didn't think I was truly vicious in the sack, I didn't even care. Being called Deddy revved me up to perform on all cylinders. We went into our room and made sure to lock the door. There was nothing worse than having to explain to not one, but two five-year-olds why you and their momma were wrestling butt booty ass naked.

Karen disrobed and laid in the bed. I followed her in my birthday suit and we melted into one another for hours that night.

The next morning, it was raining cats and dogs.

"Fuck Raphael Saadiq!" I said as I got soaked getting into Lance's car.

"Listen to you, Mr. Bernard, crying like a spoiled Californian brat," he replied in response to my griping.

"I'm just saying, here we are about to have a productive day and Mother Nature is taking a piss on us."

Lance laughed, thinking how comical it was of me having been getting all this money and not owning an umbrella. I told him from what I understood about California weather, getting an umbrella made about as much sense as purchasing a parka in Miami.

Again, Lance was amused.

I figured I must have been onto something, so I pulled out my mini recorder and restated all the things I had just tickled Lance with.

"Brother, that new manager of yours sure has you on it. It's good to see one of us still working on the craft."

"Yeah, I have this big industry showcase coming up and Lisa has me working on a *Tonight Show* set."

"Ah yes, the infamous *Tonight Show* set where urban realness is shunned and the ultra-blackness that you've cultivated is shed away so the good folks of mainstream television can accept you. Ain't that about a bitch?" Lance said, remembering his own experience of the watering down process to be welcomed into the network's good graces.

It wasn't that long ago when agents and management pitched him the fastball they were throwing my way. Lance had excelled during the process, but right before it all went right for him, he hit a wall. Lance had bought into the entire process, but couldn't figure how to regain his street cred when he performed in front of urban audiences.

This frustration was part of the reason he didn't haunt the clubs as much. He had grown tired of manufactured clowns. My being from Cleveland kept me just grimy enough to not feel that my clean-cut image was a curse. Many of my homeboys had made quite an impression on the vast comedy plain. Steve Harvey, John Henton, AJ Jamal, and Arsenio had put a dent in the game and I still had aspirations of being the next Cleveland native to be a comedy success story.

The Merrill Lynch office was in the Sherman Oaks Galleria right next to the PF Chang's where not so long ago Lance, Chris and I had divided up our spoils from our first caper. I was sure that Lance didn't give it a second thought, but being there kinda pulled at me.

We walked into the financial group's office and was greeted by a gorgeous blonde named Antoinette.

"Good morning, and how may I help you gentlemen, today?" she asked.

"We're here to see Richard Malone concerning opening two accounts," Lance replied.

"Oh, Mr. Brooks and Mr. Bernard. He's been expecting you. Give me a minute, I'll let Richard know you're here." She surprised both of us because we didn't expect such personal service.

Antoinette rose from her desk, fully displaying how blessed she was as she knocked on Richard's door to inform him of our being there. Lance was feeling her. I guess it was true when people said you are attracted to what you don't have at home. Antoinette was the complete opposite of whom he had just proposed to. Where Gwen was blessed with ass for days and B cup breasts, Antoinette was tall lean with an abundance of breasts and long legs that led to a flat ass. Blondes weren't my thing, but I did have to give her credit; she was a looker in a Cybil Shepard kind of way. She came back and told us that Richard would see us.

"Would you gentlemen like some coffee or tea?" she asked as she led us to his office.

Lance declined both offerings. I, on the other hand, told her I would take some coffee.

"Black, no sugar, no cream?" she asked me as if her words were a metaphor for her detection that I wasn't into her Nordic good looks.

"Correct, but I will have two Sweet-n-Low's if you have it," I replied.

As we entered Mr. Malone's office, we were greeted by a tanned, six foot, dark haired man with and athletic build. He extended his manicured hand.

"Mr. Brooks and Mr. Bernard, it's a pleasure to meet the both of you," he said, firmly shaking both of our hands.

"Greetings, Mr. Malone," Lance began. "As you know you were recommended by a mutual acquaintance."

"Of course you were. Sara is dear college friend. She says you're both very trustworthy and to handle you with the upmost of care." He spoke as if he and our money girl had known each other in an intimate way outside of business.

Antoinette returned with my coffee and took the liberty to bring Richard and Lance bottled water. After placing the bottles on his desk, she exited, closing the door behind her.

"Man, I would love to bury my face in all those tits," he said, reaching out his hand to high-five Lance.

I was shocked at how he shed his higher learned persona and got real with us in just a matter of seconds.

"So, what's the problem?" Lance asked him.

"She's on this 'I don't want to sleep with people I work with' bullshit."

"Then why don't you fire her ass, fuck her, then hire her back," I interjected.

"That's funny, Cameron! You don't mind if I call you Cameron, do you?" he asked as if he didn't want to get too comfortable.

I told him Cameron was fine, we might as well be on familiar terms seeing that we were about to be linked in a scheme.

We sat back and listened to him explain how having our money work for us with Merrill Lynch was better than it being in a bank, or heaven forbid, it being under our mattresses. We filled out the paperwork and were told we would receive Visa credit cards attached to our accounts. He promised to put a rush on the cards so we would have access to our money as soon as the checks cleared in about four business days.

Before leaving, he gave us packages that gave us all the information we needed to access and use our new mutual money accounts. We shook hands and exited the offices.

"Cameron, do you feel confident about this cat?" Lance ogled Antoinette for one last time as she told us to have a nice day.

"I have two questions to ask you, one being do you think you're really ready to settle down? I mean the way you looked at that receptionist made *me* feel violated."

"I'm cool. I'm just purging myself of any and all lustful urges and if I can sow my royal oats in the process, that's cool, too!"

I couldn't argue with his rational. I knew if I was going down on a sinking ship I wouldn't be wasting my last moments like a monk.

"Okay secondly, do you really trust this cat, Richard? I mean here we are about to take down six hundred thousand dollars and this white boy didn't even blink an eye about it."

"Cameron, Richard went to school to learn how to be crooked and I'm not talking about no street level shit. Those guys on Wall Street fleece folks outta millions every day. If Sara says he's cool, I'm inclined to believe he is straight."

After hearing Lance's reasoning, I left it alone and went back to our previous conversation about leaving all the hustling behind.

"So how many more dips into the cookie jar are you gonna make before calling it quits?" I asked him.

"If Sarafina gives us two more checks like this, I'm out. You, my friend, can kiss Lance the Great goodbye."

"First off, there ain't enough Power Ranger cash to make me kiss you," I snapped back.

"What? You don't find me to be attractive?" he questioned, acting as if I had hurt his feelings.

"Lance, you are one silly motherfucker. Real talk though, two more checks and its curtains, huh? I can dig it. Well, we might as well leave it like we got in it. When you head off into the sunset, so will I." I knew greed could be a downfall, and I was too smart to be dumb enough to keep pushing the envelope.

Lance dropped me off at the crib. We agreed to meet up in a few days when everything fell into place. Lance sheemed off and I went into my empty house. Karen was at work and the boys were in school. I didn't have anything to do, so instead of trying to make myself busy, I turned on the TV, put in a VHS copy of *Coming to America* and laughed at Eddie Murphy until I fell asleep.

All the things Richard promised were delivered in a speedy fashion. In just a couple of days, Lance and I both owned one hundred and fifty thousand dollars' worth of spending power on our Merrill Lynch Visa cards. The transaction was so smooth, I wondered why Sarafina hadn't hipped us to it sooner. With all the cash I had, I was beginning to run out of shit I needed. I had to come up with things I wanted just to spend some of the money.

The first thing I thought was to buy my mother a house in Shaker Heights, Ohio, but she refused the offer. Irene was too attached to and dedicated to the folks in Warrensville to consider moving.

"Mama, at the least allow me to redecorate and add on to your home," I pleaded with her on the phone.

"Look at you, trying to talk about things because you're in California and have a college education. There's nothing wrong with the house your father bought and paid for," Irene replied across the line.

"I'm not trying to be fancy, Mom, and of course there's nothing wrong with your house. I'm just saying things are going well and I want something nice for you," I insisted.

"Well, I don't know what anyone could do to the house. Plus, you have a family of your own to take care of. You need not worry about me," Irene said with humility.

"Tell you what, how about I send you a ticket to come out here for a little while? I'm sure Karen and the twins would be happy to see you."

"Cameron Maurice Bernard, you're just like your father when he made up his mind to do something," she scolded me, calling me by my full government name.

"If you know this already, why don't you just do as you did with him and just let me do what I'm going to do?" I asked her.

"Because I'm your mama boy and don't get foxy at the mouth with me."

"Yes ma'am, but let me go so I can look at the flights. I'll call you later, I love you," I told her, trying to rush off the phone.

"I love you, too, but I know you're up to something. You would have thought having Coltrane bring me over a new Cadillac after you winning big in Las Vegas would be enough," Irene said, pausing to take a drag on a cigarette. "Well, go head and check on them flights and let me know what's up. Talk to you soon, baby, and tell Karen and my handsome grandbabies NaNa loves them."

After getting off the phone, I looked up my friend from high school, Keith Durham, and inquired whether his father's construction company could get a job done on my mother's house before the snow hit in Cleveland.

"Man, it's going to be getting cold here soon, Cameron, but if you don't mind paying for the extra laborers, I don't see why not," he told me.

"I want to extend the house in the back and add another level on the patio; that way I can put in a Jacuzzi tub and widen the bathroom."

"Man, that's gonna be about forty to fifty thousand dollars' worth of work. Why don't you just buy your mom a new house?"

I explained the situation of my mother not even wanting me to do this home improvement let alone leave the neighborhood. He couldn't help but to understand. Keith had been trying to get his parents moved to Miami for years, to no avail. I obtained his banking information so that I could wire him the cash and told him I would have my mother on a plane this week and as soon as I had her onboard, I would tell them it was okay to begin on the work.

"Cool, Cameron, I'll be waiting on your call. Oh yeah, if I hear you came to the Improv again in the Grove and didn't call me, we gonna have words."

"Man, my bad. When I was there, I was a little preoccupied."

"Oh, if you're anything like basketball Cameron B, I know that means you met some exotic stallion down here and lost your mind."

It made no sense to argue with him; Keith knew me too well. The stallion's name was Lita Nuenez, a Dominican with a body that didn't quit. That fling in Miami almost cost me my family when my dumb ass brought home pictures of my conquest and Karen found them.

We ended the call and I looked at flights from Cleveland to LA on United Airlines.

CHAPTER 13

With Irene in town I found myself too preoccupied with showing her all the joys of Southern California to be concerned with anything extra, especially scooting off to Anna's. I knew even if I had Karen fooled about my comings and goings, there was no way I was going to blow bullshit passed my mama. She knew how I moved.

Of course I didn't neglect my business with Lance and Richard. Our business venture had been more than lucrative, it had been smooth and there had been no pullovers by the police. I couldn't imagine how impossible it would have been to explain to Irene why guns had been drawn on us. Forget the explanation, the shame that an ordeal like that would have brought me would have been unbearable. That never happened, though. The only thing bad that happened while she was visiting was our neighbor alerted her to the home improvements I was making on her house.

Referring to Fannie Dean as just a neighbor was a serious understatement. She had not only been my babysitter when I was younger, but she was also neighborhood watch before there was such a thing.

I could have kicked myself for not giving her the heads up about not telling my mom about the construction. But with the cat out of the bag it was easier to keep my mother around for as long as I needed for the completion of her home renovation. She complained about not having enough clothes with her to stay longer, so of course, I used this as an excuse to take her shopping.

"So you want to go on Rodeo Drive in Beverly Hills and get a few things?" I asked as we drove southbound on the 405.

"Rodeo Drive? Goodness no. Take me to a JC Penny's or a Sears and I'll be fine."

I didn't want to tell her money wasn't a problem. After being wowed by our four-bedroom home with a swimming pool, and driving around in luxury, my having a developing deal and good luck in Vegas was going to start looking suspicious. Like I said, my mother could see through me.

"Either JC Penney's or Sears is cool with me," I told her before continuing. "But at least let me take you on Rodeo Drive. I believe you'll enjoy it."

"You just aren't going to give up are you, young man?"

"Not until you agree to allow me to spoil you," I said trying my best not to be intimidated by the frown on her face.

"Oh all right, but don't go wasting a bunch of money. Fannie has already said that Durham's Construction is turning my house into something that doesn't even belong on our street."

We parked the car in front of Cartier, right behind a Rolls Royce Corniche.

When we entered the place, I was pleased to see Angela Bassett inside, busy talking to a salesperson. Irene poked me sharply in my side as she recognized the highly acclaimed actress. Before I could stop her, my mother ran over to Ms. Bassett.

"Pardon me, I just have to tell you that you are by far the best actress of this generation. My name is Irene Bernard and that tall young man over there is my son, Cameron," she said, pointing at me proudly as I tried my best to shrink into the size of a gnat and disappear.

"I thank you and appreciate the compliment. Your son is a handsome man and quite the comedian," Angela replied as my star struck mother waved me over.

I was so embarrassed I wanted to shrink and disappear but I gathered myself then headed over to the two ladies.

"Good afternoon, Ms. Bassett it's a pleasure to meet you. I want to apologize if we interrupted your shopping, my mother was just excited to see you," I said, apologizing for infringing on her day.

"Oh, it's no trouble. I appreciate all the support I get. I was just telling your mother how much I enjoy your comedy."

"Thank you. I know you were in the crowd of The Comedy Act Theater a while back. I'm surprised you remembered me."

"Talent recognizes and respects other talented people. Keep doing what you do."

My mother carried on with her for a few minutes and after receiving her autograph and having me snap a picture, she let Ms. Bassett continue shopping. I had my mother try on a couple of watches she liked. She adored one, but quickly gave it back to the salesman and led me out of the store.

"Cameron Bernard, did you see the price tag on that thing?"

I told her that I had. But if she liked it I would purchase it.

"Take me to the black mall!" she demanded.

"Well, we aren't that far from Fox Hills Mall. There will be a lot of different nationalities there, but I guess you can say it's equal to Randall Park when it comes to blackness."

The funny thing is after shopping at Saks Fifth Avenue, JC Penny's, and Sears I still ended up spending what the watch was worth.

"You know you could have gotten the watch and all of this," I told her as I stuffed the bags in the trunk of Karen's Land Cruiser.

"I wouldn't want you to waste that kind of money on me."

I kissed her on the cheek and told her to spend money on the woman who gave birth to me was no waste.

"Are you hungry?" I asked her once we got in the car.

"Yes, I could stand a good meal. What do you have in mind?"

"Well there's this great soul food restaurant in the Marina I think you would dig."

She frowned like she wasn't sure. "Real soul food or this fancy-schmancy stuff you Californians have come up with?"

I pressed my hand against my chest like I was offended. "I'm not a Californian, I'm a transplant Clevelander, thank you very much. Just how fancy-schmancy could a place named Kizzey's Kitchen be?"

Irene laughed but cautioned me about talking foxy with her, even if she did have to agree with my point that any place named after Kunte Kinte's daughter and Chicken George's mama couldn't be bougie.

CHAPTER 14

I was definitely going to have to teach the twins how to better contain their excitement. Their poker faces weren't shit.

"Mama! Mama! Wait until you see it. He is so cool," they squealed in unison.

"What are you talking about?" she questioned, wondering what or whom I was bringing into our home.

"So much for the concept of surprise. You two are worse than Paul Revere," I said, fully knowing my kindergartners' knowledge of history was limited and my reference would be lost on them.

"Cameron, why?" Karen questioned me, staring at the black and mahogany bundle of fur I carried in my arms.

"I guess the better question is, why not? I could afford it. The price was right. The boys could learn responsibility and one day this little German fellow will protect not only my property, but also the three things I cherish the most on this planet, excluding Irene," I proclaimed, putting the Rottweiler pup down on the floor. Of course my new canine companion promptly walked over to Karen, wagging his nub of a tail and piddled in excitement to meet her.

"Martin, go get me some tissue to clean up this floor."

When she glared at me, I looked at her with apologetic eyes.

"Cameron, for the life of me I don't know why you wanted to add more responsibility to me. You are not someone who needs a pet. You're a working road comedian. You don't need a fish to fend for," she replied, then looked at my mama for assistance.

I was pleased that Irene just shrugged, not coming to Karen's aid.

They knew my impulsive nature. I didn't see why my being on the road should be an obstacle.

"So what's this little piss puff's name?" she asked me as she fended for herself against the puppy's tongue attack.

I had been simply calling him 'dog.' When I suggested that was his name, all in the house vetoed it. The twins thought Spot was a good name. Karen balked at that.

"If it was a Dalmatian, maybe. But isn't this one of those demon dogs from that movie?" she questioned.

"Yep. From the Omen, but it doesn't want to invite an evil mojo into our home. What do y'all think about Pacino?" I asked the household.

The twins called to him by that name and he followed them running around the house.

"Well, I guess that settles it," Karen said, shaking her head.

"Between you and me, they could've yelled out Benji or Lassie and he would have responded. You better be glad I raised them on Scarface and the Godfather and not Walt Disney."

Cortney Gee

CHAPTER 15

"Just what do you mean, the money is gone?" I asked Lance, who was sitting in front of me at the North Hollywood Del Taco.

"Yo, hold it down," he replied, hoping that I wouldn't have everyone in the restaurant in our business.

I took a deep breath and composed myself.

"All right, explain to me what you mean, all the money is gone?" I asked in a hushed tone this time.

Lance explained that he had a habit of checking his account daily. It just made him feel good to hear that he had $450-thousand in spending power in his Merrill Lynch account. But then, last night when he phoned in to check on his nest egg, the recording informed him that his loot was gone.

"Have you checked your account lately?" he asked me.

To be honest, I saw no reason to be concerned with continually checking my funds. I had enough cash to let it just sit and not trip. Plus, Richard had been more than reliable. But while I was sitting there talking to Lance, I checked my account. I was heated when I discovered I had been fleeced as well.

"That rotten motherfucker!" was all I could say.

"Cameron, my man, we have been played." He slumped his shoulders.

"Best believe I'm not getting shut out on half a million without a fight. Have you talked to Sarafina?"

"Her phone is disconnected and last night till this morning, I staked out that broad's house and there was no movement," he told me.

"You do know they are in on this together? Richard would never make a move like this against us without her sanctioning it," I said to Lance, vexed that it was Saturday and we'd have to wait until Monday to confront Mr. Malone at his office.

If he was smart, he'd follow Sarafina's lead and get ghost. But something in the pit of my stomach told me Richard's arrogant ass would think we wouldn't dare come to his plush office and wreak havoc.

My appetite was ruined. I picked up my tray and slung my half-eaten burrito into the trash.

"Man, I can't eat this shit. I'm going over to the Big Easy and grab a stogie and a stiff drink. I would invite you, but I already know that ain't your steeze," I told him, needing something to calm my nerves.

"Yeah, ain't shit we can do now. But come first thing Monday, we are going to bring the ruckus to Merrill Lynch."

We agreed to meet at 9 am to go see Mr. Malone about our cash he had embezzled from us that we had embezzled from the Power Rangers.

***

Lance didn't have to pick me up, I was revved up and ready to go by 8 am. Instead of the smooth styling I would normally wear when visiting Richard's office, I was dressed for mayhem in an all-black hoodie, black jeans and a skullcap. The only thing missing from my outfit was a black glock, but since I possessed dynamite in my black hands I wasn't worried about being unarmed. I had a feeling that if needed, Lance would have me covered by bringing his gat, so all was well.

"Yo, Cameron," Lance said the moment I answered my phone. "Where you at, bruh? I'm in front of your house ready to go."

I informed Lance that I was already at Merrill Lynch and was ready to raise hell. He asked me to hold tight for ten minutes and not to spark shit without him. I assured him that I would stand pat until he arrived.

While I waited on him, I drank a Red Eye and finished off a half-smoked Henry Clay Rothschild.

When Lance showed up, I was already deep into character. I was mad about my cash and I had conjured up my dark side to deal with the situation at hand.

"Nigga look at you, dressed up like a boy in the hood," Lance teased me.

"I figured this educated son of a bitch wouldn't respond to a smooth criminal, so I have my roughneck thing going, ya dig?" I replied as we stepped from the parking lot to enter the office.

"Good morning, Mr. Bernard and Mr. Brooks," Antoinette said hurriedly as we busted into the office and headed straight for Richard's door.

"Is Mr. Malone expecting you?" she tried to ask us as we barged past her.

Neither Lance nor I had time for her friendly shit.

"No bitch, I don't want no coffee nor tea or fucking water. I came about my bread and if Richard don't have the right answers, I'm going to roast his ass," I barked at the stunned receptionist.

Tricky Dick was startled by our presence. Not so much that we were there about the paper, but he was shocked when we caught him powdering his nose from the line of yayo on his desk.

Since I was in goon gear, I felt the need to head our two-man brigade.

"Where the fuck is the money?" I collared and pulled Richard across his desk making the coke rail spread out all over the place.

"Oh my, God. Mr. Malone should I call the police?" asked Antoinette with a face full of fear.

Even though I still had him by the neck, Richard said, "No Antoinette, that won't be necessary. These gentlemen are just concerned about some investments. Everything is fine."

"Yeah, Antoinette, everything is cool. We're just here to collect a substantial return on our investment," Lance told her, showing all of his thirty-twos.

His calm played ying to my man-in-black-bad-motherfucker yang. Figuring I had Richard's undivided attention, I released my grip and allowed him to sit back down. With everyone in our seats, Richard tried his best to bring things back to some semblance of normalcy.

Still standing at the door, Antoinette stuttered, "May I offer you gentlemen something to drink?"

Before Richard could say anything, Lance spoke, "As you can see, my friend here has had his share of coffee. How about you bring us some orange juice, sunshine?" Lance told her smoothly, which only made me seem more menacing.

After Antoinette left to go get the refreshments, I looked over at Richard. My snatching his grimy ass up ruined any high he would have had from the blow.

"I'm sure you guys are wondering why your accounts are empty," he said, straightening his clothes and tie.

"Damn right, and you better have a keystroke on a computer to make it reappear or I can't say that this is going to be a good business day at Merrill Lynch." Lance lifted up his shirt, making sure Richard saw his weapon.

Truth be told, I didn't think Lance had it in him to pull a trigger, but with this kind of cash at stake gunplay might have been behind curtain number two for our broker.

He held up his hands like he was surrendering.

"I swear I can clear this up. That bitch, Sarafina, played me like a tune. She told me to put all the money in her account because all of you were on the run." He turned toward his computer, spit, and then began typing at breakneck speed making sure to reverse the transaction.

"So it seems that we are out of business, Richard." I said, reasoning Sarafina was in the wind never to return. She especially wouldn't come back to complain about us recouping loot that she'd attempted to steal from us.

Richard nodded, stopped typing and then pulled out a huge checkbook binder from one of his desk drawers.

When he began to write out a check, Lance asked, "Man, are you high or retarded?"

"Richard, we aren't walking out of here with no fucking checks," I told him with an intimidating look on my face.

"Do what you have to do about cashing us out."

"Of course you wouldn't. Give me some time; I'll have our account specialist get it together."

Antoinette returned with our drinks. I was surprised she didn't have the police in tow.

"Antoinette, please have Mr. Rickleman settle up these gentlemen's accounts. Sadly, they'll be taking their business elsewhere," he told her.

It appeared that Antoinette was no stranger to irate customers and Cameron figured clients were constantly complaining about how a broker had mishandled their funds. But Cameron also figured that never had she witnessed a scene like the one they had just played out.

She whisked away to get Mr. Rickleman on the job of taking care of me and Lance. We sat patiently for about 45 minutes until the account specialist returned with our money. Richard couldn't have been happier to see us leave. As we departed, we both tossed Antoinette a thousand dollars as a gesture of gratitude for not calling the fuzz.

CHAPTER 16

I wish you would reconsider staying at least until Christmas," I told my mother as we motored through traffic headed toward the airport.

"There's nothing to reconsider, Cameron, I've been here long enough," Irene replied after cracking the window and lighting a Salem cigarette.

I knew not to say anything about my mother and her beloved cancer sticks. I mean, I would have had some nerve to talk seeing that I derived such pleasure from cigars.

But Karen and my mother -- they had butted heads one too many times about my mother smoking in the house. Both of them had valid points: Karen's being that she didn't want the twins subjected to secondhand smoke, and Irene thinking she was too grown to be told what to do by somebody I hadn't even married. I thought to step in and settle the argument, but realized I wasn't going to be able to satisfy either of their needs for me to be completely on their side. So I kept quiet about it. My silence, of course, pissed both of them off with me. Karen wanted her gone and Irene didn't want to stay another day. There had been a cold war going on while the twins and I watched.

It seemed that subject was on my mother's mind, too.

"Why didn't you speak up for me? You're the man of the house and I'm your mother," she inquired after taking a long drag on her cigarette.

"I did, but you see how things are. Of course I'm the man, but even I'm not allowed to smoke in a house I paid for," I said trying to reason with her.

"Never mind; it's not your fault and that's why I'm going to my own place, where I can do whatever the fuck I want to!" she exclaimed.

"Mr. Durham said they're almost completely done working on the house. I'm hoping you enjoy it," I said trying to change the subject.

"Yeah, Fannie told me it's to die for. You know you really didn't have to spend all that money on my house. I was happy the way it was."

"Well, it would make me happy if you dig the way it is now. It's not like Mr. Durham is going to take back the Jacuzzi."

She was appreciative. Irene was just giving me the business because I had been neutral concerning her confrontation with Karen. And, I knew that when I got home there was going to be hell to pay there as well.

Other than the fight with Karen, my mother had enjoyed herself. It was fun showing her around the city. It wasn't like this was her first time in LA, but it was her first time with me as a tour guide. Being an entertainer and having some powerful connections in the business was a benefit I fully exploited while my mom was in town. Lisa virtually kidnapped her on a few occasions and had taken her to live studio tapings of the *Price is Right* and Thea Vidale's show on ABC. Irene thought Lisa's vision for my career was wise and I should put more trust and effort into trying to get my own sitcom on the air.

"Are you hungry?" I asked my mom as we neared the airport.

"No, not really; I just want to get on this plane and get home."

"You act like you have someone waiting on you," I said with a raised eyebrow.

"And if I did what business would that be of yours? Don't forget Mr. Cameron who the most grown grown-up is in this car."

We pulled into LAX's short-term parking. I grabbed her luggage and we headed over to the skycap. The diminutive Asian man strained to lift the largest of the three bags.

"You must be smuggling a body in this one," he chided.

"No, I buried the body, that's probably the saw and ax I used to dismember it that you're feeling," she replied with a deadpan look, proving that my quick wit came from her side of the family.

The skycap didn't know whether or not to take her seriously and I guess he figured that it was in his best interest to flash her a fake smile and hope for a generous tip. After he checked her in and marked her luggage as heavy baggage, I didn't disappoint when I slid him a twenty-dollar bill.

"You know you can't be saying crazy things at the airport, Mom. You could see blood drain from that cat's face."

"Ah he was all right; poor little thing couldn't even lift the luggage. I'm so blessed to have a big strong son like you," she said, trying to butter me up.

"Yes, you are blessed to have me. So who's going to help you with these bags when you land in Cleveland?" I asked.

"Wouldn't you like to know?"

"Yes, I would."

"Damn, you want to know who is carrying my luggage, using the new Jacuzzi and driving my Cadillac. Questions, questions, and more questions," she ranted as we walked through security and headed toward her departing gate.

"Look Ma, I'm serious. Are you seeing someone?"

She stopped dead in her tracks.

"Okay, I'm going to tell you this once and I don't want to hear no more talk of it." She paused for only a moment. "I am seeing someone casually. We go out, we watch movies, we dance, we dine and sometimes..."

Before she said anything else, I interjected, "Ma, okay I don't need the gory details. I think I get it."

"I mean really, Cameron, I was faithful and loving toward your father until he left us, God rest his soul. But he left me alone in this world and I have needs just like everyone else."

I felt kinda fucked up about how immaturely I was handling the thought of my mother dating, so I dropped the third degree.

"Okay, I'm going to allow you to see this who-ever-it-is, but I don't need any little brothers or sisters, you hear me?" I told her, only half-jokingly.

We got past the whom she was dating conversation. I even asked her to please accept my apology for not choosing a side in her bickering with Karen.

"Baby, it wasn't you. Two cats can't live in the same house for too long before the claws come out."

The desk agent started calling for passengers in the first-class cabin to board.

"I'm so proud of you. I love you so much," she told me as we hugged goodbye.

"I know, I love you too," I said, kissing her cheek. "Call me as soon as you get to the house; I can't wait for you to tell me how much you like the improvements."

She promised that she would and told me to kiss her grand babies one more time for her. My mother walked into the jet way and exited from my view.

I turned away, but I had a hunger pain that refused to continue being ignored. Since I was by the airport, I figured I'd call Anna and see if she cared to join me for a bite to eat. I was sure she wasn't happy that I'd been scarce for the last few months, but business and family had to come first.

I dialed her number and when she answered the phone, I said, "Hey, mami, what you doing?" as if shit wasn't wrong between us.

"Well if it isn't the man that used to love him some me. I'm about to make a run. Why, what's up?"

"Oh nothing, I was just in a neighborhood and I was hoping we could do lunch. But if you're busy, I understand," I said, ignoring the first part of her statement.

"Can I get a rain check?"

"No doubt, I'll be free most of the week. Let me know what's good for you."

She agreed that later in the week would be cool and rushed off the phone. I had to understand her not feeling me, but even in my understanding I wasn't happy that she didn't seem excited over the possibility of us spending some time together. It wasn't like I had popped out of the blue asking for some ass, even though I wanted to. Karen had drawn a picket line in our bedroom since her and my mom had been arguing, so I was definitely in the need; but I hadn't come at

Anna with my thirst. I just wanted to be in her company over a meal. Of course I would have liked some ass *after* the meal, but that was a whole 'nother something.

With Anna shutting me down, I called Lisa to see what she had brewing.

"Hey you, what's up?" I asked her.

"Oh, nothing much, just making some phone calls to get you some work and me some commission."

"Really? Would you care to tell me about it over lunch?"

"Cameron, I'm way too busy to leave the office, and plus I brought my lunch today."

Damn, within a matter of minutes I had been shut down by two women.

"Well, call me when things calm down and tell me what you come up with. I could stand some road work right about now."

"Okay, and why are you so hell bent on hitting the road? Is there trouble in paradise?"

"You've met Karen and my mother. There was no way you missed the oil and water mixture I had going on in my home."

She laughed. "You have a point there. Right now I don't have any road gigs lined up, but I have a lead on a warm up gig if you're interested."

"You mean being in front of a studio audience and keeping them entertained between takes?"

"Cameron, before you shoot it down, know that it pays fifteen hundred dollars a day. That's great stay-in-town cash. Plus, you get a bird's eye view of how sitcoms work. That way when we get yours on the air, you will have a better feel for the environment.

I couldn't deny that after Sarafina tried to fuck us and I had to kiss the Power Ranger steady funds goodbye, I was looking to have a different kind of steady money coming in. It wasn't like I was broke, hell I was far from that. But if you don't have income, everything is all outcome.

"Okay, cool. I'll also call some promoters I've worked for in the past and see if they have anything poppin'."

"Cameron, for the life of me I don't know why you don't let me handle all of that and you just concentrate on your craft."

"You know I'm a busy body and don't worry, I'll still pay you your percentage."

"That's not what I'm worried about. You've been great, but managers manage and talent shouldn't be hampered with the task of finding their own work."

I agreed to do a better job of handing over the full reins of my business. We ended the call and I found myself still hungry and still eating alone. Fuck!

CHAPTER 17

Cameron, I have some good news and some bad news. Which do you want first?" asked Lisa over the phone line.

I always wondered why people found it necessary to inquire which news you wanted first instead of just dropping the bomb, then giving you some hope in its aftermath.

"Give me the bad news first," I said, bracing myself for whatever she was about to lay on me.

"Well, I talked to the producers of BET *ComicView* and they aren't going to let you perform this season."

"Why? What did I do? I mean I haven't fucked anyone over at the network. This is so fucked up. You know I use *Comicview* as a commercial for my fans and promoters to see that I have fresh material," I stated, pacing back and forth.

Lisa sensed I was about to go off the deep end so she interrupted my tirade.

"Cameron, don't you have any interest in the good news I have to share with you?"

I was really tripping. I needed to do a breathing exercise to keep from passing out before I could refocus on the conversation.

"Yes, please, do tell me the light at the end of the tunnel isn't a train."

"The reason why you aren't going to be on the show this season is because they've hired you as a staff writer for *The BlackBerry Inn*."

I didn't know how to process the information she had provided. I mean sure, it was great that I had landed my first writing gig in Hollywood. But on the other hand, I knew on-staff writing was a job and I was allergic to employment. One of my inhibitions about working was that folks expected you to be somewhere every day at the same time. My being an artist and one who was sitting on a considerable lump of cash wouldn't lend me to being barked at.

"Well, that is some good news, good news indeed. I'll get the opportunity to sharpen my writing skills. So just how much is this good news going to be paying?" I asked, eager to hear how much my bondage was worth.

"Well, Curtis Gadson offered us two thousand dollars a week, but I mentioned to him that you were going to gripe about not appearing on the show and he counter-offered twenty-five hundred dollars a week and your very own thirty-minute comedy special on the network."

"And you wonder why I let you handle the negotiations," I chided. "My dumb ass would have settled for the two g's a week."

"No, to be honest, Cameron, I think we both know why you chose to work with me."

"And what might that be?"

"Well one, because I'm a hungry go-getter who knows how to maneuver in a tank filled with sharks and two, I'm a white girl who's not intimidated by black business."

I admitted that she was correct. If I was going to succeed in the business I needed someone who didn't see things out of the same set of eyes as mine.

Lisa fit the bill perfectly, plus she was cool as fuck to boot.

"Sounds to me like you have Hollywood's newest staff writer in your stable. Congrats, Ms. Noonan."

"Congrats to you, Cameron. It was your unique sense of humor that got you hired. I just brokered the deal. You have a meeting with Curtis Gadson at BET after the Tyson fight, don't forget it."

I got off the phone with Lisa, then I called out in the house to Karen and informed her and the boys of my new opportunity. We all got dressed up and went to Spago's in Hollywood to celebrate. After a long wait to be seated, we enjoyed an incredible meal. Karen had the California Wild King Salmon. I dined on the Grilled Dry-Aged New York Steak and for the boys we kept it simple, they had grilled prime beef burgers with aged cheddar and smoked bacon. After we finished dining and were headed home, I received a call from Lance the Great.

"What up, Lance, what it do?"

"Shit is cool, but it's complicated. Can you meet me in an hour?"

I told him that I had to drop Karen and the boys off first but I could make myself available.

"Well drop them off and meet me at the crib."

I told him that I would be there, but from the looks of things the 101 heading east was jammed, so he needed to give me some leeway.

Karen wasn't feeling the out-of-nowhere need for me to meet Lance and thought I was up to some sneaky shit.

"So are you going to be long or are you coming right back?" she asked suspiciously.

"I don't know, Lance didn't say what he wanted, but whatever it is, he didn't want to discuss it over the line. You know how paranoid his ass can be."

She wasn't happy that I was calling a premature ending to our celebration. From her attitude all evening, I deducted that the picket line in our bedroom had fallen down and the pussy had been set free. The thought of me having to wait to be dipping into her dark depths frustrated me. That nigga Lance had no idea how good a friend I was to be leaving those promises to see what he needed.

After I dropped my family off and promised Karen that I'd be back as soon as I could, I dashed over to Lance's upscale condo. He buzzed me in and I parked in the visitor's section of the lot. They didn't play at his complex. If you fucked around and parked in an owner's spot, they would tow your shit with no remorse.

I took the elevator up to the ninth floor, exited, and walked down the hallway to Lance's door, 9G. I noticed it was slightly open, which was peculiar seeing that Lance was paranoid to a point leaning toward lunacy.

I rapped on the door and announced myself. "Hey Lance, it's me, Cameron, pimp. Is everything cool?"

"Nah shit ain't right, but we gonna make it right," I heard Lance speak from the dining room.

I walked into the door and was surprised to find Lance's crib in complete disarray. There was women's clothing flung all over. Something had to be wrong because not only was my friend paranoid, but he was a clean freak that suffered from OCD.

As I journeyed further inside, I witnessed Lance doing something that shook me. He was sitting in a chair, knocking back slugs of vodka with his gat on his lap.

"What the fuck are you doing?" I asked, without taking my eye off of him or the weapon.

"I'm having a celebration drink, what the fuck does it look like I'm doing?" he replied sarcastically.

I just stood there before him in silence, knowing shit was bad because Lance never ever, never ever drank.

"Lance what's wrong, bruh? Why are Gwen's things all over the floor?" I asked him.

But he just sat there, spaced out, neither here nor there with one hand on his drink and the other hovering near his gun. I walked slowly toward him making sure not to make any sudden movements that might startle him into a defensive reaction.

"Lance, where is Gwen?"

He looked up from his drink and then poured some liquor into an empty glass on the dining room table.

"You gonna make me drink alone or are you gonna join your boy?"

"No brother, I'm good. Where's Gwen, Lance?" I asked him, more focused on what was going down than on a drink.

"She's in the bedroom." He paused and gave me a cold stare. "I think you better have that drink, Cameron."

The way he said it, I knew Gwen's condition wasn't for sober eyes. I lifted the glass filled with Skyy vodka and asked him what we were toasting to.

"You being a man of your word, that's what the fuck we're toasting!"

"No doubt, son, my word is bond," I told my friend who had kept me off the back of a fruit truck and gave me entrance into a world of thievery.

"Yeah, my man, Cameron, my nigga. So your word is bond, I heard that shit."

Then suddenly, he stood.

"Come with me," he said, walking toward the bedroom.

I figured that I would see Gwen's swollen face from an ass whuppin', but instead I saw a vision that made me weak in my knees and threatened to make the drink I had just consumed come back up.

Gwen was laying in the bed, lifeless. Her limp body was slung on her back and her eyes were locked in an eternal stare upward.

"I had some questions that needed to be answered and she refused to cooperate," he said like he hadn't committed hell felony number one.

"Lance, what the fuck do you mean you needed answers? Was whatever the fuck you just had to know worth her life?" I was horrified.

"Look, Cameron, I ain't doing all this hustling, putting me at risk for felony charges just to have some bitch, no matter how fine she was, steal from me."

I couldn't believe my eyes or my ears.

"Nigga, how much money could she have taken to deserve to be slumped?"

"It could have been a dollar and that would have made it justifiable, dog. I was going to marry this worthless lump you're looking at."

I slammed my fist into the wall. I felt like I was in the middle of some bad movie. "How much, dammit?"

"Three hundred thousand dollars. Not all at once, but she had been piecing me off. I thought my shit was short but I tried to give her the benefit of the doubt."

"Damn."

I paused and stared at her body for a moment.

"So, what are you going to do?"

"Fuck you mean, what am I gonna do? You mean what are *we* gonna do?"

Shit, I knew one day my big mouth, word-is-bond ass was going to write a check I couldn't cash. But you could have never told me a promise would have me as an accomplice to murder, or at the least, involved in the criminal disposal of a corpse.

"Lance, I know I owe you man, but this goes against some ten-commandment type shit, bruh."

"And coveting your neighbor's bitch ain't?" he replied, effectively destroying any doubt that he was oblivious to Gwen's and my tryst in Vegas.

What he said paralyzed me internally but instead of showing my fear I fronted with bravado.

" So what you want me to do? Apologize? Because I can do that. What you wanna kill me, too? Just know I ain't nobody's bitch and I'm gonna fight for my life!" I spat at him, not knowing where this massive rush of courage was coming from inside of me.

He shook his head.

"Cameron, you're my brother; I would never step to you about no broad, man. I set myself up for the shit that went on in Vegas. I knew Gwen was hot for Anna. If I wasn't so preoccupied with fucking Terri, I would have hipped you to it." He looked at the dead body sprawled across his bed.

With the chance of Lance retaliating against me diminished, I asked him what he had in mind about what he would do with Gwen's body. I was open to helping him, but I wasn't about to be party to no gory dismemberment.

"First, we need to clean up my shit in here."

He put his gun down, then began rolling his fiancé into the comforter.

I watched as he finished that task, then started bagging all traces of her being in his home. I just stood there; I had seen enough *America Justice* on TV to know I didn't need to be touching anything. DNA had a funny way of showing up from simple shit like dropping sweat from a brow. And since I was sweating like a motherfucker, I was probably leaving a plethora of evidence for the authorities to find.

"Here, put these on with your scary ass. You sure are shedding that goon swag you displayed a minute ago," Lance taunted as he finally turned to me and gave me some gloves.

That jab pissed me off, especially since I was way outside of my hook-up helping him cover up his animalistic way of dealing with a problematic relationship. I was cool with helping him sanitize his crib, but I was drawing the line when it came to touching Gwen's rigid body. I had already enjoyed it when it was warm and full of desire. It would have been pure sacrilege to touch her in the state she would be in for eternity.

After an hour of making sure that Lance's condo was spotless, I asked him what our next move was.

"We're going to take her to the marina, put her on my boat and Gwen will be sleeping with the fishes."

"Okay, so just how are we supposed to do this because I'm not touching her?"

"I'm going to put Gwen in her truck, you're going to follow me in my Porsche. We'll dump her and then I'll leave her truck in South Central."

Though this was no laughing matter, I couldn't stop laughing. This fool had concocted a plan that sounded like a fucked-up Lifetime Channel script and I was following his lead like Lance's plan didn't have holes in it.

"Okay, just so I got this shit right, you intend to take that dead body on the elevator of a well-secured and heavily populated condominium community, wrapped in a comforter. Then, dump the body into the back of an Expedition, drive to Marina Del Rey, get on a boat in the middle of the night, hope by coincidence that a hungry great white shark has the munchies enough to devour all of that dead ass that Gwen has. Then after all of that having to go right, we drop off her truck in Watts and hope a Blood or a Crip takes it?"

He grinned. "Yeah genius, ain't it?"

"Only if we don't get caught it is, but if not, we are going to be viewed as the dumbest inmates in Folsom."

Lance tried his best to convince me not to worry, like he had done this shit before. I mean, he really said the shit like it was going to be a walk in the park or better yet a romp in the ocean.

The biggest hole I saw in the plan was that fucking elevator. The probability of someone happening upon us as we removed a corpse was too high for me to just brush off. Luckily, I was able to convince him to take the stairs. If this fool hadn't helped me touch my first million dollars and taught me the game, I would have given him the peace sign minus one finger and bounced. My dumb ass knew better, but I had made an oath so I helped.

Much to my surprise, everything went off without a hitch. I was amazed how emotionless Lance was toward the remains of the woman he supposedly loved. He was so cold that before he tossed her overboard, Lance removed the huge diamond ring he had given her.

After he tossed Gwen and her car away, we headed back to his spot. It was getting late and I knew Karen would be worried so I called her.

"I had to make a run with Lance, baby. I shouldn't be much longer. You need me to bring you back anything?"

"No just bring your ass home," she demanded, satisfied I wasn't out whoring around but still impatient with my absence.

I thought about trying to catch up with Anna being that I was on her side of town, but seeing that I had put enough bad in my karma bank, it was best that I went home.

When we returned to Lance's spot, he pulled his car up next to mine. I lit a cigar to calm my nerves. After puffing a huge plume of smoke, I broke the silence between us.

"Now you know if you get pinched, this is your load to carry, right?"

"Yeah, I feel you," he replied in a listless manner.

"If I was you, I would get conveniently lost somewhere, as far away from this crime scene, ya dig?"

"Yeah, I was thinking of going to Vegas."

"Vegas? Motherfucker I said as far away from here as possible. Venice might be an option but Vegas? You have to be fucking kidding me. There is no way your flamboyant ass can be low key in Sin City."

"You might have a point there," he replied, knowing I was right.

I took another long pull on my MonteCristo #2, got out of his Porsche and opened the door to my Jaguar. As I was about to sit in my seat, I turned and said to Lance with all the seriousness I could muster up, "Oh yeah, and we are even!"

Lance nodded, but I didn't feel he completely agreed with me.

"Say it, we are even," I demanded.

"Yeah no doubt, we are even, blood."

I sat in the car, slammed the door, and cranked up The Wu Tang Clan's "C.R.E.A.M."

Just as I was pulling off, Lance asked, "Hey Cameron, you looking to own some real estate and a few new toys?"

"It depends on what you're offering and how much it's going to set me back."

"Obviously for me to disappear, I can't take none of this shit with me. I'm talking about the condo, the cars and the boat. I'm asking for two hundred thousand and I'll turn over the deed and the titles."

With those words, now I was sure he saw my point about doing a ghost move. I told him that I was down.

"Let's link tomorrow and settle up."

Pulling off, I was already missing dude, but I couldn't wait to get him that cash and seeing his ass off into the wind.

CHAPTER 18

My sleep had been disrupted by nightmares starring Gwen on several occasions. Today's subconscious feature film was a perverse dream of me making love to her cold corpse while her lifeless eyes stared holes into me. Nothing like nocturnal necrophilia to cause you to wake in a cold sweat.

My rustling in the bed woke Karen.

"Baby, are you okay?" she asked, snuggling up to me, pressing her warm chocolate body into mine.

"Yeah, I'm fine, it was just a bad dream," I told her, hoping she would fall back asleep.

"You wanna talk about it?"

I paused. "Nah it was stupid really. Now that I think about it, I don't remember what it was about." I kissed her on the forehead. In no time she was back asleep and I laid in the bed staring at the ceiling. I feared going back to sleep, there was no need for a sequel. So I just stayed there and thought about how overjoyed I was that Lance had taken my advice one month ago and got ghost.

I had no idea where he was and it was best that I didn't. The only problem was I didn't have anyone to discuss the guilt I had about my involvement in the crime. It didn't take a rocket scientist to know that the people who got caught were those who ran their mouths about their illegal activities. I was hoping Lance was following the same code that I was... loose lips sink ships. I stared at the ceiling until I fell back asleep, praying that Gwen wouldn't make a reappearance.

When I awoke, the house was quiet. Karen was off to work, the twins were off to school, and I was left alone to handle whatever business I had. I checked my emails and saw that Brian Mouton had left me a message concerning an upcoming date and wanted to know if I was available. I was surprised he contacted me via email, but then it dawned on me that he was used to hiring me through my old management. I called the number he left and Brian answered on the second ring.

"Cool Mou Promotions, how can I help you?" he said like he had an entire staff working for him.

"Nigga, do you still live in your grandma's house?" I chided him.

"Who the fuck is this?"

"So quick to ditch your professionalism, Brian, I'm surprised. It's Cameron, brother, I received your email, wassup?"

"Cameron B, my nigga, if you don't get no bigger. I heard that you and Tony weren't working together anymore, but I still wanted to pull your coattail and let you know I had a three-day run up here in Da Town. You open?"

"I saw the dates you offered and I'm good to go. I could stand to bask in the loveliness of the 510 and 405. You still paying a nickel a night or did I get lucky and your stingy ass has bumped up the budgets?"

"I'm still paying five hundred a night, but I would think with the added amenity of Tasha's ass thrown into the mix, you won't be complaining," he said, knowing my saying that I needed a Northern Cali excursion really meant that I wanted to hook up with my half-black half-Japanese side piece. We shared an on and off again relationship that was magically activated whenever my comedic career found me in the Bay Area.

Brian informed me that he had been trying to get in touch with Lance to no avail and asked me had I heard from him.

"Nah man, I haven't heard from dude, but check it, if you need someone else on the bill how about you book Marc Howard?"

Marc was another DC product who had come to LA pursuing the dream of hitting the big time. He was the polar opposite of Lance. Where The Great One wouldn't be caught dead without being casket clean, Marc was happy and most comfortable onstage clad in blue jeans, Nikes, and a jersey. He was still signed to my old management, but that didn't get in the way of me occasionally throwing some cash his way. There was a time when Lance and I considered Marc as someone we might add to our fraudulent fraternity, but we decided against it because he was so square.

"Cool," Brian said, "tell him that it's three hundred a night flight and hotel." He had saved two hundred dollars by hiring a lesser-known talent than Lance.

"All right, well lock my number in and if anything changes let me know."

"Oh dude, as far as I'm concerned, we solid. I'm going to start promoting the shows and don't worry, you're going to dig the spots," he told me before hanging up.

After finishing the conversation with Brian, I immediately contacted Lisa to inform her of the booking.

"Cameron, I wish you would let me handle things."

I could tell she was exasperated.

"Here it is I'm getting ten percent of a fee I didn't negotiate."

I reasoned with her that I had handled dealing with Mouton because he was much more like family than a promoter. As a gesture of apology, I offered to bring over her commission instead of making her wait until after the gig.

"It's fine, I can wait until after you have made it. But I thank you for the offer, it's very noble of you."

Again I promised to do a better job of letting her handle my comedy business and disconnected the call. After talking to Lisa, I had to contact Marc to see if he could actually do the gig. When I got him on the line, he let me know that the Oakland gig couldn't have come at a better time.

"Man, I would have been staring down an eviction notice if you hadn't thrown this my way, good looking out."

"It's all good, man, just make sure to clear this with Tony and get him his due. I don't need any flack for bypassing him," I told him to avoid the wrath of my ex manager.

A week later on a Thursday morning, Marc and I found ourselves aboard Southwest Flight 254 headed to The Town. Oakland was the only city in California that reminded me of Cleveland. Where LA was Hollyweird and plastic, Oakland was Hollyhood and real. Our first show was going to be at Sweet Jimmy's, a nightclub infamous because of its player clientele and being featured in the black exploitation classic *The Mack*.

Mouton used the spot to gauge the abilities of the comedians he booked. If a comic could grasp the attention of the loud and bawdy crowd, the other two nights were a breeze.

On the flight, I kept reiterating to Marc how important it was for him to put his best foot forward at tonight's show. Even though I had proven myself under fire at Sweet Jimmy's

152

time and time again, I knew the audience wasn't to be taken for granted. Many a comedian had left that spot with their egos deflated and tails tucked.

We touched down at OAK and after debarking the 737, we made our way to baggage claim and retrieved our luggage. Marc ribbed me because of the large rolling suitcase I brought along.

"What are you doing? Running away from home?" Marc asked as he grabbed his gym bag off of the conveyor belt.

"No, unlike you I have outfits and matching reptilian accessories for each night. You might want to upgrade your wardrobe, pimpin', and then you could demand more money," I said already knowing he was feeling a certain kind of way about the difference in our pay.

"Fuck you, Cameron, the only reason why you're making more money is because you hooked up the gig," he fired back.

"No, Mr. Howard, I'm making more money because I command more money," I responded, knowing his competitive spirit would fire him up to perform at his best.

Truthfully, I wasn't trying to rub his face in shit. The fifteen hundred dollars I was being paid he could have had. I was still sitting on a small fortune. I was merely raising the bar so that he didn't give a half-hearted performance. I knew if he fucked around at Sweet Jimmy's, just going through the motions, Mouton would have no problem sending his ass home.

We gathered our things and headed outside. Brian was already standing beside a GMC Suburban. Brian Mouton stood out no matter where he was. Not only was he high yellow with curly red hair, courtesy of his creole heritage, but he was also 6'3, 245lbs and loud as fuck.

A sexy airport police officer was attempting to get him to

move the truck, but to no avail because he was too busy trying to invite her to one of the upcoming shows for her to get in a word.

"Yeah, tonight it's Sweet Jimmy's, tomorrow Mexicali Rose, and Saturday it's Geoffrey's Inner Circle," he told her.

"Well, my girl and I might just come through to Geoffrey's, but we ain't even about to be at Jimmy's tonight being sweated by men old enough to be our dads," she told him, looking over the flyer.

She was directing him to move the truck when Mouton spotted us. "There goes my comedians right there," he said, waving us down.

We introduced ourselves and put our things into the back of the SUV. Marc and I sat in the back because Mouton had a male passenger in the front.

"This is my man, TMB, he sponsored the flights and tellymo rooms."

"You two are some funny cats, it's my pleasure," he said, extending his balled-up fist giving us the pound.

Mouton looked into the rearview mirror and asked if we were hungry.

"Shit yeah, you know Southwest don't give a nigga nothing but peanuts and coke," Marc replied.

"Yeah, what do you have in mind?" I inquired.

"This is The Town, we got it all, it's your call," TMB chimed in.

"How about Everett and Jones? Their BBQ and sauce is da bomb," I said, looking at Marc.

"As long as they have beef or chicken that sounds cool," he told the two in the front.

"Oh yeah, Marc you're converting to Islam?" asked Mouton.

"I wouldn't say I'm converting, but I have been studying the Koran for about a year," Marc replied.

"Good, that means all the ribs and white women in the place I can claim without competition from you," I quipped.

The truck burst into laughter; even Marc couldn't help but to laugh at my swipe at his religious choice. Not that I was clowning Allah or Marc's seriousness about his faith. I just saw an in for a joke and I took full advantage.

We found a parking spot in front of Everett and Jones and had to wait a good fifteen minutes to be seated. You knew from that fact alone that this was no ordinary barbecue joint this was an upscale soul food factory. The patrons inside represented the multicultural community that made Oakland such a cool place to visit. Mouton was outside hustling off flyers about the comedy shows while we waited on our orders to be prepared. I had the mixed meat sampler with candied yams, collard greens, macaroni and cheese as side orders. I just knew that they must have had the last of government cheese in all of America.

TMB and Mouton ordered the same meals as mine while Marc ordered the BBQ chicken dinner. As soon as our lovely waitress, Ebony brought out our drinks, we all began complimenting her on her good looks. Though our entire table was being flirtatious, Marc seemed to have the inside track for her affection. She kept commenting on his green eyes and how much she had enjoyed his appearances on ComicView. When she left, Marc couldn't help the urge to pop his own collar.

"Don't hate because light skin is coming back in style."

"Whatever, she probably has a classroom charity assignment to flatter an endangered species or some shit," I said giving TMB a high five.

"Damn Cameron, that's cold. I'm with Marc, don't hate because she likes high yellow niggas."

"Ah Mou, that's high yella nigga, you didn't get no play either," I replied, causing TMB to send more dap my way.

Ebony brought out our meals and other than a few 'hand me the salts' and 'pass me the butters,' it was a quiet feast. After we finished eating, TMB footed the bill and I left Ebony a hefty tip. Mark swore up and down that I was flashing my bankroll to get her attention from him to me. He was right, but I didn't have a need for her on this trip. I was in hunt for someone with blended genetics.

Even though she'd given him her number, Marc talked about how much of a hater I was until we arrived at the Marriott. Brian and TMB told us what time we needed to be ready for transportation to the venue. Mou handed us our room keys and we got on the elevator. Marc said he needed to make a few phone calls. I was tired from the trip and the itis that I caught from that good food. I planned on crashing as soon as I got in the room.

I set the alarm for nine-fifteen, allowing myself plenty of time to wake up and get myself together for the show. I hoped that Gwen haunting my dreams again wouldn't disturb my rest.

I rested well and a few hours later, we pulled up to Sweet Jimmy's. Surprisingly, the place was jammed pack for a Thursday night. The crowd, which consisted mostly of old school playas and young chicks looking for a sugar daddy were seated in crushed velvet burgundy chairs popping bottles and anticipating the entertainment. Mouton hired the Bay Area's favorite master of ceremony, Daniel Dugar to host the show.

The female portion of the audience hung on every word he said. Not only was Dugar hella funny as a comedian, but he sported looks that rivaled a male model. At 6'2, 170 lbs. with chocolate brown skin, he served as the perfect maestro for the evening. The men respected his homegrown swagger and all the ladies were itching to be down.

Marc was the featured act, but there was another Oakland native who was in attendance and asked if she could perform a guest set. It would have been criminal to deny Luenell's bawdy ass a crack at the stage. Her raw in-your-face delivery and slurred speech, tempered by what I assumed were a few drinks in the parking lot, had the crowd in tears.

"Yo, just ride her wave and you're going to smash it," I told Marc after taking a swig from my double Jack. I suppose he had already figured that out, but suspected that seeing Ebony (our waitress) in the front row looking fiercely delicious might have distracted him.

Luenell had pummeled the audience with a fire set that made the crowd stand on their feet in ovation. Dugar had to calm down the crowd to even introduce Marc. Once they settled in, Dugar went on to give Marc an introduction that was worthy of a comic of a much higher profile, but the effect was what was needed to polarize the crowd. Marc pounced on stage clad in a Chester McGlockton number 91 Oakland Raider jersey and black jeans and went right to work. The gauntlet that I had presented to him, fueled him to show what he was made of. His material attacking cultural icons had the audience doubled over in laughter. After his allotted thirty minutes had expired, he exited the stage to thunderous applause.

"Now you ride that wave, homie," he told me with his ass on his shoulders.

I polished off my drink and ordered another from the lovely half-breed bartender, Tasha, whom I planned to thoroughly polish after the show. As I straightened my collar on my crisp white, French cuffed shirt and made sure my gun metal grey custom made suit hung properly on me, I asked her politely to bring it to me onstage.

"Marc, that was no wave; it was just a mere ripple in the water, playboy. Sit back, take notes and learn something."

Our friendly professional rivalry was in full effect but there was no bitterness between us, mostly we tried to push the other to excellence.

Dugar did a few jokes after Marc's set and got the crowd extra hyped with his ghetto superhero bit, My Nigga. He then introduced me to the audience.

"Ladies and Gentlemen, it's star time and you know how we do here at Sweet Jimmy's. Cool Mou Promotions brings you the best in urban entertainment every Thursday night and tonight we truly have one of the best in the game. You've seen him on *Def Comedy Jam*. He's a BET *ComicView* All Star, he plays colleges and concerts all over the world. All the way from Cleveland, Ohio give it up for Cameron B!"

I made my way through the cheering crowd to the stage where Dugar was awaiting to give me dap and exchange the microphone like a well-tuned relay teammate passes the baton. Tasha met me at the stage with my double jack neat and I started into a blistering set about how much I loved the Bay Area and its Midwest playa appeal. The retired pimps all cheered when I talked about macking and how Sweet Jimmy's was the only club in America where you could smack a bitch and the first question asked would be what the fuck did she do?

I riffed about now and later flavored gators and sugar daddies tricking for about thirty minutes. The audience was eating it up, laughing loudly and slapping the tables in amusement. I took a few sips from my drink so that they could compose themselves. Then a complete silence came upon the room when a medium size mature black man with too young voluptuous blondes sat down at the lone reserved table in front that had remained empty throughout the show. I recognized the gentleman immediately and realized why the crowd was so in awe of him.

Before me sat Ike Turner, R&B royalty with a look on his face that screamed 'entertain me'. Immediately, I switched gears and did my Laurence Fishburne impersonation.

"Now, now look I, I, I done kicked that narcotic, Anna Mae."

Mr. Turner roared out in guttural laughter that filled the room, giving everyone the cue that all was good and they followed suit. The rest of my set was dedicated to drinking, fucking and other mindless debasements, just what the crowd wanted. By the time I wrapped it up, the entire room, including Ike and his blonde companions, were on their feet as I took a bow and exited the stage.

"Fuck your wave, how you dig that tsunami, nigga?" I asked Marc as I stepped up to him at the bar.

"That shit was tight, Cameron. I'll be gunning for you tomorrow, trust and believe" he replied before going into conversation with Ebony who was dressed in a leopard cat suit with a black blazer and black pumps. If I didn't know why Marc had pushed up so hard to her before, I damn sure understood now. Her fat monkey was poking out making her crotch look like a huge camel toe. I considered challenging

Marc for her attention, but the opportunity of spending the evening with Tasha held too much promise. So instead of pissing him off by sliding up to his companion, I let him win. Letting him win wasn't a bad thing. I knew by morning I would receive his play by play and know her vicariously through his conquest.

We signed autographs and mingled with the crowd while the staff removed the tables and chairs to transform the area to a dance floor. Marc and Ebony went to dance while I sat at the bar talking to Mouton.

"Damn, Cameron, that was a banging set. Word is going to get around town and folks will be piling into Mexicali Rose tomorrow," he told me.

"Thanks, man, I was just doing what I do. Ike Turner walking into the place with those big breasted white girls was bananas!" I replied.

"Yeah, I didn't know if he was going to laugh or kill you when you did that impression," he replied, referring to the tense moment before the huge roar of laughter after I poked fun at the Rock and Roll Hall of Famer. "But on some other shit, Cameron, my man TMB has the hook on flights, he thought you might be interested in doing business with him. It's sweet, two hundred dollars for coach class and five hundred for first class roundtrip."

"Damn, you can't beat that with a bat. I wish I would have known that when I flew my moms out here awhile back. Is that price good for anywhere?" I inquired as TMB rolled up with the take from the door.

"Yep the price is the same across the board, ain't that right, Beezie?"

"No doubt; if you wanna go somewhere just give me a call." He handed me his card.

They had an excellent night at the door and were in good spirits when it came time to break bread. I wasn't pressed to take the loot, so I told TMB to just keep it and put it toward my first class trip when I buzzed him.

"Damn, this nigga Cameron on some big willy shit. Normally you be hounding a motherfucker about your scratch."

"Nah, Mouton, I'm not trying to be a baller, man. I just hit a big lick in Las Vegas and got a job writing for BET so I can afford to pay for TMB's services in advance. You say your man is slick with the flights and I'm tired of riding coach. It's a perfect arrangement the way I see it."

"Oh, I got you. I like the way you get down. Mou said you was cool and because you handling me with trust, this five hundred gets you two-for-one first class."

Mouton ordered another round of drinks that Tasha was more than happy to serve us. When she brought me mine, she inquired if we were still on to hang afterward or had she been upgraded.

"I'm hungry, sweetie; if you want you are more than welcome to come along and cum afterward."

"Cameron Bernard, don't act like you don't know what comes after that, over and over again," she replied before she walked away to handle other club patrons.

I have to admit she was right; an evening with Tasha consisted of fucking, sucking, groaning, moaning and good sleep.

"Cameron, you still getting all up Tasha's sushi? Damn, you been hitting that since your first show in the bay," Mouton said.

"Well, what can I say? She commands a repeat performance."

"Well, it's best you get her out of the way tonight. Tomorrow night and Saturday there's going to be some high-class breezies at The Rose and Geoffrey's. Believe me, you aren't going to want to be bogged down with old news."

I felt him but it wasn't like Tasha was some ratty hood chick that every dude in town had a story about even if they were lying. She kept it tight, fresh, and didn't bug me about my life in LA. All she demanded was that I was respectful of her while I was in her midst. I didn't know how I was always blessed with side-pieces who knew how to play their positions, but I was thankful for it. It was my belief that my honesty upfront didn't leave room for grumbling. I made it a point to always inform women about Karen and my two sons and that I had no intention of leaving. This truth made it impossible to build false hope and I made it a point to never make promises I knew I couldn't keep.

The cool thing about Tasha was that most chicks dug her. The ones who didn't were only hating on her Japanese heritage. That hate would only cause Tasha's black side to rear up to check them. Needless to say, we rarely had any problems when we were out together.

We practically closed the joint down, shooting the shit at the bar with Dugar and Luenell while I waited for Tasha to end her shift. Marc and Ebony had long gone off to the hotel after he received his pay. I figured by now he was knee deep in her guts or begging his ass off to be doing so.

Mouton and TMB had met a couple of honeys and invited them to join us for breakfast at The Denny's in Emeryville. Tasha cashed out and all of us left to feed the liquor we had consumed.

The all-night eatery was busy, but there was still more than enough room to seat our party of eight. We ordered our food, waited for it to come out, and then smashed it when it arrived at the table. Right when we about to leave, we were forced to remain inside while Oakland's finest administered some 'act right' to two rowdy customers. The Taser therapy we witnessed was enough to end the late night laughs; we were all ready to bounce.

"Cameron, do you ever think of doing anything else besides comedy?" Tasha asked as she drove me back to the Marriott in her Volkswagen Jetta.

"Well, of course I'm focused on being the best comedian I can possibly be, but I do have other interests I've been pursuing like writing short stories and screenplays. As a matter of fact, I have just been hired by BET to write for their show."

I could tell from the toothy smile across her face that she was delighted by my news.

"That's marvelous, Cameron, I mean really, that's really nice and deserving of a celebration."

"And how do you propose we celebrate?"

"By me putting all of this hot wet cat on you."

"Tasha, you were going to do that anyway."

"Well now I don't have an excuse not to!"

That was one of the things I dug most about Tasha, she was witty on top of being exotic and drop dead gorgeous. We parked the car and headed to my room to celebrate.

I was awakened by Karen when she called me at 7:30 AM, right before she left for work.

"Somebody must have really had a good time for you not to call and check in," she sarcastically said into the phone.

I slipped out of the bed so not to disturb Tasha and walked into the bathroom.

"Ah yeah, baby, my bad. We shut the club down and went to get something to eat afterward. I didn't want to wake you up, babbling all drunk and shit," I said to her as I released a steady stream of pee into the toilet.

"Will since you put it that way I guess I'll forgive you." She sounded less irritated.

Karen told me the boys had asked about me before having to get off the phone because of some emergency at the VA hospital. After her abruptly ending our conversation, I went back into the room and took in the visual of Tasha in deep slumber. This chick even slept cute. She didn't snore like Karen but in Karen's defense, her job was a lot more demanding than running drinks in a bar so I couldn't compare or complain. What really turned me on as I gazed at Tasha was her long lush black hair, a gift from her mother's side of the family, that cascaded over the pillow.   I climbed back into bed and drew her to me so that she could feel my morning wood stiff against her thick nakedness.

"Good morning, baby, I see you want to celebrate some more," she said to me with her eyes half closed.

I didn't utter a word; I just let my body do all the talking for me as I rolled on top of her and pressed myself between her parting legs until I found the heat I was seeking. We celebrated until each of us climaxed, were sated, and drifted back to sleep.

CHAPTER 19

It was around noon when Marc came to my room to brag about his conquest.

"Damn, Cameron, it smells like badussy up in here."

"If you were doing the work that I put in up in here, your room should be smelling the same way," I told him as I sprayed Lysol in the air.

"Oh, I handled my business, you can believe that," he boasted.

We exchanged war stories for a few minutes before Marc said some shit that made me put a halt to the conversation.

"Man, the only thing that was jive whack about the evening was that she didn't give me no head."

I froze for a few seconds. Just to make sure I heard Marc right I had to ask.

"What do you mean she didn't give you no head?"

"She didn't go down on me."

"Did you go down on her?"

"Yes and she came so hard, she squirted," he said.

"So you're telling me you went down on her until she busted a liquid nut and you didn't even ask for the favor to be returned?"

"I did, but Ebony said she wasn't comfortable doing that so soon. I didn't want to press the issue."

"Man, you let a waitress in a rib joint treat you like you were a common worker and she was the one with television appearances?"

"It wasn't like that; she says she does do it, she just has to be comfortable."

"And squirting in-your-face, trembling in orgasm ain't comfortable? That sounds pretty fucking comfortable to me."

"Man, you don't understand."

"That might be the first thing you said we can agree on. I don't understand," I said to him. In my way of thinking it didn't count if she didn't suck his dick. I mean any woman could spread her legs to a man, but to put a dick in her mouth was personal.

"So you're telling me you ain't never ate a chick out and she didn't return the favor?"

"What I'm telling you is, Marc, if I dine, she dines."

Marc figured out that it was pointless trying to convince me to see things his way. Instead of continuing to argue, he chose to change the subject to something he knew I wouldn't object to, food.

"So you hungry or what?" he asked.

"Hell yeah, I'm starving. What do you have in mind?"

"Let's catch a cab to Nations and get some burgers."

We caught a cab, grabbed the food and grubbed. We didn't have to meet up with Mouton until 9 PM. I had some writing Lisa asked me to do on my laptop. Mark told me he was going to watch SportsCenter and crash.

I went into my room, checked emails and chatted with some local online friends who I'd met on AOL. My boy, KappaCrimson and the flirtatious ITSGOOOOD requested some tickets for the show at Mexicali Rose and I agreed to grant their requests before shutting down the online conversations. I didn't see any harm in inviting ITSGOOOOD, whose real name was Thelma.

She was a cool cutie and let her tell it she could burn in the kitchen. Even though we had flirted with each other via the Internet for months, we had never met face-to-face. So in my mind there wasn't going to be any expectations between us. It was just going to be good to finally meet. After signing off-line, I attended to the task of writing characters' descriptions and a synopsis of my pilot *Barely Standing*.

Lisa had two producers interested and they were waiting to see more than just a pilot script. Since the show was my creation it wasn't going to be difficult to hammer it out.

It was times like these when I thanked God for English teachers like Sandy Talley and Valerie Weaver who hadn't allowed me to be a dumb jock and cultivated my grasp of the language and writing skills. I finished the synopsis of most of the character descriptions before my eyelids became too heavy to complete anymore. I saved the WORD document, shut down my Apple computer and called the front desk for an 8 PM wake-up call before drifting into a deep slumber.

It felt as if no time had passed when the phone rang.

"It's 8 PM, Mr. Bernard and this is your wake-up call," said the front desk attendant, waking me from some much-needed rest.

I rose out of the bed and went to the bathroom for shit, shower, and shave time -- in that order. After handling my human and hygienic endeavors, I exited the bathroom with an oversized terrycloth towel wrapped around me. I pulled out my hounds-tooth wool blazer and black French cuffed long sleeve shirt and black wide leg trousers. I grabbed a pair of black silk socks and my black alligator belt that matched my David Eden alligator loafers. I considered donning a black fedora that I had purchased at *The Hat Guys* on Broadway, but decided to throw some Murray's grease into my hair so I could make folks sick with my waves.

I checked over the entire outfit and concluded I was dressed properly to impress, then headed downstairs to see what crazy casual look Marc would wear and to be picked up by Mouton.   When I exited the elevator, I was surprised to see Marc dressed up. Well not exactly dressed up, but enough to make me have to say something.

"So who died to get you to be funeral formal?" I didn't give him a chance to answer. "So I guess you figured out that wearing a Raiders jersey isn't get-your-dick-sucked attire so you might as well try shirt and slacks, huh?" I commented, knowing I would spark a debate.

"Damn, Cameron, you just can't let shit go, can you?"

"Nope, sure can't, not even if I tried!"

"Don't hate because I'm looking too suave tonight."

"What? Did Ross Dress for Less have a sale on leisure suits and shoes?" I questioned.

Marc knew he couldn't down my style, so he changed the subject.

"So yo, is Tasha going to be there tonight?"

"No, I'm solo, she had to fill in for someone at the bar. I'm glad, it saved me from pissing her off by telling her she couldn't come."

"Damn, I knew I shouldn't have asked Ebony to attend tonight."

"You should've told her she couldn't attend last night right after she didn't suck your dick," I said before breaking out into the Funkadelic classic "No Head No Backstage Pass."

"How did I know you were going to find a way to bring that shit back up?"

"Because I'm a predictable asshole probably."

Mouton and TMB pulled up to the front of the hotel in the Suburban.

"Wassup fellas?" Mouton asked, as we entered the vehicle.

"Marc ate that waitress's pussy last night and she didn't go down on him, that's what's up," I told the front passengers before Marc hit me with a light jab to the side.

"Damn, she played you like that?" Mouton asked.

"Man, fuck what Cameron is talking about. The only reason he got laid last night is because he and Tasha been kicking for years. Ebony just wasn't comfortable doing that on the first date. I'm sure she'll be more secure tonight," Marc replied.

TMB looked into the backseat like he knew something we didn't. "You told her to come tonight?" he questioned.

"Yeah, we had a good time minus the extracurricular activity that Cameron keeps joking about."

"First of all, if you eat a broad's pussy until she pops on your face, her sucking your dick is not extracurricular; it's a mandatory requirement," I interjected.

"Wait a minute, Ebony is a squirter? Nigga, I thought Larry LaLa was lying on his dick when he told me that," Mouton said like he owed this Larry an apology.

"Yeah, she told me that they dated awhile back," Marc explained.

"Dated him awhile back? Nigga, Larry was last week's headliner. He met her just like you did when we took him to eat. The way he tells it, she sucks dick, licks toes, elbows and assholes," TMB said to Marc, making everyone else laugh, but him.

When we pulled into the packed parking lot of Mexicali Rose, the subject changed. I said, "Mou, you and TMB are pimping the promotion department folks. I dig how many people you have turning out."

Right before we stepped inside the club, Mouton asked, "Marc, you have any more guests besides Ebony? What about you, Cameron?" He wanted to make sure so there wouldn't be any hang up at the door.

Marc said that he was cool and I told him about Thelma and Eric as we entered the large club space filled with sexy Latinas and black women. There probably were a bunch of guys too, but I wasn't checking for them so there wasn't any need for me to take inventory.

Mouton led us to the dressing room that was downstairs. Luenell was already in the green room sipping on some cognac. She was in conversation with a diminutive man who wore a long perm and was sporting a fedora perched on his head like it was a crown.

"Cameron and Marc, this is 'Katt in The Hat'; he's doing a guest set tonight if that's cool," Luenell said to us as she introduced her friend.

We shook hands and I told him it was all right by me especially when he told me he was a fellow Ohioan. While we were talking, Mouton informed us that we had another special guest in the house. I asked who that might be.

"I was told not to say shit so I ain't saying shit."

I wasn't about to trip; it was obviously someone I knew who had serious juice to shut down Mouton.

The crowd was getting restless. Seating had begun an hour before show time and the mixture of liquor and anticipation had them chanting, "We want the show!"

Mouton dimmed the lights and had the DJ play "I'm Every Woman," Luenell's intro song.

The crowd went wild as she took the stage as the host and MC. If I didn't know better, I would've sworn that Luenell had bused in her entire family and fan club the way they responded to her antics and comedy. After she had the room nice and hot, Luenell brought Katt in The Hat to the stage. He performed fifteen minutes of material that had audience rolling. Not only were they laughing at his cultural observations, but also his high-pitched voice and slow cadence.

Luenell returned to the stage and announced that the crowd was in store for a special treat.

"Ladies and Gentleman, your money spent tonight just doubled in value. Coming to the stage is the former host of Showtime at the Apollo. Born and bred right here in town, he has his own hit show on ABC. Please welcome home, Mr. Mark Curry!" she said as the crowd got louder with each credit until finally they erupted in applause.

This wasn't just another celebrity comic. Mark was one of them, their homeboy had done well. What was really cool was that the writers of his show had situated the sitcom in Oakland. So each week the city was showcased as a character as well.

I marveled at Curry's incredible standup abilities and improv skills as he performed at a high level with off-the-cuff wit. I noticed Marc was paying Curry's set close attention as well because he was up next and I could only imagine how nervous he must've felt having to follow the homegrown superstar.

I was glad Marc was going after Curry; he was the one being offered to the crowd as the sacrificial lamb. Curry closed out his set and left the stage to a standing ovation. Luenell didn't waste any time as she brought Marc Howard to a hot stage that Curry had just set ablaze. Again Marc was being baptized through comedy fire as he had the previous night at Sweet Jimmy's. He handled the pressure with a cool that was admirable.

Ebony was by the bar watching him intensely, laughing along with the rest of the crowd that was really enjoying his performance. I was scanned the room to see if I could spot my friends, Thelma and Eric. As I looked the place over, I got a glimpse at a vision that caught my attention. There was a very light skinned lady with flaming red curly hair and freckles standing across the bar from me, sipping a drink through a straw that was being sexually assaulted by her juicy pink lips. I tapped Mouton who was standing nearby and asked him, "Who is that thick redbone over there?"

I made sure to point in her direction blatantly so that she would notice I was flirting.

"Oh that's Jessica, she's a bad broad, right?"

I agreed with his observation, then asked the question, "What's her story?"

"We call her Jessi the Body, for obvious reasons, or Jessica Rabbit. She comes every week to support the show. From what I know, she lives in a condo on Lake Marin and stacks racks and racks of dough."

My eyes were still on her when I said, "I appreciate the intel."

"Are you going to step to her?"

"No, I'm going to do what you have paid me to do and if she's still here when I'm finished, I'll holla at her." I got the bartender's attention and instructed him to get her whatever she was drinking on me.

While I was admiring Jessica, Curry came over to where I was standing.

"What's up, nigga, you know better than to come to my town and not holla at me."

"My bad, dude, I was preoccupied last night and was recouping all day."

"You still fucking with Tasha when you come up here or have you found something new to play with?"

"Yeah, but I might be looking to trade her in for a newer model," I said, raising my glass, acknowledging Jessica who was thanking me for her drink.

"Oh, I see you have aspirations of moving up from triple A ball to the majors if you get that one."

We chatted it up for bit and shot the shit until too many folks were vying for his attention. There were too many for him to ignore.

It was cool; Marc Howard was wrapping up his set and I had to get my game face on anyway.

Luenell went back on stage and did a few minutes before bringing me up. This was a different clientele compared to the one at Sweet Jimmy's, so I changed up my material and talked about relationships and when love goes wrong.

The men were cracking up at my baby-mama-drama material while the women were digging my-men-ain't-shit jokes. I kept the crowd at odds as I went through material that had each sex laughing at the other's shortcomings.

When I exited the stage I didn't get a standing ovation, but really, that wasn't my intention. I was flexing my change up game instead of bombarding them with high heat.

Luenell closed out the show and we all met at the bar to celebrate another great night of comedy as the club staff moved tables and chairs so that patrons could dance. I looked all over for Jessica so I could put a bid in, but there was no sign of her.

I was jive sulking about my missed opportunity when Eric and Thelma walked up and thanked me for the tickets. Much to my surprise, they both looked like their online profile pictures. They hung out with the comedy crew and had a couple of drinks with us. Eric was a computer programmer who lived in Berkeley and Thelma was a San Francisco native who worked in the banking industry. They fit right in with our clique. TMB got my attention and pulled me to the side.

"Cameron, homie, you are the geese that lays golden eggs. We have far exceeded last night's take; I'm thinking we should do a little tour of the West Coast. Are you interested?" he asked as he pulled off a thousand dollars from his bankroll.

"Yeah I'm down, but I'm only owed five hundred, pimp," I replied.

"You and I are going to be partners. My friends and family fly free, ya dig?"

I tried arguing with him that we had a deal and it was cool. But he wasn't hearing it. I went back to the bar so that everyone else could get broke off.

As we were all standing there, the bartender came up to me. "The redhead told me to give you this," he said, as he handed me a folded note.

I opened it and it read the message: *Thanks for the drink. You are a very funny and handsome man. Give me a call if you're free for lunch tomorrow Jessica 510-311-4579.*

If I hadn't been in public and in the company of the very sexy Thelma, I would have been jumping for joy, celebrating like I had scored a touchdown. Instead, I fist pumped the air and returned to the gathering of my comrades.

After Marc got paid, he was ready to dip with Ebony back to the hotel.

"Don't end up with the glaze face again doing the 68 where she owes you one," I chided as he left.

He didn't even dignify my jab. He just shook his head as he exited.

I hung out with Thelma and Eric until Mouton and TMB were ready to take me back to the hotel. I knew better than to try my hand with Thelma since she was going through a bitter divorce with her ex because of his infidelity and the best I could offer her was the same shit. I didn't feel the need to wrangle a stray. Tasha would more than likely be calling to creep by. Even if I was to spend the night alone, I was cool. I had already won the grand prize when I scored Jessica the Body's digits.

CHAPTER 20

As predicted, Tasha came by for another celebration. What we agreed to celebrate I didn't know, but I remembered the festivities.

She had tried her best not to disturb my sleep while she readied herself, but all of her efforts were in vain because I was wide awake when she came out of the bathroom.

"Baby, I'm sorry, I have a dentist appointment and some errands to run," she said, sitting on the bed, putting on her boots and zipping them up.

"So you don't have time for another celebration I take it?" I pulled back the covers revealing my rock hard dick as an offering.

"Cameron, you don't play fair. I really have to go, boo."

I wasn't really trying to do the do. I was just playing the role. Because all I could think about was Jessica. I was itching to call her.

I played it cool so Tasha didn't sense me rushing her off. I was glad she had things to do. It would free me up for my lunch rendezvous.

She kissed me goodbye and was off.

After releasing my morning constitution and showering, I called the red-headed, freckled face vixen that captured my interest at The Mexicali Rose.

"Hello may I speak with Jessica?" I asked in my smooth baritone voice.

"This is she and who's calling?" she asked because she didn't recognize my number.

"This is Cameron Bernard. I bought you a drink last night and I'm calling per your lovely note."

"Of course it's you, the humorist. Thanks for calling. I wasn't sure if you would or not. You seemed to be preoccupied with a throng of fans."

"Actually, I hadn't seen Mark Curry for a while and we were chopping it up. Those fans were his."

"If you say so, I'm not about to allow our first conversation to be an argument, but I beg to differ with you. During your performance the ladies at the bar were all commenting about the things they would do to you if given the chance."

I laughed. "That's funny because I was totally oblivious to it. I was too busy being enchanted by you."

"Enchanted? That's an interesting way to put it. You make it seem as if I casted a spell on you or something."

"I'm not saying it for conversation sake. I'm sure you're complimented on your beauty all the time."

"I've been told that once or twice."

"Humbled beauty is a very sexy trait to possess, Jessica, if you don't mind me saying so."

"No, I don't mind. So are we going to do lunch like I suggested or are we going to stay on the phone blowing each other's egos up?" she asked.

"I'm down to do lunch; that way we can stroke each other's egos face to face."

"You, Mr. Bernard, are quite the charmer. So what would you like to eat?" she asked.

I paused before answering, causing her to reconsider her wording.

"Maybe I should rephrase that, Mr. Comedian. What type of food would you like to dine on for lunch?"

"What? I didn't say anything," I replied, even though we both knew that she'd caught me in my dirty thought.

"You may have not uttered a word, but I can already tell there's a bad boy behind the smooth exterior, sir."

Jessica had pegged me perfectly. I had been thinking of her in a lustful manner since my first glimpse. Even while Tasha and I were engaged in our carnal celebration, I couldn't get Jessica out of my mind.

I told her that since it was her city and she had me invited me out to lunch, I was open to whatever she fancied me to share with her.

"My call, huh? Okay, I like that. Just remember that when I come to visit LA," she said, making it known that she planned on seeing me again.

"So it's 10 am now, what time would you like to meet?"

"Lunch is from noon to three universally. How about we link up in an hour, that way we won't be rushed for time."

"I'm not driving. I would appreciate you picking me up at the downtown Marriott, if you don't mind."

"Oh, I don't mind, but please be downstairs so that I don't have to come up and get you. We wouldn't want to miss lunch, now would we?"

I ignored her innuendo. "Okay cool, so what's the attire?"

Jessica told me there was a brisk breeze coming off the bay and she was dressing in jeans and a blazer. I told her that I would follow her casual lead and meet her downstairs at eleven.

Since I had already taken care of my hygienic needs before I called Jessica, all I had to do was throw on some 501 Levis, a black V-neck sweater, and my Baco Bucci loafers.

Before leaving to go downstairs, I knocked on Marc's door. I wanted to check in with him to see if he was cool.

"What's up, are you by yourself?" I asked him as I walked inside his room.

"Yeah, Ebony been gone. Where the fuck you off to all dressed up and smiling?"

"Yo, did you see that cutie across the bar last night with the curly red hair?"

"You mean the tall journ with the tight black dress on?"

"Exactly!"

"Nah, I didn't see her."

"Man, you trippin'. You know damn well you peeked. A blind motherfucker couldn't have missed her fine ass."

"True dat. Shorty was off the chain; I don't remember seeing you approach her. How did you pull that off with the Thelma chick around?"

"Well, first off, Thelma is going through a divorce and we are just friends."

"But I assumed you brought her back to the hotel with all of the squealing I heard coming from your room."

"Oh, that was ol' faithful. But peep this, I sent the redbone a drink before I hit the stage, then after we got paid, the bartender slid me a note from her." I sat down in the computer chair.

Marc leaned against the wall with his arms crossed. I could read the skepticism all over his face.

"So are you gonna tell her the truth about your family or are you gonna be jive slick and omit that from your lunch conversation?"

I didn't know why he would question my style. I thought he knew how much I prided myself in keeping it one hundred with women from the jump. I only reserved lies of omission for Karen, but even she, at one time, had to endure being the other woman.

"So do you think Karen believes you're being faithful when you're out on the road? Better yet, do you think she's being faithful to you?"

I explained to him that Karen knew I was faithful -- to my urges and desires. I didn't try to convince him that she approved of my ways, but I did point out that she wasn't complaining about the new truck or house with the swimming pool that I provided for her and our sons.

As far as the question of her fidelity, I told him the plain truth. I was too busy enjoying myself to even be concerned.

"Damn, Cameron, I didn't know your pimp hand was so strong man!"

"Marc, we're in our thirties and one day, not too far from now, all we'll have are the memories of our youth. And I'll be damned if I'm gonna be in my rocking chair with Karen as the only piece of pussy I can recall, ya dig?"

Marc just shook his head. I guess what I said left him speechless. With no real retort, he changed the subject.

"So, you aren't curious about Ebony's performance last night?"

"No, not in the least bit." I paused and laughed. "I'm just fucking with you, do tell."

"Well, let's just say she is comfortable with me now and she has swallowed her fears," he replied.

I told him that I would have to get the gory details later. I needed to head downstairs since I didn't want to have Jessica waiting.

Marc threw on his shoes and came along. "I want to see how fine she looks in the daytime."

"That's cool, but don't be all ogling and shit; she'll know what's up. Just hang back like we're discussing some business.

Dealing with Lance and his promptness had taught me to be early and ready when folks came to pick me up. That thought made me pause and think a little longer about my accomplice. I wondered what he might be up to and where he had gone.

Marc and I were outside acting as if we were in deep conversation when in actuality he was just bragging about Ebony's profound oral proficiency.

Jessica pulled up in a blue Mercedes S500 sitting on chrome dubs. She put the car in park, exited, and walked over to where we were standing.

"Hey, Cameron, I'm sorry if I'm late," she told me, looking at her watch.

I told her that she was on time and that Marc and I were just talking about the show last night. Then, I introduced them, "Jessica, this is Marc; Marc this is Jessica."

Jessica told him how pleased she was to meet him and how she had enjoyed his performance.

"The pleasure is all mine," Marc smoothly replied. It was as if Ebony's head game had awakened within him a newfound swagger. If Ebony hadn't already had him riding high, being complimented by my Amazonian companion sure did the trick.

"Cameron, I like her already, it's obvious that this lady has an eye for talent. Now why she is bothering herself with you is beyond me, but you two have a great time." He said goodbye, then walked away without giving me an opportunity to respond.

Jessica and I walked over to her luxurious ride and I opened the door for her. When I entered her passenger side, she leaned over and asked, "So did I pass the test?"

I pretended that I had no clue what she was talking about. "What test are you referring to?"

"The is-she-cute-when-the-lights-come-on-and-the-drinks-wear-off test."

My eyes opened wide as if her words shocked me. "There is really a test like that? That must be a West Coast thing."

She chuckled. "Okay, Mr. Bernard, if you wanna start off this relationship not being real, it's doomed to end that way."

That was the second time that she'd mentioned us having a future. I didn't say anything about it, but I did make a mental note.

"So where are we off to?" I asked, once she started the car and took off.

"Well, I was thinking we could go to San Francisco or make our way to Napa Valley. Which would you prefer?"

"As long as I'm in your company I don't care if we eat at Alcatraz," I said, trying to be clever. But the reality was that I didn't want to see no parts of anyone's prison. It was always perplexing to me when folks talked about going on guided tours there. What motherfucker in his right mind would pay to be at The Rock?

Jessica was amused with my statement and as we rode in the car, I checked her out. I saw why she was tabbed The Body or Jessica Rabbit; she was comic book cartoon voluptuous.

Thick up top, wide in her hips, but she had a slim waistline that defied belief. Not only was she a physical marvel, but she owned a pretty face with light brown eyes, which had a greenish tint. And then, there was her mouth -- pouty. Talk about being sexy, ooh lawd.

Fuck yeah, she passed the test.

From now on the test was going to be graded on her curves.

"Seeing that the vineyards are at least fifty-two miles from here and you have a performance tonight, let's just point this car in the direction of Golden Gate Bridge and see where we find ourselves," she said as we pulled onto Broadway headed to interstate 880.

Jessica turned up the volume of the CD player loud enough to fully enjoy the SADE track, "Taboo."

"That's the jam. I love this song." She snapped her fingers and accompanied the sultry artist.

I listened to her sing for a moment, and was surprised that she could hold her own. "Yeah she is a marvelous songstress and from the sounds of things, so are you."

She glanced at me out of the corner of her eye. "Why thank you, Mr. Bernard."

"Please call me, Cameron, Mr. Bernard was my daddy's name."

She laughed. "Fine, Cameron it is, but I'll reserve the right to call you daddy if I so desire."

Damn!

She continued, "So tell me something about yourself."

I went right into what I told all the ladies. "I'm sure you gathered from my act that I have twin sons and I'm currently in relationship with their mom. I'm originally from Cleveland, Ohio. I'm a thirty-year-old ex college basketball player who stumbled upon my comedy career. I'm an only child," I paused for just a second, "and I'm very attracted to you even though that might be considered improper after all that I've told you."

She didn't hesitate. "Well, Cameron, I believe I would be more upset if you didn't find me to be very attractive. That would be improper, especially since I go to the gym at least four times a week to maintain this figure."

"So did I pass the test?"

"What test would that be, sweetie?"

"The is-he-going-to-lie-to-kick-it test. I believe that's universal," I responded.

"Yes, with flying colors. I told my girl who was with me last night that you'd be honest. She, on the other hand, begged to differ."

I nodded. I understood her friend. "I make it a point to be real from the jump in most of my personal and business dealings. When you lie you have to keep remembering the false shit you've said. I have too many important things to remember to be thinking about some stuff I've made up."

She agreed with her silence.

"So tell me some things about you."

"What would you like to know?"

"Now you know it's rude to answer a question with a question," I teased.

"Well everybody in this car doesn't do interviews all the time. I guess what I meant to say was, my story is fairly simple."

"Please feel free to bore me."

"Well I'm an only child, too, raised by a hard-working single mother. I grew up in Vallejo, but I've been living in Oakland since I graduated from San Jose State seven years ago with a Business degree in Finance and Money Management. Oh yeah, and I like to swim naked and take long walks on the beach watching the sunset."

I commented on the two things that stood out most. "Really, naked swimming and beach walks?"

"No, I'm playing, I don't walk the beach. I just read that in *Playboy* and guys eat that shit up." She laughed a little. "I'm sorry, Cameron, I couldn't help but throw it out there to see how you would react."

"That's hilarious and too bad it's too cold to swim. That would have been interesting," I replied almost ashamed to admit that I was a devout *Playboy* reader, and found the articles to be truly some of the best in publication. It was just an added bonus that they were packed between pages of pussy.

I had to admit to myself that I was not just feeling her as a physical specimen but also as a genuinely cool chick.

"So just out of curiosity, Jessica, what made you leave the note last night?"

"Like I said earlier, I respected you at work and your fans had obviously paid good money to be up close and personal with you. I didn't think it was right of me to get in the way of that. But I was intrigued. You were handsome, funny and charming so I took a shot."

I told Jessica how appreciative I was for her leap of faith. We continued to probe each other through our conversation. I was surprised to find out that last night wasn't her first time seeing me perform. She informed me that she had caught me when I opened up for Don DC Curry and DL Hughley at the Paramount Theatre. I asked Jessica why she hadn't said anything to me then.

"I had difficulty getting backstage and when I saw you at the after party, you were preoccupied with some mixed chick."

The more she talked, the more I could tell that she had a genuine interest in me that had been brewing for quite some time.

We crossed over the bridge after paying the toll and Jessica suggested that we head over to Chinatown for some authentic Chinese cuisine rather than the American version. Considering the company and how Chinese just so happened to be my favorite, I didn't complain.

We parked the car in front of the Hong Kong Clay Pot and I went over to the driver's side to open her door. Jessica truly was every bit deserving of her nickname. The way her jeans were fitting her, even gay men that we passed on the street took a second look at her ass.

I was taken aback when I saw dead carcasses hanging in the window of the restaurant. I didn't know who told the proprietor that this was a way to draw motherfuckers in to dine, but it wasn't working for me. It reminded me of summers spent at my Uncle Louis and Aunt Sus' farm in Alabama.

My uncle used to forbid me from becoming attached to and naming the livestock. Secretly, I named my favorite rooster, Red. One day Red went missing and I looked for him all day, only ending my search because hunger had overcome me and the scent of fried chicken enticed me to go back in the house to eat. It wasn't until after I had already smashed the food that my aunt told me that I had eaten Red. I was stricken by the realization but Red tasted too good for me to mourn over his demise.

But, I was thinking about Red right before we stepped inside and Jessica must have sensed my apprehension.

"Don't worry, they won't bite."

I gave her a half-hearted smile, opened the door, and we walked inside.

"You are quite the gentleman, Cameron. Either you were raised by southern parents or you're fattening me up for the kill."

"My father was from Cleveland and my mother is from Tuscaloosa. I guess politeness is one half of my DNA."

"You said your father was from Cleveland, that's past tense. Is he no longer with us?"

"Unfortunately no, he passed a few years back from lung cancer."

Jessica expressed her condolences for my loss and wished peace for my dad's eternal soul.

I thanked her as our hostess escorted us to the table.

Our waiter brought us ice water and hot tea, then left us with menus so that we could decide on our meals. I already had an idea of what I wanted to eat, so while Jessica perused over the offerings, I continued to fulfill my need to know more about her.

"You mentioned earlier that you saw me out with a mixed woman. When you said that it was as if you aren't of synergized heritage. Is that the case?"

"Well, my mother is Irish and my father is as black as coal. They met at UC Berkley during the 60's. Obviously, she was a liberal and he was a revolutionary. Let's just say that my father taught my mother what true Black Power was all about."

It all made sense to me. Her green eyes, red hair, and the freckles I was so smitten over.

Jessica had comically explained it all.

When the waiter returned, Jessica ordered lamb in a clay pot and I asked him to bring me ginger lobster. We both ordered wonton soup and spring rolls.

By the time that the waiter returned to our table with our meals, we were both more than ready to dive in. We were hungry, so looks were the only things we exchanged until we finished dining.

I sparked up more conversation after washing down my food with a diet coke. "Do you have a nickname that your family calls you?"

"Yes but unfortunately, I'm not very fond of it. I believe I have far outgrown it."

"Let me be the judge. I promise not to laugh. How can I? My mother's nickname for me is Reesie. Do you know how many kid's asses I had to kick growing up?"

She laughed. "Reesie is cute, Cameron, hell I might even call you that. At least you didn't grow up being called Carrot."

I almost broke out into laughter, but being the man of my word I suppressed the urge by biting down on my lip.

"My man, Mouton calls you The Body and Jessica Rabbit. Were you hipped to that?"

She nodded. "Yes, Brian refuses to stop even though he knows there's much more to me than my body."

"I feel you, but I would be lying if I didn't say the name is befitting. You are justifiably fine as fuck," I told her bluntly for a lack of a better way to put it.

"Well, I guess I'll just have to take that as a compliment, won't I, Reesie?" she replied as our waiter returned with our bill and placed it in front of me.

I instinctively reached into my pocket to whip out some cash. But before I could do anything, Jessica reached over the table, grabbed the bill, surveyed it and pulled out a crisp one-hundred-dollar bill from her purse, then handed it to the waiter.

"I could've taken care of that, sweetie," I told her.

"I'm the one who invited you out for lunch. It's on me."

"Thank you. But at least allow me to leave the tip."

"Okay, if it will make you feel better about it, but know it's not necessary."

I left a ten on the table and we bounced. I was full as a tick and happy that we had parked close to the restaurant. As we were headed toward the car, out of nowhere a fully nude man walked up the street, then suddenly stopped, kneeled and prayed. Jessica acted as if nothing was out of the ordinary. What was even more peculiar was that all of the pedestrians paid as little attention to him as Jessica had.

I, on the other hand, couldn't believe my eyes. There before me was actually a booty-ass naked man on a public street and not one motherfucker had shit to say about it. Talk about freedom of religion and expression. I was sure the founding fathers didn't intend for this to be protected by the Constitution.

Once again, Jessica read my expression. "This is San Francisco, baby; believe me, you are bound to see just about anything. They truly live by a different set of rules here."

"This could have had never happened in Cleveland, dude is wildin'."

Jessica shook her head and told me I was a mess. That was true, but dude walking around in his birthday suit was a *hot* mess.

Once we were back in the car, I was curious as to what else we were going to get into. I still had plenty of time to be back at the hotel and chill before my show.

Jessica suggested that we head back to the hotel and have a drink. I liked how she suggested things that I had thought to ask, but feared would have been considered being forward. The last thing I wanted to do was come off as being pressed or hurried.

Luckily for me, Jessica wanted to be in my company, so it seemed.

The Golden Gate Bridge was congested as we headed back toward Oakland, which lent for more conversation time between the two of us.

"So are you glad that I left that note?" she asked, though she kept her eyes on the road.

"Of course, the question is, are you happy that we had the opportunity to be in each other's company today?"

"If I tell you something, you promise not to freak out?"

"Okay, I promise," I replied, anxious to hear what she had to say.

"I've had a crush on you since your first appearance on *ComicView.* Every time I saw you on TV, I would tell my girl how you could get it." She chuckled a little, like she was embarrassed by her confession.

I wasn't freaked out at all. In fact, I was quite flattered. Lust at first sight made perfect sense to me. I had been thinking about jumping her bones since I sent her that drink and her revelation only served to intensify the desire that was building within me.

"You aren't saying anything," she said, breaking into my thoughts as we pulled up to a red light. "I guess you think I'm some kind of weirdo?" I thought to say something to ease her curiosity and anxiety, but instead I leaned over from the passenger side and gave her a warm wet kiss.

Jessica responded by parting her perfect mouth and allowing my tongue to wrestle with hers. The only thing that ended our kiss was the sound of horns blowing behind us as the light turned green.

We continued back to the hotel without saying another word.

When we arrived at the hotel, we stopped by the bar, ordered a bottle of Riesling, asked the bartender for two glasses and had him charge it to my room.

But even though I'd given the bartender that directive, Jessica pulled out another hundred-dollar bill. "You keep trying to pay for my date." Then, she said to the bartender, "Please have room service bring us some strawberries and cheese and you can keep the change."

We boarded the elevator heading to my room. The elevator was empty and I wished that Jessica had worn the dress she had on at the Mexicali Rose so that I could have had easier access to her wares. With her wearing blue jeans that fit her snugly, I had to be content with the passionate kisses shared as we ascended.

"You just wait until I get you all to myself," she told me.

I like Jessica's aggression and confidence and even though I didn't know what she had in mind for me, I knew it was going to be all good.

When the elevator reached my floor and the doors opened, Marc greeted us. When he saw us with wine and glasses, I knew his mind was racing with ideas about what was going to take place. I could only imagine how guilty I must have looked with Jessica's lipstick smeared all over my face.

"I'll assume that lunch was enjoyable," he said sarcastically.

I didn't have anything to say...it was written all over my face, literally.

"You can assume what you will about lunch, but you can't even begin to imagine how things are going to be after this wine," Jessica said to Marc as we walked to my room and left him standing at the elevator, awestruck.

Jessica held her composure until we entered my room, then she busted out laughing.

"Did you see the look on his face?" I asked her, not knowing if she even heard me over her laughter.

"So you liked the look I put on his face?" she asked, putting the glasses down and removing her jacket.

"Hell yeah; he was stupefied. It was priceless," I told her, pouring wine for the both of us.

"Priceless, huh?" she asked as she took off her shirt and unbuttoned her jeans.

I stood with my mouth open in awe, marveling at her green undergarment-clad physique.

Jessica took a sip from the glass and kissed me, running her tongue across my lips, feeding me the sweet nectar of the grapes. Only the knock at the door interrupted the passion brewing between us.

"Room service."

Jessica darted off into the bathroom to hide her nakedness as if we were in Eden and God Himself was looking for us.

I opened the door and allowed the Hispanic bellman to bring in a tray filled with cheese, crackers, melon slices and strawberries.

I reached into my pocket to pay for it, but he informed me that he had already been taken care of.

"Have an enjoyable afternoon, Mr. Bernard," he said as he exited the room.

When I closed the door and locked it behind him, I tapped on the bathroom door, then said, "Ollie, Ollie Oxen Free."

Jessica stepped out of the bathroom, naked as the day in which she was born, save for her high heels. The moniker Mouton had dubbed her with was more than well deserving. Jessica's 5'10" sculpted figure was perfect.

Now I know there is no person or thing on this planet that is worthy of such a lofty description, perfection is reserved for celestial and heavenly beings. But if Jessica had a flaw, I was unable to see it.

Lionel Richie was wrong when he sang about the measurements of a brick house. His interpretation was missing some concrete. Before me stood a brick skyscraper, 36-24-40 and I held the winning hand.

"So, are you going to stand there gawking or are you going to join me?" she asked, grabbing our glasses and taking them over to the bed.

"Oh yeah, of course I'm joining you," I replied, ripping off my jacket, shedding my sweater, letting my pants and sports briefs drop to the ground, then kicking off my shoes.

"Quite impressive, Cameron." Her eyes roved all over my exposed body hungrily, before settling on my stiff pole.

I walked over to the bed and leaned over to kiss her. As I did, she drew me into her arms and guided me down into and between her long parted legs.

"Let's save the rest of the compliments until after we've finished."

"Cool, I'm sure they'll be well deserved afterward," I told Jessica as I kissed her mouth and then her neck.

It was only two-thirty in the afternoon and there was no rush for me to be anywhere, so I took my time becoming acquainted with every inch of the treasure that laid before me.

"Is there any place in particular that you like to be kissed?" I asked.

"You are doing fine; you'll figure it out," she replied in a throaty tone.

I put up no argument and followed her instructions.

I began first by kissing Jessica's left breast while cupping the right one. My pecks on her titties were just like the ones I placed on her cheeks. My kisses morphed into licks and my licks evolved into sucking as I enjoyed her large erect nipple in my mouth.

"Ooh," she groaned.

Her moans let me know that I had discovered one of her erogenous zones. Armed with that knowledge I switched from the left to the right nipple.

Jessica licked her lips and told me not to stop. Again I complied with her demands, knowing that it was in my best interest to listen to my lover rather than to go about making love from my own playbook.

I lowered my face down her body, placing kisses on her abdomen. Jessica was brewing with excitement as she raised her hips and gently guided my face toward her well-shaven mound. Again, she found no struggle from me, but I did take my time, like I said, there was no rush.

I glided down, kissing softly all of the areas surrounding her womanhood. Her inner left thigh was my first target, then I glanced over her glistening box as I attended to her right one.

Anticipation was mounting within Jessica.

I kissed and tongued her thighs until she could take my teasing no more. She responded by forcing my face into her wanting nether region.

The warmth of her longing reached out to me as I licked and lapped at her labia.

"Awww...right there, baby, oh yes!' she exclaimed as I darted my tongue in and out of her at a deferred speed.

Then, I turned all of my attention to her throbbing clitoris, sucking on it with my lips and assaulting her pearl with my wet flickering instrument.

With all the commotion that Jessica was kicking up, I figured if Marc was back in his room he was either being treated to or tortured by all the noise.

Jessica responded to my applied pressure by hurling her pussy toward my face. "Don't stop, don't stop, don't you dare stop!" she pleaded as her body rippled in orgasm.

I kept the pressure on even though I could tell she was nearing the point of not being able to take my tongue-thrashing any more.

Jessica went limp and released the grip she had on the back of my head, then pushed me away in complete surrender.

My attempts to go after her again were thwarted as she closed her legs, locking them, while she still quivered in climax.

"Cameron, you have to stop, wooooo!"

I lifted myself up, reached over to the nightstand and grabbed both of the wine glasses.

Jessica took a generous sip, quenching her thirst. I sat with my back against the headboard, sampling my wine, wondering what else was going to transpire between the two of us and praying that this wasn't going to end up as something Marc could clown me about.

Jessica curled up next to me, captivating me with her gaze. I swear I felt like I was drowning in the depths of her sparkling green eyes.

"You are so wrong, Mr. Bernard. When someone taps out, you're obliged to stop."

"I'm sorry, I didn't hear a plea or you saying uncle. My hearing was impeded by your luscious legs," I told Jessica, rubbing her still-shaking thigh.

"You just remember what's good for the goose is good for the gander." She put down her emptied glass and grasped my swollen member.

I could only imagine how Jessica planned to repay me for torturing her beyond her threshold of pleasure.

Jessica rose up and kissed me deeply, without releasing my tool, slowly stroking it with expertise. Again our tongues danced a forbidden dance.

"Mmmm, I taste delicious," she said, savoring a sampling of her own sexuality that lingered on my lips.

Jessica descended upon my lap and began licking the helmet of my rod, wetting it properly as she stretched her lips to accommodate me. She bobbed her head up and down, relaxing her jaws, taking in all of me, inch by inch until my entire shaft disappeared.

No words could describe how good it felt. My vocal chords were paralyzed in appreciation of her determination to orally pleasure me. It was criminal not to release my seed and show her just how I was enjoying myself. But I refused to climax in this manner.

I wanted to be inside her.

Playing with her fat clitoris and sliding a digit into her well moistened hole drove me to pull her up and into me.

"You don't play fair, Cameron. You knew I wanted to feel you explode in my mouth," she whispered in my ear while I reached over to the nightstand and pulled out a three-pack of Trojan ENZ's, hoping she hadn't noticed that the box was already opened.

"That's because I'm not playing. I'm seriously about to put in work," I told her, unsheathing the condom and putting it on.

Jessica straddled me and guided me inside her saturated slit.

"I don't need you to exert yourself, I can handle it all from up here."

"Well, you're the one up there, no need to talk me to death. Show me what you got," I prodded her.

Being ridden was not my favorite sexual position, mostly because I hated being underneath my mate, at her mercy and being dominated. But I let Jessica do her thing, and she ground her goodness into me, in a slow motion, losing herself in her own ecstasy and motivated by my moaning.

"Talk to me, Cameron. Tell me how good this pussy feels to you."

I would have been lying if I didn't admit that Jessica had the bomb and she was working it with expertise. But I kept it quiet, hoping my silence would inspire her to put in an even greater effort and more focus on her horsemanship.

"I know the cat doesn't have your tongue, that was minutes ago. Tell me how good this pussy feels to you," Jessica panted as if she were determined to make me voice my approval of her skills.

"Yeah baby, that's it throw it on Daddy," I obliged.

Jessica, finally satisfied with my response, bounced up and down, taking me to the hilt, then lifting almost completely off of me while holding my head captive for the next plunge into her.

As much as I was feeling the physical aspect of our pairing, the vision of her relishing her own work was even more gratifying.

Jessica's perfectly shaped breasts glistened from the beads of sweat which formed on her chest. They bounced beautifully as she ran her finger through her auburn curls, losing herself in the moment until she convulsed in full ecstasy and fell into a heap upon me, breathing heavily.

I turned Jessica over onto her back while I was still lodged in her canal.

Jessica had won a round that I had been a mere party to. Her catching a nut before me wasn't even selfish in my book. I dug the freedom in which she fucked me and showed no inhibition.

"Now it's my turn and best believe I brought my hard hat," I declared.

Jessica stretched out her long legs, wrapped them around my waist and arched her hips to give me full access to prove my point.

"Don't tell me shit, Daddy, I'm from Missouri, show me!" she told me and even though I knew for a fact that she was from Vallejo, I got her point.

Jessica readied herself for the ravishment I had promised, but instead of going for the beat-up, I finessed the situation. I took long strokes into her cramped space until I was balls deep comfortably. Jessica responded to my presence with a low moan and a quick catching of her breath.

"Ooh Cameron, you are all up in it, baby. It's yours if you want it. Make it yours, daddy," she encouraged, smacking me flush on the ass.

I felt the sharp sting and I quickened the rate of my thrust.

"Ooh, ooh, Cameron... don't stop. Get it!"

I was thrashing myself into her body with my face nestled in her neck when I asked her if my being on top was her favorite position. Jessica told me how much she was enjoying what was transpiring between us but if I really wanted to take her, I should dog it from the back.

I believed there were really only four real sexual positions; on top, on bottom, on your side and from the back. Anything else was just a variation of the aforementioned, unless of course, you were one of those Karma Sutra motherfuckers, which to me was more yoga than fucking.

Of the four positions, burying my bone from the back had always been and would forever be my position of choice. Call it just the dog in me if you like, but make sure to do so before your face was in the pillow like Jessica's was now. Even if she did have an objection, I wouldn't hear it.

Oh my, God, did this woman have an ass on her. I marveled at its splendor while she spread it before me.

I grabbed Jessica by her small waist and drove myself into the sweetness she offered as a sacrifice to my desire and debauchery.

She grunted as she felt the length of me coursing through her space.

Finally, I was in the driver's seat and readied to release my seed.

"Woah! Woah!" Jessica shouted as she unsuccessfully attempted to restrict my pounding by putting her hands back. But I was too far gone to be restrained.

Jessica had faded out of the room. There was only her pussy, me, and the rhythm and her pussy was playing my song.

"Here we come, walking down the streets, get the funniest looks from, everyone we meet. Hey, hey we're the Monkees."

I grunted, heaved and let the silver back go go rilla out, then slumped over unto Jessica's moistened back and stayed that way until my prophylactic clad snake went flaccid and slipped from her cave.

CHAPTER 21

The crowd at Geoffrey's Inner Circle was everything that I thought it would be. The upscale club catered to the shot callers and real ballers in the Bay. My homie, Shannon Reeves, the NAACP's youngest regional director, who I attended Grambling with, was in the house as well.

We chopped it up with fellow Gramblinites, E-40 and B-Legit, at the bar.

The Golden State Warriors had played against the Seattle Supersonics and 'The Glove,' Gary Payton blessed us with his presence.

"Don't go up there acting bougie just because you see niggas wearing suits. Keep it real, this Oaktown," he told me, ordering a round for everyone who was in the immediate area of the packed bar much to the delight of the patrons.

"You know bitches are gonna be ordering shit they can't even pronounce because you're footing the bill, GP," I told him.

"Hey, anyone order a Marlot or a Courvoiseur will be a thirsty non-pronouncing motherfucker, believe that," he said, loudly laughing.

GP was wondering why I was hanging back at the bar instead of cruising the club for a new conquest.

"The way y'all spanked the Warriors tonight, I thought I would let them get first crack at some pity pussy."

I had made the quip but honestly, my reason behind me being posted at the bar wasn't my generosity, but because the bar offered the best vantage point to see who entered and exited the front door.

After my date with Jessica that literally ended with a bang, I knew I had set myself up for disaster. Tasha was definitely going to be in the building with hopes that we would be spending the rest of the evening together. Which was the furthest thing from the truth as far as I was concerned. Our last tango had already occurred and my new side piece was more than likely on her way to the club.

Marc was having a ball hanging out with Ebony, but he was finding the possibility of me being cold busted even more entertaining.

So far, there hadn't been any fireworks to amuse him, but even I knew that the sparks weren't far from igniting. As far as I knew, the gunpowder was just waiting for the other participants in my lust triangle to arrive.

I was pressed but the Jack Daniels, courtesy of GP's generosity, took the edge off.

Dugar had begun the show, so instead of concerning myself with what might go down, I turned my attention to what I'd been paid to concentrate on, my set.

Because the clientele at Geoffrey's was a mixture of professionals and street CEOs, instead of beating them over with topical humor, I chose to perform my *ComicView* TV friendly set and see how far I could push them to the edge.

Dugar had them eating out of his hand.

His performance was a clinic for anyone aspiring to learn how to be a true Master of Ceremony. He tiptoed around subjects so that there was room for those who followed him to put their own personal stamp on the current events. This was especially necessary for a comedian like Marc because he got a kick outta sticking it to people and places in the news.

"So have you been paying Doogie attention or have you been too preoccupied about how fucked up my night might turn out?" I asked Marc.

"As much as I would like to see the sky fall in on your uppity ass, my performance is first and foremost on my mind."

Maybe I was putting too much on it.

Marc was due up on stage and I had yet to see Jessica or Tasha.

For all I knew, I was the one being cold played and was going to be dateless tonight.

Dugar had just dropped one hell of an opening set and brought Marc up to the stage.

I had to admit Marc didn't seem one bit concerned about what I was going through. He was at the top of his game firing off a Kirk-Franklin-falling-from-the-stage bit that had the crowd in stitches. I had to admit the flavor of his material was on point.

I was so caught up in his performance that I had stopped chicken-hawking the door.

That was my first mistake.

Then, when I realized that Tasha and Jessica were standing next to me, I knew that was my second mistake. My third mistake was inviting two bad bitches to one club to see me at the same damn time.

I should have just told Tasha not to come. I mean, we had enjoyed a good run but The Body had replaced her, plain and simple.

Mouton must have sensed some tension between the three of us because he rushed over and laid down a sacrifice fly for me.

"Tasha, what's up, girl? I'm glad to see you. If you don't mind, I need to holla at you for a few ticks," he told her, pulling her away to discuss some Sweet Jimmy's business that could have waited but he made it seemed urgent.

"Nothing like having friends who will play Captain Save a Hoe, huh?" Jessica questioned.

I was sure that she had recognized Tasha from that after party, so I was in no position to argue a point.

Instead, I complimented her on how good she looked in the fitted basic black dress that made her body look anything but basic.

"Why thank you, Reesie, and I dig you in that pinstripe suit."

I wasn't casket-clean, but I was confident the brown suit with cream pinstripes was slick. I was just glad she noticed.

"Well, thank you. Let me apologize for the scene that almost happened. Can I offer you a drink?" I asked her, turning toward the bartender.

"I'll take a screaming orgasm."

Of course she had left a window wide open for a sarcastic reply, but instead I chose to order the vodka with Baileys and Kahlua like she had asked for.

After the bartender had prepared Jessica's creamy concoction and freshened up my double jack, I guided her to the table designated for the acts.

Dugar was already seated in the company of a gorgeous chocolate woman named Ursula whom he introduced to us with great pride. She seemed to be quite smitten with him and happy to make our acquaintance. Ebony was also at the table. She sat up proudly, pleased to be the companion of the act the appreciative crowd was currently enjoying. I guess some chicks are just like that. They get excited being close to talent. I was happy that my libido wasn't attached to or dependent upon the fame of whom I was involved with. If Ebony's pussy pulsed because she was in the company of my feature act, it wasn't my place to judge.

I was getting my head together to perform, but I was still mindful of Tasha being in the building and having to be dealt with at some point. Sure, Mouton had put his finger in the dyke, holding back the water, but she and I had wrestled naked too many times for her to let me walk away without some form of struggle. Honestly if she did, my feelings would have been hurt.

"Looks like your boy is wrapping it up, you ready to work?" Dugar asked excusing himself from the table and preparing to relieve Marc of the microphone.

"Shit I was born ready, Pimpin'. Let's do this," I told him, feeling quite cocky.

It was funny how being in the company of a drop-dead gorgeous chick could boost your self-esteem. After thinking about it, I couldn't really say anything about Ebony and how she felt.

Marc exited the stage to what was becoming common -- a well entertained crowd. I was digging the friendly competition between the two of us. He was raising the bar and I kept meeting the challenge. Tonight wasn't going to be any different.

After Dugar introduced me, I approached the microphone with plans of talking about something that was completely different than what came out of my mouth. When I went into my material about my father passing and his funeral, the artist within me was awakened. I wasn't concerned about the laughter from the crowd. I had a need to get something off my chest about what was real. Sometimes it was the stuff that you dreaded or loathed most that made for conversation that transcended jokes. When I talked about my father's will and how the shit he requested wasn't covered by the insurance, folks were howling in their chairs. The laughter only escalated when I spoke of family members fighting over shit we'd wanted to throw out, but had to wait for Pops to die to do so. I guess universally black folks be on bullshit when it came to burials because everyone was feeling what I was putting out.

I free-styled my way through a forty-five-minute set that had people on their feet clapping, smiling, and congratulating me. Everyone in Geoffrey's inner circle seemed to be happy with me, all except Tasha who was standing next to the comic's table. She had her arms folded in front and her weight resting on one hip.

When I stepped over to her, she said, "Cameron, we have always been bigger than you ever coming here and playing me close. I'm not mad about your choice, I'm just disappointed on how messy you handled this."

There wasn't anything to say and I refused to lower my head. That move wouldn't have gone with the suit and alligator shoes.

I had made up my mind about the direction I was headed. All roads led to Jessica and crocodile tears weren't on the menu. I gave Jessica a look of apology and excused myself to have a more private word with Tasha.

"Look T, you know I have dug you for a long time. When we started this, we mutually agreed that when it had run its course either one of us could pull the plug with no regrets."

"That's true, and to keep it real, I'm probably only mad because you beat me to the punch. I found someone who I believe I can have a real future with. I was planning on telling you tonight after I gave you some goodbye ass."

The way she said real future kinda fucked with me, but she deserved to get that off without me saying shit. I mean I was getting off without any real incident.

We shared a hug and a peck on the cheek. I knew Jessica was probably peering and I wasn't about to fuck up what I had to appease that which was exiting from my life. Tasha freed herself from my arms and vanished into the crowd.

I reflected on the fun times we shared for a moment, then turned and headed back to the table.

Marc was heading out with Ebony.

"Cameron, I don't know how you do it, but you always find a way to come out of a hairy situation unscathed."

I could tell he was disappointed shit wasn't more heated between me and Tasha. If we weren't in a crowded club that had just lost one of its loveliest members when Tasha vacated, and if Jessica wasn't marinating over at the table, I might have made an effort to give him a clue. But we were at Geoffrey's, I had just told my side chick goodbye, and my new person of interest was waiting on me with a screaming orgasm that I was sure was in need of refreshing.

"Yeah lucky me, Tasha came here to bid me farewell," I told him, conceding a victory for his delight.

What Marc didn't understand was that my being completely honest had saved me the embarrassment of Tasha losing her cool. Sure, I hadn't mentioned Jessica to her, but what she knew all along was, I wasn't her man. Of course she could be irritated, but deep down inside Tasha knew we were both free to pursue whatever adventures we could imagine.

As I walked over to the table I thought about how happy I was Tasha found something concrete.

"I'm sorry about that little interruption; please allow me to make it up to you," I told Jessica, bending down and planting a kiss on her neck.

"She's gone and we're leaving together; there is no need to apologize, Reesie."

With her calling me by my nickname and stating the obvious, I knew everything between us were cool.

Marc had left because we had an early flight to catch in the morning. My plan had been to wait until we were alone to surprise Jessica with the news that I had made plans to stick around for two extra days, but I saw this as a better time than any to spring it on her.

"I talked with Karen and explained that I had some pressing matters to attend to here with TMB and Mouton, so I guess we can spend some more time together if you're available."

"Do you really have to spend time with those guys or was that a rouse you concocted to be with me?"

I admitted that it was a little of both. I could have easily talked over the details of the proposed tour with TMB over the phone, but I was really feeling the necessity to spend more time in her presence. The issue of Karen was handled by explaining the tour opportunity. And since I always packed more clothes just in case I got stuck somewhere, Jessica and I were clear for take-off as far as I was concerned.

We hung out for a while, shooting the shit with the movers and shakers of The Bay area. Marc's pussy-whipped ass would have done himself a great favor by sticking around and networking. That night, I got booked for shows in San Jose, Sacramento and San Francisco by promoters who were in the place scouting for talent. My impending business with TMB and Mou caused me to steer the conversations toward them and as a courtesy to my boy, I made sure they had Marc's best interest as well.

"Lisa is going to kill me!" I said as Jessica and I exited the nightclub.

"And who the hell is Lisa? I mean, I know about Karen and I just watched Tasha leave. Cameron, you can't really be telling me there is another woman to worry about?"

"Carrot, you got it all wrong, sweetie. Lisa is my manager and she hates it when I leave her out the loop. Now I'll have to explain to her how she is entitled to three commissions that she didn't negotiate."

From the fact that she kept her grasp in mine, I figured Jessica was satisfied with my answer. I couldn't even be mad with her suspicion; I was asking an awful lot from a chick this fine, to understand my domestic situation and extra-curricular activities. It wasn't like she could have told me she was renting out space in her crotch to all comers and I would have been comfortable with it.

My stomach was growling when we got to her ride. I was hungrier than a runaway slave. We were only minutes away from the hotel and room service, but Jessica and I hadn't discussed whether or not she was planning to continue the night with me. And after already pushing the limits of our new arrangement, I saw no reason to be more imposing.

"Do you feel like grabbing a bite to eat?" I asked, giving her the option of going to Denny's in Emeryville.

"Would you mind if we just went to your room and ordered something? I've had enough of crowds and my heels have expired."

Pleased that I had given her the driver's seat when it concerned our destination, I agreed that room service was perfect with only one catch -- that I was allowed to foot the bill. It was the least I could do after that ordeal at Geoffrey's.

"Reesie, can I tell you something?"

"As beautiful as you are, and as long as it's not that you began this life as a baby boy, you can tell me anything," I replied.

Jessica was too amused to dignify my stupidity with an answer.

"What I was going to tell you, Mr. Bernard, is that our relationship isn't going to be normal. I'm not going to trip on your home life, complain about your work or be concerned about your comings and goings."

I nodded my head even though I wasn't sure where she was headed with this conversation.

"So since we're in agreement that this is not a basic arrangement, baby, you have to stop trying to treat me like a basic bitch."

As we pulled into the hotel parking lot, I agreed to do a better job of not putting whatever we were embarking on into the basic box. With her hand in mine, I proudly escorted her through the lobby and to the elevator.

There was just as much passion between us as our first journey upstairs. This time, though, there was less mystery and our real hunger was felt more in our stomachs than our loins.

Jessica and I were greeted by the sensual sounds of the savagery taking place between Marc and Ebony as we exited the elevator.

"Sounds like someone is having fun tonight," she said with a broad smile.

I agreed with her and thought that we would be causing the same amount of auditory ruckus immediately after we calmed the rumble in our bellies. Keeping with my gentlemanly ways, I opened and held the door for her so not to lose points and also to get another gander of that incredible ass in her form-fitting dress. I considered dismissing the idea of sinking my teeth into a T-bone and instead, taking in the luscious sight before me, but my stomach grumbled, winning the argument away from my swelling member.

While we ordered our food, we were serenaded by the constant thump of Marc banging away in his room right next door to ours. Ebony was howling obscenities. Letting all on the floor know he was hitting her spot.

"She must have watched the *Devil in a Blue Dress*," Jessica chided.

"After we finish with this food, I'm going to be like Lucifer getting you out of that little black number you have on."

Jessica was more than aware of my skill level and didn't bother questioning if I was keeping it real or if I was talking myself up. I wasn't just talking.

She called room service and ordered chicken fettuccini for herself and a medium rare steak for me.

"Baby, would you like red or white wine?" she asked me to complete the order.

Though I wasn't much of a wino, I ordered dark wine so

I wouldn't go against my rule of never mixing dark and light alcohol.

***

I was awakened from my deep sleep by my phone ringing. It was Marc telling me to get a move on so we could make our way to the shuttle and be on our way to the Oakland airport.

Jessica was nestled near me and I rose, so not to disturb her.

"Yo man, I'm not going to be making that flight, I have some business to attend to here in town," I told him in a hushed tone.

"I would have thought that you would have taken care of that business like I did last night, Cameron," he replied.

I allowed his sarcastic remark to slide and explained to him that no gash would have me extending my stay, but a real opportunity to make some cash was my reasoning for not leaving the Bay. It wasn't like I was equating the beauty that I was sharing my time with to a simple piece of ass, but I found it necessary for my friend to know I was more about my paper than some pussy. Before getting off the phone I congratulated him in his conquest of the dark beauty Ebony, and wished him safe passage back to LA.

Jessica stirred when I was hanging up the phone, but I settled her from waking by squeezing her gently in my arms.

I would have liked to think that my powerful lovemaking made her slumber in such a manner, but I knew that this was the kind of sleep brought on by a heavy meal and too much wine. My ego had to take a back seat to that realization as I fell back into the throes of peaceful rest.

When I finally awoke at ten, I was treated to the sweet aroma of lavender and the tranquil sounds of the shower. The scent was so enchanting that I followed it to the bathroom finding her enjoying a reinvigorating refreshing shower.

"Mind if I join you?" I asked, pulling back the shower curtain somewhat startling the half-breed beauty.

"Reesie, you know good and well if you get in this shower we will be under this water until our skin wrinkles. Give me a few minutes and the bathroom is all yours," she replied, effectively thwarting my attempt for morning glory.

"That's cool, you want me to call downstairs and order us something to eat?"

"No need, I already took the liberty to have some eggs, bacon, toast, orange juice and coffee to be sent up," she told me as I relieved myself into the commode.

"And don't you dare flush that toilet, Mr. Bernard."

I laughed as I exited the bathroom, wrapping the plush white terry cloth robe provided by the hotel around me in preparation for room service to arrive. By the time our food was delivered to the room, Jessica had joined me, adorned in the matching robe. She had a towel wrapped around her crimson mane and a smile on her face that could have lit up a black hole.

"Well good morning, Reesie; the food smells delicious."

"Yes it does, but it can't rival the scent of you." I enjoyed the floral assault on my olfaction.

We enjoyed our breakfast and plotted the course of our day.

I knew I had to meet with TMB and Mouton to figure out just what the proposed tour dates and locations would be. I also wanted to Western Union Lisa her commission even though she insisted that I waited until my return from Northern California.

"I need to head to the house and grab something to wear. Daddy, you can come with or hang here until I return."

I told Jessica to handle her business, that way I could tie up my personal loose ends and get some writing in. I knew she understood without me saying it -- I had to check in with my real life before I would be free to continue fantasizing with her. I appreciated that she didn't judge me nor put up a struggle. She knew that putting up an argument would have only found our fantasy at an end had she done so.

I dialed Karen first and as soon as she picked up she said, "So just when do you intend to bring your ass home, Cameron?"

That was Karen suspecting I was on trash, but not willing to fuel any fire I might have had blazing by pressing too much. I was glad that Jessica had taken all of that body away from my room so she didn't have to witness me being punked by my babies' mamma.

"I'll be back by Tuesday evening. Mouton and his partner, TMB, are trying to put something together that's going to be very profitable."

A few months ago, this conversation wouldn't have been questioned, but the fact that we were sitting on a grip of cash made Karen call bullshit.

"I don't know who you think is a fool, Cameron, but just remember I'm sitting here in this house and I know the combination to the safe."

I didn't even dignify her threat with a response. I just kept it pushing like she hadn't said some shit that would find her sleeping with the fish like Gwen.

"Hey, I gotta get ready for this meeting. Tell the twins that I love them and I love you, too."

Not going for the sucker shit, Karen hung up without acknowledging she heard or cared about what I had said.

The meeting between Mouton and TMB was simply three brothers getting together over a few delicious Nation burgers, French fries, and some cokes. The succulent flavor of those beef patties couldn't rival the tasty opportunities we had before us. TMB had concocted a righteous plan. I would grab three recognizable acts and tour the Wild Wild West first class. He and Mouton explained to me how they were scamming the airlines out of airfare and how fail proof it was.

"The shit is so sweet, Cam, I didn't even hesitate to put my grandmoms on a flight to see her sick sister in Louisiana, and you know I wouldn't fuck around with Granny," Mouton told me in efforts to convince me of just how solid the hook-up was.

After being in cahoots with Lance, I didn't need much prodding to get ahead by doing dirt. I didn't need the details of how they did what they did, I just wanted the safety exit strategy. My lesson learned from the Great One was to always have paperwork handy to cover my ass.

"You're an entertainer and that works for people who don't know you until you get to your destination. That fact alone and saying that you are traveling to perform, should be enough to keep you out of harm's way."

That sounded about right enough for me. I knew that I could put on an Oscar award winning performance in front of any airport worker so my fears were at a minimal.

"I'm down. I just have to pick the talent and make sure our schedules are available for the dates and everything should be smooth."

There wasn't much to haggle over. We had chosen the west coast as our initial targeted region of the country. TMB suggested that we put on a show in Vegas during the Tyson vs. Seldon fight. I didn't balk at it; I saw the earning potential. The only real challenge that we anticipated was taking the show to the 50th state. I assured TMB that my man, Pierre Cockrell, had Anchorage on lock and we had no worries as far as that was concerned.

"So they have a black population that will support a Def Jam kind of concert?" asked the rotund broad-built brother.

"I don't know how many black motherfuckers live there, but I can tell you they so bored in Anchorage that you could promote a grudge boxing match and three thousand folks will pay to see it." I explained to them how Pierre came up with the event when he had a dispute with a mechanic and challenged him to fist to cuffs. He was making a killing once a month with bouts between everyday Joes and Joans who had a score to settle. If he could get three thousand folks to see nobodies slug it out, I knew he could get at least a thousand more folks to watch me and my friends from TV slang jokes.

Pierre was a slick cat from Tacoma, Washington. He had been splitting his time between Hilltop and Anchorage. Just to give him shit, I asked him which witness protection agent had he pissed off to be sent to Alaska. When I went to visit him, I realized why he dug it so much. Anchorage was a place where an in-shape caramel brother blessed with the gift of gab could flourish. There, he had found his Shangri La and with his help, I was going to put on the biggest black comedy show The Wilderness of America's last untamed state had ever seen.

"It must feel good to have one of the baddest broads in the town sporting you like a new bracelet," Mouton chimed in as Jessica pulled up in Jack London Square ready to whisk me off in her shiny black Benz.

"I dig being displayed in public, but the private privileges are even better," I replied.

They both gave me dap and we concluded our meeting. We had discussed all the details of the proposed seven-city tour and I was geeked about the possibilities. Lisa was going to be upset about the fact that again, I had earned her commission.

I left my boys and went outside to join the company of my newfound friend.

"Good afternoon, sweetheart, and how are you doing?" I asked as I entered her German luxury sedan.

Jessica was casual but chic in her black leather coat white turtleneck sweater black denim pants and patent leather ankle boots. I loved the way her crimson curls cascaded over her collar and how her sensuous mouth was painted in a fiery orange that complemented her mane.

"Yes, the afternoon just got better with you in my midst, Daddy. Seeing that you have just eaten, I don't have to rush to feed you," she replied, making me feel quite welcome. "So were you able to tie up all your business or do you require my services in aiding in their completion?"

"Well, I still need to get to a western union to get my manager her loot, but after that I'm free."

"So you don't need to handle any business pertaining to your home?"

I wasn't going to allow her being sprung on the dick and now acting insecure, to get in the way of us enjoying the last couple of days together. So I played it off and assured her that my home life was situated.

"How 'bout you and I worry about my road life while we're together."

"I dig it, Daddy, let's."

We darted off to a bodega on 15th street that was being held under siege by the scent of patchouli. The store owner wasn't very fluent in English, but it was obvious he was familiar with my female companion as he blurted out Spanish pleasantries. *"Asi buenas tardes señora atractiva y cómo puedo ayudarle?"*

I guess he must have thought I looked like I had flunked Spanish in junior high school. I mean I had, but that didn't mean I couldn't translate that he was flirting with my peoples right in front of me. I wanted to swat the nervy silver front-toothed bastard from behind the counter, but instead I played it cool.

"Estoy bien señor pero no creo que mi compañero apreciaría la naturaleza ligona en la cual usted me ha hablado."

Jessica checked the man behind the counter, then respectfully introduced me. Though he was still smarting from being blasted, the storeowner assisted me in sending a thousand dollars to Lisa.

I was sure that when she received the money, Lisa was going to argue that it was too much. But I already had it in my mind to explain to her it was an advance for the work she was going to do for the Cameron B Wild Wild West Comedy Jam I had concocted along with Mouton and TMB.

After concluding my business with TMB and Mouton, then making sure Lisa was taken care of, Jessica asked if I would mind accompanying her on a quick mission. How could I say no? I agreed so we headed over the bridge to San Francisco.

My mind had drifted, lulled by the beautiful Bay weather and before I knew it, Jessica had me standing in front of some dude who looked like someone had pissed him off two minutes ago.

"Cameron, this is Kwan. Kwan, let me introduce you to Cameron Bernard," Jessica said.

Less than two hours ago, we were in the bodega and now, here was another man who despised me because I was in the company of this mixed beauty.

Kwan Tran didn't even make an attempt to conceal his contempt toward me as he shook my hand. I could tell that he and Jessica were never lovers, but that didn't get in the way of his love for her.

From the looks of things, the two of them not being together had nothing to do with his appearance or his possessions. Kwan was what I guessed to be an attractive Asian man. I said I guessed because I wasn't attracted to men and I couldn't fucking really say which Asian tribe he belonged to. My being from Cleveland kinda hampered me from being able to distinguish the variations, but my guess was that he was Korean.

He was 5'8, well-muscled, and kept an outwardly clean appearance. If he had been wearing a suit instead of sportswear, his tattoos would have been hidden and I would have figured him for just another cat working in corporate America.

That much about him I had right. He was a corporate dude, but the twist was he was a tech boy. Kwan didn't have to be confined by the normal suit that company's outside of Silicon Valley demanded of its employees. He was a printing software guru and a genius graphic artist who had talent that caused rival companies like Apple and Hewlett-Packard to woo him like college coaches promised high school seniors the world to join their programs.

But Kwan Tran didn't plan on making someone else wealthy and wasting twenty-five years of his life to only to be given a gold-plated watch. His intention was to be just as wealthy as the company executives who were courting him and Kwan had the necessary talent to make his own money.

"May I offer you a drink, Mr. Bernard?" Kwan asked me after releasing his firm grip on my hand and walking over to a fully furnished bar.

It was too early in the day to get twisted, but seeing as how I'd had the greasy hamburger lining my stomach and only Jessica's business dealings to consider, I accepted Kwan's offer.

"I'll take a vodka and lime with two cubes."

"That's one vodka lime with two cubes coming up," he said while he made my drink and showed just how familiar he was with my companion by pouring Jessica a glass of white wine without so much as asking her. I made a mental note of it but because I was only two or three days into enjoying the sweetness of Jessica, I wasn't going to be pulling the jealous territorial card.

After pouring himself a stiff double bourbon, Kwan went into why he had asked Jessica to bring me along to his plush loft apartment in the financial district of San Francisco.

"Mr. Bernard, I'm in the business of making money and from the looks of things so are you. I can't speak for you, but I've tired of pimping my talents for others to make money. I've changed the game, so to speak, and decided to make money for myself." His pissivity seemed to be tapering off and he was all business.

Kwan slammed down a grip of at least ten thousand dollars' worth of crisp one hundred dollar bills.

Now that I was no stranger to having loot, the ten racks weren't impressive until Jessica explained to me that Kwan wasn't being matter of fact when he proclaimed he *made* money.

Kwan was *really making* money.

"Reesie, I'm sorry if I blindsided you with all this, but I knew from the moment we were together you would be a perfect fit."

Here I was again being set up to play a part in someone else's hustle for the second time today. Both were no different than how Lance had enlisted me. I received before I had to bite: TMB was offering me free passage. Jessica had already provided hassle-free loving, and Kwan topped it off with ten thousand dollars' worth of high quality counterfeit cash plus a refreshing vodka lime with two cubes.

Again, I was a willing pawn in another person's game against big business. Irene hadn't raised me to be a criminal, but nonetheless that was exactly what I had grown up to be. My only rationale was that the big businesses were just as guilty as I was.

Neither Jessica nor TMB had to twist my arm to join them in their endeavors. I saw they had a solid hustle and I was ready to dive into the deep end.

"So how much of this can you deliver on?" I asked, ready to negotiate my terms.

"I'm better than the US mint, man. I don't make my money dependent on how much gold I have in the reserve. All I worry about is ink and paper."

Jessica was sitting on the couch, sipping her wine, letting Kwan and I haggle out our business. I felt like I was her Anna. Here I was sitting on enough hard earned cash and had a job opportunity that should have warranted my not being thirsty for more, but it occurred to me she must have smelled a greed in me that I didn't even realize existed. That could be the only reason for her bringing me into her and Kwan's circle of counterfeiters.

"Cameron, I have three million dollars right now that will stand up against any scrutiny. I'm willing to part with a million for three hundred thousand. If you need more I can supply it at a moment's notice."

"Man, how am I going to unload that kind of funny money?"

"You can do it one bill at a time, which would take forever or mix it in with real money and spend it freely without conscience."

"Yeah, it's only been three days but it feels like an eternity, Carrot," I replied, not letting on about my other more prevailing thought.

It wasn't that I didn't really desire to be in her presence, but my hustle hand was itching and that sensation dominated any lustful thoughts I harbored.

We were wrapping up our conversation when Lisa surprised me by tapping on my window. Luckily, it wasn't a good weather day where I would have had my top down and her hearing my exchange about crimes of the heart and of a fraudulent nature.

I quickly ended my call without saying another word. Jessica wouldn't be upset; she had become use to my abrupt termination of our contact once I'd returned home and I appreciated the lack of pressure on her end. That lack of pressure made it easy for me to lead a double life between her and Karen.

In the instant before rolling down my window, I pondered how much longer before Jessica's patience would wear off or how long before Karen would figure out my mind was on someone else.

"Well, things must be going well at home because Karen has you smiling from ear to ear."

Instead of lying to my manager, I just continued to cheese like a cat whom had eaten the canary.

"Hey, Lisa. You hungry? I'm starving; let's go grab a bite."

She walked around my British automobile and got inside. She was in her regular grunge attire. The baggy jeans, the cotton t-shirt, and blue jean jacket were in complete contrast to the polished look I wore.

"Cameron, you might be the only client I've had who's overpaid me and has sprung for my meal."

"Who said anything about paying for you to eat? I just offered to give you a ride," I chided in reply.

I was kidding around, but we needed to have a serious conversation. Lisa had been cool about the tour idea, but again my negotiating without her input had my manager infuriated.

"Seeing that I'm paying for it, then I'm picking the spot. You cool with that?" I asked my lanky Nordic passenger.

I had never steered Lisa wrong when I invited her out to lunch, so she didn't argue my point.

I had the taste for corned beef and I knew a trip to Jerry's Deli just might be the trick to calm Lisa's intensity as it concerned her chastisement of me.

"I was thinking we could grab some Sky High Corn Beef sandwiches and negotiate the terms of my surrender," I said flashing my pearly whites.

"It's going to take a lot more than your smile and some food, Cameron. I'm at wit's ends with you. I mean, normally my

clients overwork and underpay me. You overpay me and refuse to let me do shit. What am I to do with you?"

"Well, seeing that I'm good for your finances, keep meat on your bones, and probably save you from complete boredom, I'd suggest we make a mutual agreement to keep working together until either I surrender to your will or you quit fighting me in my being so generous."

"You are incorrigible!"

"Our partnership wouldn't be fun if I was any other way, now would it be?"

As much as Lisa hated to admit it, I was right and she knew it. But my taking her out to lunch was just one part of my attempt at apologizing. I had arranged for her office to be fully remodeled by the good folks at OfficeMax, courtesy of Kwan's prowess. I figured it would be a proper thing to do some good with the bad cash. Not that I was superstitious, but it couldn't hurt my juju and Lisa's office could stand modernizing.

I pointed my blue automotive elegance westward on Wilshire Blvd. and raised the RPMs when I gunned the V12 engine. Lisa and I sped down the city street at a comfortable pitch while the Bose speakers pumped the sounds of R. Kelly's "Bump and Grind."

"Who is this guy? He leaves no room for imagination, does he?"

It amused and saddened me at the same time how you could be a superstar in the black community but totally unrecognized in mainstream society. That was why I hadn't fully turned over my bookings to Lisa. I knew that when she contacted booking agents outside my black scope, she was selling an unrecognized or ignored entity. I had honed a following and fandom among my own that didn't need her expertise.

"Damn, you never heard of R. Kelly? The 12 Play CD is responsible for the spike in African American pregnancies and abortions. This ain't your father's R&B where the Temptations sing about "My Girl." R sings about that raw shit."

"My father didn't listen to Rhythm and Blues, but I get your point. It's definitely raw, but it's infectious and it's catchy. I need to pick up a copy of this," she replied, bobbing her head to the beat.

"You damn right it's catching, you might get a yeast infection just listening to it. You're more than welcome to this one, I'm sure I've gotten more than my money's worth out of it. Plus, Karen and I have already made our contribution to the black community." I ejected the CD out of the stereo and handed it to her.

She handled the CD with caution like my remark about it being communicable was true.

While at the stop light at Wilshire and San Vicente, I took the opportunity to pop in Stevie Wonder's "Innervisions" and the classic recordings played until we arrived at our destination.

When we pulled up, I realized this was the first time I had ever been to the establishment sober or in the daytime. Jerry's was the after hour's diner for the club crowd; it was The Club Part II. It was the place that if you hadn't scored with a honey, this was overtime and extra innings.

It also was the place to grab a bite and catch a glimpse of many of Hollywood's stars in the wee early hours of the morning. My comedy crew and I had peeled out of there right before the sun rose many mornings.

The deli had a different feel, though in the daytime. Bobby Brown and Tyson Beckford weren't holding court at any of the large round tables. While they slept and recharged, business professionals on lunch break took their places in the establishment.

While we waited to be seated, Lisa and I took in the fresh deli fragrance. All of the offerings were behind a glass case. Though we had made up our minds about what we were going to eat, it was tempting to see the luscious desserts on display.

"With shit like this I don't know how women keep in such good shape in LA."

"Vomiting and exercise. Sometimes they skip the gym altogether," Lisa quipped.

I was glad that I wasn't a woman in the Hollywood rat race after hearing her frank remark.

After what seemed like forever but really was only about a seven-minute wait, our less than glamorous hostess came and took us to a booth. The drab brunette handed us our menus and went away to get us some water after telling us to take a few minutes to look over Jerry's massive menu. I purposely stalled, making my order even though I knew exactly what I had a taste for. But I was conscious of the workers needing time to pull off my surprise at Lisa's office.

"I think those young ladies are trying to get your attention," Lisa said, referring to the group of twenty-something year olds seated across from us.

I saw their looks of recognition when we walked in. Of course Lisa didn't realize that I was getting my Hollywood front on and acting like I wasn't me.

I had learned that trick hanging out with the comedy big boys like Jamie Foxx and Eddie Griffin. Even though everyone in the place knew it was them, they could find a way to make people second guess the truth their eyes were telling them, which only made folks curious enough to introduce themselves.

When I saw the three young ladies getting out of their seats and heading over to our booth, I knew my ploy was successful.

"Oh my, GOD. Aren't you Cameron B from *Def Comedy Jam*?" asked the brown-skinned cutie who could have easily doubled for Lark Voorhees.

I looked up from the menu and smiled and acknowledged that she was correct.

"I told you that was him, I told you," she said to the light-skinned member of the trio.

She wasn't any celebrity's twin but owned a body that was very athletic and a brilliant smile that made her plain face light up.

"I didn't say it wasn't you," she said to me. "I just said I didn't believe you were as tall as you are."

"Yeah on *ComicView* and Def Jam; it's just me and I'm not next to anyone to gauge how tall or short I am."

"That ain't it," the first one said. "Cynthia just has a little ass TV; shit, she would think the Jolly Green Giant was aa midget on that itty bitty screen," quipped the darkest of the three, causing all of the ladies, including Lisa to break out into loud laughter.

They introduced themselves: Monica, Cynthia and Sabrina.

"We are sorry for disturbing you and your lady's meal, but would you mind if we took a picture?" Monica asked, whipping out her camera like she wasn't going to take no for my answer.

"Oh, I'm not his lady," Lisa said. "I'm his manager and I'm sure Cameron would love to be photographed with you wonderful ladies," Lisa added as she passed along her business card.

Lisa was right. I didn't hesitate to rise up and oblige them. After taking a few photos I asked what had brought them to the City of Lost Angels. They told me that they were a singing group and were in town looking for employment and a place to stay.

"A singing group ... so can y'all sing?" I asked.

Instead of answering, the three belted out EnVogue's "Never Gonna Get It" in such perfect harmony that if EnVogue had been there, they would have gone back in the studio and worked on their vocals.

"Well, damn, I don't have to asked that dumb shit again. That was fantastic," I said, blown away by their talents.

"I know a few folks who might be able to help you get your foot in the door. That is, if you don't already have things set up." I wrote down my contact info on a napkin.

The trio shrilled in excitement and took my number, promising to call. The young ladies excused themselves, elated that they had met someone from television and a possible aide in the business.

Once we were alone, Lisa said, "Cameron, what on earth was that all about? You just had three attractive ladies audition for a record deal you don't have in place."

"It wasn't about what I had. They know I know someone who does and they were flexing their vocal cords to show they were worth a hook up."

Our drab waitress finally returned to take our order.

"So have you two decided?"

"Yes, we will have three sky high corn beef sandwiches and two lemonades. Please put one in a box for me to carry out, thank you," I told her, without looking up. It made no sense to waste my charm on her miserable ass.

"Our lemonade isn't very good; you could save that money by just asking for more water and I brought you out some lemon wedges."

I was irritated by her insinuation that I couldn't afford to pay for some punk ass lemonade. "Thank you, but I don't feel like laboring over my beverage and money is not an issue." I decided right then and there her tip would reflect my agitation.

Making sure that I wasted more than enough time for the office to be finished, I explained to Lisa that I needed to drop off Karen's lunch, if she didn't mind.

I wasn't surprised that Lisa agreed to me doing right by my girl; she dug Karen and thought it was admirable that I displayed concern.

Laura, our nondescript server, must have sensed my unhappiness with her. She returned with our food and drinks in a speedy fashion and much to my surprise, a smile that bitch must have had stored in the kitchen.

"I hope you two enjoy your meal and if you need anything just let me know," she insisted before walking away to handle her other customers.

"Well, that was a complete change of attitude. What do you make of that, Cameron?"

"I don't know, maybe Patti LaBelle works in the kitchen or she knew her tip was going to be 'smile bitch'."

Lisa laughed hard. She always laughed at my wisecracks and her laughter was genuine. I guessed that was why we were at a lunch and I was stalling. I wanted to do something nice as a token of appreciation for her believing in me.

"Hey, I know my shit is kinda raggedy with you, but I feel this tour is going to be big fun and we'll both make some scratch off the deal," I said to her between bites of my sandwich and a sip of the lemonade that was as bland as Laura had warned.

"Cameron, really you and I are okay. I was just trying to do my job but the problem is you won't let me." She paused, then added, "And what is scratch?"

"Scratch is money." I laughed. "Lisa, you are such a white girl and that's what I love about you. We are the perfect Ying and Yang. In the mainstream world, you move in a way I can only dream of. On the other hand, on the urban landscape of entertainment, I walk like a giant. Did you see how those girls reacted to me?"

"I did, but you're an attractive man. I'm sure that you get approached by women all the time."

"I appreciate the compliment, but that was all about me being a somebody enough to them that I could help them achieve their dream. If that were three white girls from Iowa, they wouldn't have thought enough of me to say a word and that all has to do with recognition. That's really where I need your expertise. I need to be showcased on some mainstream television and you, my great white hope of a manager, can get me there."

By the time we finished our gigantic mountains of meat and bread, Lisa and I had agreed upon a working relationship where she loosened on her demands of complete control and I made a better effort of getting out of our way.

Laura returned to our table several times, making sure we were satisfied with our meal. I couldn't help but to keep prying about her changing attitude.

When I asked her, she told me, "I've been here since last night. Everyone has been calling in and taking off and I'm tired as shit. Again, I apologize for acting like a zombie earlier."

I actually felt bad for judging her without knowing her story. Before we left, I made sure to gift her with one of the Bay Area's finest hundred dollar bills.

The girl group was piling into a Honda CRX, a car that could have doubled as a circus automobile, when Lisa and I made it to the parking lot. Monica made sure I knew how appreciative they were to have met me and told me she would be in contact.

The temperature had risen enough to pop the roof off my cat. Lisa and I made our way to the VA hospital with the brains blown and the sounds of Method Man and Mary J Blige "You Are All I Need."

CHAPTER 23

It wasn't a normal occurrence that I showed up at Karen's job unannounced, so I wasn't tripping when she was surprised to see me bearing the gift of grub. What did take me aback was the chumminess between her and a male co-worker when I exited the elevator to deliver her lunch. They weren't touching but the proximity between them was enough to catch me off guard.

"Hey, baby," she said, gathering herself. "I didn't know you were coming by; what's up?"

"I tried to call but whoever answered the phone said you were tied up." I eyed the six-foot sandy-brown brother standing near her. "I just left Jerry's with Lisa. She's downstairs in the car, but I brought you a corned beef sandwich."

"Oh, thank you. Baby, I was just telling Dr. Allen how hungry I was. Cameron, this is Dr. Simon Allen."

I was cordial in extending my hand. If there was something going on in dude's mind about what was mine, I was sure my firm handshake let him know that he would be best served to proceed with caution. The fact I had fucked around and presently had a side piece in Oakland didn't change the fact that I was marking my territory with him.

"Pleased to meet you, Dr. Allen. I'll let you two get back to what you were doing. Karen, I'll see you when you get off, boo." I kissed her and headed to the elevator.

I wasn't about to clown at Karen's gig. Truthfully, I didn't even know if there was a need to be tripping.

When I got back into the car, Lisa asked, "Did you tell Karen I said hello?"

"Most definitely and she told me to tell you hey. You know hey is hello in Georgian."

CHAPTER 24

Lisa was still gushing over her remodeled digs. She had called me at least five times in the past couple of days expressing her gratitude. It made me feel good to bring her joy. I was happy to be in good graces with anyone right about now.

Karen and I had mixed words at a high enough volume for the neighbors in the cul de sac to be informed of my unhappiness with her concerning Dr. Allen. She argued that it made no sense for me to be acting so jealous about nothing.

Truthfully, I wasn't even tripping; I was just arguing to make space so I would have an excuse to be out and about without trouble. I knew it was a sophomoric ploy, but it was the best I could come up with in order for Jessica and I to enjoy undisturbed time together while she was in LA.

I had three hundred large in my trunk as I rolled southbound on the 405 Freeway.

My mind was bubbling with ideas about moving the millions of funny money Jessica was hauling from up north. Knowing she was close to being in my company had my loins on fire as well. Though Kwan and I had agreed to do business together, it had taken two weeks for the deal to come to fruition. The time apart from Jessica had born a longing in me that I could no longer ignore. The crimson coiffed, freckled-faced vixen's entry into my world had developed a chasm with Karen that I didn't know if I even wanted to build a bridge over.

With Karen and the twins, I had a solid home life, especially since we had enough money not to worry about the bills anymore. But what Karen couldn't offer me was the excitement and thrill that being involved with Jessica did. I couldn't blame Karen for being the southern born plain beauty she was nor could I ignore my desire for exotic adventure.

There was no way for me to explain to anyone how I wished I could split myself in two. Marc wouldn't understand, Lisa would be shocked, and my mother, even if she weren't very fond of Karen, would insist I wasn't raised to leave my family behind. This was definitely a time when having Lance around was needed.

Shit, with Lance still in the mix, I would be doubling down on my investment. He would have moved that shit with a quickness and just one look at Jessica would have justified any decision I would have made, contrary to popular belief.

Jessica surprised me by already being outside waiting when I pulled up to the arrival area at LAX. The statuesque beauty was stunning in sunglasses, an Oakland A's jersey, some form-fitting Levi jeans, three-inch green pumps and her red mane tucked underneath an A's baseball cap.

"Carrot, I thought you got in at three," I said, looking at my watch making sure I was not late.

"I was, but our captain was on some super-duper I'll-get-you-all-there-ahead-of-schedule stuff. It's nothing, I've only been out here for a few minutes."

I walked around my car to help Jessica with her two bags. Before I could grab them, she wrapped her arms around me and gave me a kiss that would have made soap opera stars blush. It caught me off guard, not because we hadn't shared more intimate moments, but because we were expressing our affection for each other in public in my own backyard.

After the kiss and the clearing of my head, I looked around to see if our public display of affection went noticed by anyone. In my own city and on my home court, there were a different set of rules.

Jessica sensed my discomfort and pulled back.

"Reesie, I'm so sorry. I couldn't help myself, I've just missed you so much."

I wasn't going to flip on her for the warm greeting. I had been desiring those juicy lips of hers on mine as well.

"It's all good, beautiful. You just never know who is watching, who's in this town, ya dig? Are these the only bags you brought?"

"Yeah, I'm traveling light on clothes and heavy on paper."

I had enough room in my trunk for the heavier of the two bags, which was the business, so I placed it next to the duffel bag I intended to give to her and placed her smaller bag in my back seat.

"You ain't lying about traveling light as far as clothes are concerned. You must have every intention on being naked for the next two days."

"That's my plan exactly, Daddy and guess who I intend to be naked with?"

I was glad that I had caused that riff with Karen. If I hadn't, the adventure that Jessica presented would have been too difficult to be enjoyed.

We drove off and I took Jessica to the Airport Sheraton and checked her into a luxurious suite. I thought we would go grab something to eat in Long Beach, far out of the investigative eye of anyone Karen might know.

Instead, Jessica kept good on her word. She disrobed and had her way with me all over the room.

Our ravaging of each other left DNA on the sink, the couch, the floor and against the wall. The only piece of furniture we hadn't tainted was the king sized bed.

"Reesie, you must have thought I was playing. My pussy has been throbbing since I started packing my bags," she told me as we cuddled in each other's arms, spent on the floor.

"Not at all; I just thought you would be hungry for more than a nut after being served Southwest Airlines idea of inflight cuisine. But of course I'm never going to argue with you about making love."

I called downstairs and ordered some lasagna for the both of us from the highly praised in-house Paparazzi Ristorante. While we awaited the delivery of our meals, we made the exchange of the monies. Kwan had delivered the cool million we had agreed upon and Jessica was satisfied with the real cash I had tucked away in the leather Cleveland Browns' bag I brought along with me.

"Reesie, you must be crazy if you think I'm taking this bag to The Town. You must be trying to get me robbed and murdered by Raider fans."

I knew she was right, plus the prospect of explaining her carry-on to Karen was in no way appealing to me. We agreed that that I would go to the gift shop and float Kwan's currency to obtain luggage that would be safe for her.

I made a call to Marc and Speedy and told them that we needed to link up at The Comedy Act Theater. I wanted to gauge if they had an interest in aiding me move some of the paper.

Two soldiers weren't going to be enough, so I planned to enlist Anna and the three singers from San Diego as well. I wasn't absolutely sure if the trio would be interested, but I'd bet real money that they would be.

CHAPTER 25

After an amazing show in Leimert Park, Jessica and I joined Marc and Speedy at Larry Parker's, another one of our late-night haunts in Beverly Hills. The all-night diner was a small restaurant where club goers got their grub on and parking lot, and pimping was in full effect until the sun rose. The walls of the place were adorned with the stars of our day in comparison to the black and whites of celebrities from the past that graced the walls of Jerry's Deli. That's what made Larry Parker's so hip. My own autographed eight-by-ten was sandwiched between Larenz Tate and Sinbad.

"It's really simple, I give you fifty-thousand of this and I need fifteen back," I told Speedy, who sat across from me eating a full stack of pancakes.

I knew Speedy would be down. He was a LA native and he had done some time for receipt of stolen goods. I was sure the contacts he had in the streets would make it easy for him to be successful in my army of counterfeiters.

"So I make ten g's off of every fifty? I can do that!" he replied in between bites.

I knew that Marc was going to be the weak link in my crew. Not because he was a fuck-up, but because he was going to have to move any amount I gave him one bill at a time. Where Speedy could sell the paper in weight to underworld folks he knew, Marc was going to have to break the bills and collect change. Marc was my boy and I wanted him to get it while I had it, so I went against my better judgment and included him.

"Marc, of course, if this is something you don't think you can do, brother, by all means don't involve yourself. This is some straight FED shit."

Jessica was kind enough to give Marc pointers on establishments that would readily accept the bills and not draw attention.

"You can purchase fifty dollars' worth of gas and keep the change a thousand times if you like, but that shit would be tedious."

I had already devised a few ways where we could rid ourselves of a ton of the loot and have some fun at the same time.

"I'm a rollercoaster enthusiast and there might not be a more money hungry place in our country than the theme park industry." I told them.

Speedy stopped eating and ogling at my fine companion and let out a loud laugh.

"So you telling me that you are going to gorge Mickey Mouse with this play money?" he asked.

"Walt Disney prints his own dough and passes it off to his patrons; it only makes sense that we buy his bullshit with our bullshit. Plus, Disney isn't the only place this will work. There are over seven hundred amusement parks in the world."

I could tell from how she was squeezing my hand and smiling that Jessica was impressed with my ingenuity.

"Cameron, I have to admit that's a cold blooded plan.

You know if you put this much effort into hustling Hollywood they would give you a star in front of Mann's Chinese Theatre," Marc quipped.

I knew he was right, but if things happened the way I hoped with the tour and our hustling, I felt I would be able to buy me a star of my own.

CHAPTER 26

I had been so preoccupied with handling business and pleasure with my Bay Area connection, that I missed several calls from the 619 area code. The singing trio had shown their interest in what I could possibly do for them and I had inadvertently blown them off. Today found me in North Hollywood at what I called the condo of horrors. Lance's place had been vacant since the awful night of Gwen's disposal. When I purchased the two-bedroom condo, I had intended to keep it as my fuck pad bachelor spot. My nightmares, starring the strangled beauty, thwarted those plans in an instant. The only reason I could stomach being here was the addition of the cleaning crew and moving company I hired to get the spot in order to be occupied.

As the movers packed Lance's personal articles to be transported to a storage facility, I was struck by the idea of leasing the condo to the girls.

"May I speak with Monica, please?" I spoke into the phone loudly because there was a ruckus on the other end of the line.

"Don't y'all see I'm on the phone? Damn, y'all are rude." Monica screamed at whomever was making all the noise.

"Hello?"

"Hello? Is this Monica?"

"This is Monica speaking. Who may I ask is calling?"

"My name is Cameron. We met at Jerry's Deli." There was a pause and then, deafening silence over the line.

"Hello? Are you still there?" I asked, making sure we still had a connection.

"I'm still here. I guess you just go around getting people's hopes up for kicks, huh?" she spat.

I didn't owe her an explanation, but an apology was in order.

"I would like to apologize. I've been swamped with writing and preparing for some tour dates. I hope all of you will forgive me."

Monica accepted on behalf of the entire group. She explained to me that when they had been trying to reach me, the group had depleted their funds and couldn't afford to remain in Los Angeles. When I hadn't responded, they packed it in and went back to San Diego.

"So have you ladies given up on your dreams of making it or do you still aspire to succeed?" I questioned.

"Oh, we still believe we can make it. It's just that we can't finance our dream anymore."

I was sitting on enough cash to help out. The Kwan currency was too much for me to enjoy alone. I figured that if I enlisted the hungry trio in my crew, it could be a win-win situation for all of us.

"What if I told you that your financial problems weren't a problem anymore and you ladies had a place to stay?"

"I'd say you were full of shit."

"I can understand why you would feel that way. Again, I'm sorry to have not been available, but I'm able now to help."

"And you want what in return for your assistance?"

"I don't want any more than what I'm willing to invest in your careers. And I have a business proposition I'd like to run by you."

"Hmmm. A business proposition? Is that what folks in L.A. call giving up some ass now?"

"Oh, Monica, you got it all wrong," I corrected her. "If you and your friends will come to North Hollywood, I can better explain myself."

Monica was the spokesperson for the group, but she couldn't assure that the other two would be interested. I told her to run it past them and to call me back.

While Monica was conferring with Cynthia and Sabrina, I took the liberty to draw up a leasing agreement on Lance's desktop computer before the movers packed it up for storage.

I wasn't surprised to receive a call back from Monica confirming the ladies were willing to hear my offer. Monica wasn't playing when she told me their funds had been completely depleted. In good faith, I wired her three thousand dollars. If they were going to fuck me over, this was their chance.

"You are giving us each a thousand dollars and you don't want no ass?"

"Nope."

"And you aren't gay? I hear Hollywood is littered with brothers on the down low."

"Nope. I like pussy as much as I need air," I said, telling her the complete and honest truth.

CHAPTER 27

After the cleaning crew and the movers left, I exited the condo as well. Not that I was superstitious but I wasn't chancing it. Instead, I sat in the black 911 I purchased from Lance when he departed town and awaited the girls' arrival. I had the roof blown, a cigar lit, and Sly Stone's greatest hits playing on the system. I was sure Lance's neighbors could appreciate Sly's psychedelic funk much more than the go-go beat that had once banged over these very same speakers.

"Que Sera" was ending when the girls pulled up to the eight-story building in a yellow Honda CRX. I flagged them down and exited the car, motioning for the ladies to park in the space beside me.

"It's a pleasure to see you three ladies again," I said, greeting the three San Diego natives. "I appreciate that you made it in such good time."

"Monica almost killed us three times driving like a maniac, but here we are," said Sabrina, the sexy dark-skinned singer who was now rocking braids.

"I'm glad you ladies made it in one piece. If not, my initial investment would be blown," I chided with a wide smile.

"Thanks for believing in us and for the advance," Cynthia told me before walking over and planting a kiss on my cheek.

Sabrina followed suit and thanked me with a kiss. Last to get out of the car was Monica. She was looking good in black stretch pants, a blue jean shirt and sandals.

"I don't know why you bitches are complaining. Y'all wanted to get here just as bad as I did. Hey, Cameron, I appreciate the G. How about telling us what's up?"

"So much for small talk. Well ladies, if you will follow me, I can better begin the process of informing you," I replied coolly. The lovely vision of the trio made the thought of hitting all three cross my mind.

As instructed, the young ladies followed me inside the building and we took the elevator to the condo. Cynthia suggested we take the stairs. I, of course, shot that idea down and it had nothing to do with fear of exercise.

When we opened the door and entered the fully furnished apartment, Monica turned to me with rage in her eyes. "Cameron, I don't know what you think this is, but our voices are going to get us to the top. Not the talents we have on our backs." The other two girls crossed their arms and nodded their agreement.

"You have me all wrong. This condo belongs to me and I was showing it to you to see if the three of you would be interested in moving in."

Each of the women looked over the spacious dwelling. After the inspection, it was time to talk business. I showed them the lease and told them that it was already paid for.

"All I ask of you ladies is that you practice your craft with extreme diligence and not get caught up in the nightlife of L.A."

"But isn't that when all the deals get made?" asked Cynthia.

"Oh course they do, but most of what happens at night is under the table. The meetings I'll try to get for you will be legitimate."

"Okay, so let's say we move up here and practice our asses off. How are we supposed to make money to live on?" questioned Sabrina.

"Yeah, explain that to us, Mr. Bernard," chimed in Monica.

This was the time to spring on them the opportunity to join in on my counterfeit endeavors. There were two ways to handle it. One would be to finesse it or the other would be to be as blunt as kindergarten scissors. I chose to keep it one hundred and tell them the real.

"Ladies, you can do a few things in this town. You can wait tables, maybe substitute teach, get a job with a temp agency or take on the oldest profession in the world. From what I've gathered, the last option is beneath you all, so just strike that I mentioned that. But if you really want some serious loot, you got to have a little hustle about yourselves," I told them as I unrolled the knot of 100's I had in my pocket and placed it on the table.

"Whatever it is that has you in a Porsche, owning a sweet pad like this, and keeping a wad of cash like that, I'm sure I can speak for all of us that we would rather do that," Monica stated.

I had them inspect the bills and asked them which one's they thought were legit and which ones weren't.

"They all look real to me and I used to work at a bank as a teller," Sabrina stated.

Monica was fingering the Kwan currency and comparing

it against one of the hundreds she received from Western Union.

"Shit. I can't tell but if you can produce this kind of quality, I know some bloods in my neighborhood that would take a boatload."

Cynthia was the only girl who hadn't examined the cash. She didn't care to know the difference. She already had decided that she would be blissfully ignorant.

"I'm hoping you ladies decide to join me. If you're against it and still want to stay in the condo, the rent is twenty-five hundred a month. All I ask of you is that you don't make mention of what we've discussed today."

The group was eager to join in. I was happy to have them in the fold.

"You know, Cameron; it's not like Monica was totally against getting with you," Sabrina remarked.

"From what she told me, I would beg to differ," I said.

"What I told you was I wasn't going to just be giving up no ass. The thousand dollars you sent was a deposit. The actual price was going to be much more," Monica said with a smile.

CHAPTER 28

The girls had been doing their thing, grinding out the dividends and bringing me what was owed in speedy fashion. Anna was becoming more and more of a distraction. She wasn't happy with her banishment from my inner circle. Her feisty Latina ways had rubbed my hummingbirds wrong. Monica told me that if Anna was going to be on our upcoming trip to Vegas to move some money, they would rather not make money than be in her company. The good history that existed between Anna and I was no longer in play and there was no way for me to fix that. Jessica's existence in my life was making my home life difficult enough; there wasn't any room for a fling with my once steady south of the border delicacy. I thought I was being kind enough allowing her to be party to my money-making schemes.

I wasn't about to fuck up my crew to satisfy Anna's increasing demands of more profit and my attention. Being cold toward her was hard though, so instead of terminating our business relationship over the phone, I thought it would be best that I paid her a visit.

My folks at Statewide Auto had just laced me with a salvaged 1995 Jet Black Range Rover. The truck had fallen off the delivery truck and the dealer collected the insurance claim.

My people called me and informed me that they had something special I might dig. I had enough cash to walk onto any lot and cop a brand new one, but my loyalty to those who fucked with me when I was down and dirty hadn't wavered. The fully loaded SUV filled a need that my association with Mario in Memphis provided. It wasn't like the Jaguar was designed to haul around the electronics he was hooking me up with and at the price of twenty-five thousand cash, it was too sweet of a deal for me to walk away from.

When I pulled up at Anna's apartment, I lit a Cuban Hoya de Hoya before exiting the British 4x4. She never complained about the large plumes of smoke and I needed that cool high I knew Fidel's tobacco would provide to carry out my task.

I was surprised but not shocked when she opened the door naked as the day in which she was born. Not too long ago, in what seemed like forever, Anna being ready for me to stab her with my phallic lance would have been a welcomed sight, but today I was unmoved by her curves.

"Come on in, papa. I was trying on some outfits for the fight," she said, ushering me into her lair.

"Hey Anna, I don't have a lot of time. I have to run to Encino to drop off some merchandise, but I needed to holla at you."

"Do you want to holla at me or make me holla?" she asked, drawing near me.

"I'm here about business," I replied, sidestepping her and thwarting her advancement.

"It's about those bitches, huh?"

I nodded, answering her question.

Anna walked over to her couch and grabbed her burgundy robe adorned with cream flower prints. I was thrilled that she did so. It was going to be a battle to remain calm and not accept her invitation to ecstasy if she hadn't covered herself up. She slouched down into the furniture I had purchased when this apartment was my leisurely escape from the reality of my home life.

"So what's up, Cameron?" Anna asked with her eyes devoid of any affection and her tone even more distant.

"This is not going to work out between us."

"If you're talking about those girls, I can handle them. They are just on some territorial stuff and trying to position themselves. I'm not worried about them at all."

"That's not really what I'm even concerned about. I'm talking about you and me dealing with each other. I brought you in because I thought you would be an asset. You handled yourself well when we were mashing with Lance, but since you and I aren't involved anymore it seems you have every intention on disrupting the flow."

"Cameron, did you come to my home to cut me off? Isn't it enough that you flaunt that cinnamon-haired bitch in my face?"

"I came by to talk with you and give you this." I reached into my computer bag, retrieving a bundle of cash and ignoring her derogatory statement about my lover. I gave her the five thousand dollars she would have made and another five thousand I decided was appropriate to give her as a parting gift.

"I'll assume this is legal tender," she spat, accepting the offering.

It offended me that Anna would even consider that I would give her some work as compensation considering the good times and friendship we had shared.

I assured her the cash was legitimate.

Every good thing has an ending and our good was gone.

"This thing I have going has to be harmonious and to be honest, the change in the dynamics of our relationship is just causing too many ripples."

"I can try and be better, Cameron. I can be a good teammate. I could be even more than that if you would just let me," Anna begged.

"That's just it, Anna. There isn't any other position open in this organization. It's best that we be done with it all."

Anna sat on the couch with tears welling in her eyes. I knew that my words had hurt, but I was surprised when she broke her silence.

"Get the fuck out of my house and lose my number!"

I was in no mood to argue and I was already out of her home and her life before she'd made that demand.

I grabbed my computer bag, took a long drag on my cigar, and left her without saying a word.

CHAPTER 29

Damn those television appearances must be finally paying off," said Henry Arnold as he plopped down into the passenger seat of my Range.

Henry was my ex-college teammate who played power forward for the Cleveland Cavaliers with an emphasis on the word *power*. The six-foot-nine athlete was in town to play the Clippers and then, the Lakers.

"Yeah, things are finally popping for me," I replied, not telling him the truth about my illicit gains.

It was cool to see my friend. It was even better to be finally able to afford the damages that we would incur while dining and hanging out. Over the years, Henry's generosity toward me when the bill came was appreciated, but tonight his money was going to be no good.

"So what do you have in mind to eat, my brother?" I asked, already knowing the answer.

"The same shit I always have in mind, steak and side orders, bruh!" the hulking giant exclaimed.

With Ponderosa and Golden Coral beneath the standards of my millionaire buddy, I suggested that we head over to George Hamilton's restaurant and cigar bar in Beverly Hills.

"I heard that George actually hangs out there and mingles

with the patrons," I told him as we pulled away from Hotel Nikko and headed to Jed Clampett's hood.

Maze was flowing over my system. My Louisianan passenger was singing "Joy and Pain" note for note with Frankie Beverly when he paused to say, "You will never guess who I ran into after the game in Dallas."

Henry was right. There was no way in the world I could surmise who the fuck he was talking about. I mean he was only talking about one of the most densely populated metropolitan areas in the country's biggest state.

Dallas, where folks thought JR Ewing really existed and the place where my ex-girlfriend, Chandra Chones, called home.

"I don't know, who Steve Harvey?" I asked, feigning dumb.

"Nope, I saw Chandra from Monroe," he told me, awaiting my reaction.

"Oh, Chandra, yeah I heard she was staying there. How is she doing?" I questioned like her name alone hadn't pierced my once-wounded heart.

"She's still fine as frog's hair. The cute country college girl has given over to a sophisticated executive, but all and all, she's the same."

I wondered had she asked about me. But I knew better than to give Big Henry that much ammunition to riddle me with for the rest of the evening.

"That's good. I'm happy to know things are going well for her."

"I bragged about how you were out here in Hollywood doing it big, rubbing elbows and shaking hands with the real players in the industry."

"I remember her telling me I wasn't going to be shit without her," I replied, unable to contain my contempt.

"Man, it's folks like that who we used to fuel or inner fire to succeed. People told me before the NBA Draft I was too slow and not athletic enough. I worked my ass off to improve and now, while all those guys drafted before me are either overseas working in inferior leagues or out of basketball altogether, I'm looking to sign a max contract this summer. I applaud my naysayers and embrace my haters as should you," he told me as we pulled up to the valet.

I couldn't have agreed with him more. Of course I had a few folks I wanted to show that they were wrong for doubting me. Even though I didn't think Henry would judge me for hitting a few licks, I still hadn't confessed it. His thinking that comedy was the goose I was retrieving golden eggs from suited me just fine.

"I have reservation for two under Bernard," I told the maitre'd.

He looked inside a leather covered book, then ushered us through the dimly lit room to our table.

"It's dark as fuck in here," said Big Henry as we navigated to our seats.

"It's called ambiance," I quipped.

"Then ambiance must be the polite way to say dark as fuck."

I laughed at my friend's retort as we reached our table.

"You know we played up in Seattle the other night and I ran into GP," Henry stated as the waiter filled our glasses with water.

"Yeah, I saw the game. You did more than run into him. I can't believe you argued that charge call, he was definitely planted and in position."

"I'm not talking about during the game. I'm talking about afterward and just to answer your lack of loyalty, that motherfucker's feet were moving. That blind ref cost us the game," he spat.

Our conversation was put on pause while the waiter took our drink order.

"I'll take a Jack with a splash of coke and my friend will have a Seagram's 7," I instructed.

"So as I was saying I ran into GP and he tells me you have one of Bay Area's finest chasing behind you."

I nodded to affirm his statement.

"You doing too much, youngster. If Karen finds out, she is going to skin you alive."

"The operative word is *if.* That's a powerful little word. If my aunt had a dick she would be my uncle."

As we laughed at what I had said, the waiter returned with our beverages and took our requests for Porterhouse steaks and loaded baked potatoes. Satisfied that he had us together, he darted off to the kitchen.

Henry was right about how dark it was in the establishment. I speculated that the clientele dug it because of how it hid the famous and influential faces who dined there.

I amused myself by trying to figure out who else might be in our midst. I was sure Henry didn't share my same pleasure. He was too busy filling me in on his latest road conquest.

"I heard you two gentlemen ordered the best we offered, so I took it upon myself to personally deliver your meals," said the handsome well-tanned man with his hair combed back and not a strand out of place.

Both Henry and I were surprised to have the iconic 80's actor serving us.

"Mr. Arnold, I assure you my cooks, who are fanatics about the Lakers, did nothing to you and your friend's meals. So as a show of returned courtesy, could you go easy on our boys' tomorrow?" Mr. Hamilton asked, flashing his brilliant white smile.

"I wouldn't expect anything but impeccable service from someone of high class like yourself. I have to admit though, I get a kick out of giving it to Elden Campbell, so I can't make any promises."

"Understood. Well, you two enjoy your meals and when you are finished, please feel free to join me in the cigar room. I would be honored to be in your company," he said with a wide smile.

We both thanked him for coming to our table, accepted his invitation and dug into our delicious entrees.

After dinner, I instructed the waiter to bring me the bill.

"What, you trying to start a new trend or something? You know I can handle the damages," Henry huffed.

"It's all good, Big Fella. You're my guest and it's a pleasure to take care of one bill out the hundreds you've handled," I said giving the waiter two hundred dollars to settle the bill and slid him a fifty for himself.

We gathered ourselves and walked through the "ambience" to the connected cigar bar.

Mr. Hamilton had quite an impressive walk-in humidor. The walls were stocked with all the brands Cigar Aficionado had highly rated.

"Well, I see you two decided to take me up on my offer. I hope you find the selection up to par," said the slick proprietor.

"Your inventory is amazing. As a habit, I tend not to smoke during the season or better yet, I don't smoke anything but Cubans when I go against my general rule," Henry replied.

"I wouldn't expect anything less of you," Mr. Hamilton said, ushering us to another room.

"For only the most discerning of guests."

I was enjoying riding the wave of my good friend's celebrity as we hobnobbed with Mr. Motherfucking Hollywood while we smoked Fidel Castro's illegal offerings.

After forty-five minutes of puffing stogies and tossing back glasses of dark liquor, Big Hen and I thanked our gracious host, then left to get our boogie on.

It was Friday night and the happening spot was Tilly's Terrace in Santa Monica.

My boy, Spike, promoted the night and I had already alerted him to my bringing Big Hen with me.

"You sure you can hangout for a while? I don't want you to miss curfew or no shit like that," I told Henry as we pulled into the parking garage.

"It's all good. First off, I'm a veteran and secondly, coach told us to enjoy ourselves within reason."

I didn't know what the coach considered too much fun, but if there was such a thing as too much, Tilly's Terrace was definitely the place to find it.

Spike and his promotions team set the place out.

There was a comedy show on the heated patio with grilled food and drinks offered to the patrons. Inside the restaurant, General Lee and Fred Loc kept the party jumping with all the latest jams.

The security was super tight and the doormen were ultra-selective. Spike gave them orders to drag out whomever wanted beef and to disallow anyone who wasn't sexy.

"What's up, Cameron? I see you brought your homie with ya." Spike greeted us, extending his meaty mitt for a pound.

"Tonight is off the hook, bitches are in there dressed like it's June instead of January."

Most people would be taken aback by a six-foot-two, two hundred and sixty-five-pound dark-skinned brother with the pension to refer to women as bitches and hoes. I didn't judge dude because I realized that his verbiage was just a byproduct of his 5th Ward upbringing in Houston.

"Spike, I don't know how you do it week in and week out, but this joint never disappoints. Let me introduce you to my big brother, Henry Arnold."

"No introduction is needed man, you practically shitted on my Clippers last night. Please just do me the favor of dogging the Lakers tomorrow."

"That's funny you should say that. We were just dining at George Hamilton's and he begged me to go easy on the purple and gold," Henry replied.

"Leave it to Cameron to have you chillin' with Tinsel town royalty. Right now I can't say we have any Hollywood starlets in the building, but there are some broads who were extras in movies and a couple fluffers in here tonight," Spike told us as he ushered us into the party.

Spike hadn't lied. The place was littered with a plethora of prime pussy.

"Damn, it's like The Mirage to the tenth power up in here," Henry said, comparing Tilly's to Cleveland's top urban nightclub.

"This ain't shit; wait until you see the dance floor. It's so many bad bitches grooving, you're going to think you're on Soul Train," added Spike.

We walked by the heated patio that had sixty chairs facing Buddy Lewis, a brilliant biological engineer turned comedian. He was serving as the host for the comedy show.

"Ladies and gentlemen, I would bring up the brother who's walking by, but he's too busy to bless the microphone," Buddy said, causing the crowd to turn in their seats.

I didn't want Buddy's sarcasm to have people thinking I was bougie, but I really wasn't in the mood to perform either.

"Go ahead and give them a taste, Cam as a favor to me. The crowd will appreciate you for it," Spike said, nudging me in the ribs.

I hadn't prepared a set.

My training over the years had me in perpetual readiness, though. To my advantage, the clientele at Tilly's didn't take to the heady material. They dug the down and dirty stuff and I had a full armory of blue jokes to spray them with at my disposal.

While I walked to the microphone, the audience buzzed with anticipation. With each step I made, I was determining what my verbal assault would consist of.

"I appreciate the warm welcome. Obviously y'all recognize me from my recent television appearances or y'all think I'm someone else. Being recognized ain't always a good thing. I took out a girl the other day and she flipped on me. She told me because of my being on *Def Jam* and *ComicView* she needed at least five hundred dollars to fuck. I was like, 'a whole five hundred dollars?' Then she said, 'Yup a whole five hundred dollars.' So I told her obviously you don't know the blue book value of your pussy." I paused long enough for the crowd to calm down from the shock of my words and the laughter. "Because you're trying to sell me some used pussy for new pussy prices."

My punchline caused the sixty people in the audience to erupt into uncontrollable laughter. Though I had their approval the only two folk's reaction I was concerned about was Big Hen and Spike. To my delight, both of them were doubled over cracking up.

I continued on for fifteen minutes more, conscience of the other comics who were actually booked, and I was also anxious to get my party on. By the time I finished with my set, Spike had already introduced Big Hen to one of the fluffers in attendance.

I was hoping that Spike had at least explained to my boy exactly what the doe-faced, raven haired vixen did for a living.

"Big Hen, this is LA; what happens here can stay here, ya dig? But do not kiss her."

"Your man already filled me in, I got it."

"Good, 'cause I don't want you to get it."

CHAPTER 30

It was a surprise. Karen had no idea I had bought Lance's boat.

"Cameron, what does your Midwest raised ass know about boating in the ocean?" she asked.

I could have told her that Lance and I had dumped a body somewhere between Los Angeles and Catalina Island, but loose lips sink ships.

"It's no different than sailing a great lake. It's great with larger waves and sharks to contend with, but other than that, it's relatively the same," I replied as my family approached the Marina. It was an excellent day for leisure boating. The ocean was as blue as the sky and the surface was smooth as a sheet of glass. The thirty-one foot Rinker powerboat was part of the liquidation sale Lance had when he bolted town. I still hadn't made up my mind whether I was going to keep "Go-Go Gal," but I was certain I would be rechristening the white and burgundy water vessel with a new name.

The twins were excited to be on their first boat ride and even though Karen was being apprehensive, I sensed that she was equally stoked.

"Good afternoon, Mr. Bernard. I've stocked the boat

with the provisions you instructed. We're ready to sail when you give the instructions," said Captain Grant.

I hired the fifty-three-year-old seaman with the recommendation from Lance. The Captain stood six-foot-tall and had a build that suggested if we got into a rumble, he could hold his own. The salt and pepper bearded man helped Karen and the boys board the boat.

I hopped onto the dock brandishing an envelope with five hundred dollars.

"Your fee of five hundred is all there. If my family is pleased, of course there will be a hefty tip at the end of the voyage," I said, handing him the envelope.

Karen and the boys had already headed onto the lower deck of the watercraft. Before joining them, I asked the Captain if he needed anything of me.

"No, sir. I have it all handled. Go join your family and enjoy the ride," he responded.

"Cameron, this is too much. I mean just a few months ago we were facing starvation and eviction. Now we have a home, luxury vehicles, and a friggin yacht," Karen said as I entered the lower deck of the Go-Go Girl.

Yeah, I was definitely going to change that name.

If Karen thought we were doing it big because of the things she knew we had in our possession, the knowledge of the two Porsche sport cars and condo would have blown her mind. I had decided to keep that close to the vest.

I didn't see any reason to hip Karen to the fact the girls were staying in my North Hollywood hideaway. I couldn't burn enough sage and sweet grass in that place to use it for my own carnal purposes.

Karen was enjoying the white wine that Captain Grant brought aboard. I could tell she was getting buzzed because she kept inviting me to show her the bedroom.

"So this boat has two bedrooms?" she questioned.

"Yep, and a shower as well."

"That means we can be frisky and wash off the scent of sex," she whispered back.

I had the twins put on their life jackets and told them if they wanted they could go up and see the dolphins swimming alongside the boat. Just the mention of dolphins excited the two mini me's and they bolted upstairs.

Then, I said to Karen, "You just follow me. I have some trouble I need you to get into."

CHAPTER 31

There is nothing on earth like a Mike Tyson fight to entice black folks to congregate together. The Honorable Louis Farrakhan had made a call to a million black men to gather in DC. If he had said Iron Mike was going to be in combat that day, Washington Mall wouldn't have been large enough to accommodate the seven million motherfuckers who would have shown up. But they had shown up here in Vegas. The city was on fire with anticipation over the WBA and WBC unification bout and the merchants were looking forward to the opportunities of being bombarded with tourist dollars.

I was looking forward to the concert, after party and the illegal gains I stood to gain.

TMB had provided me with the perfect getaway excuse by booking Cameron B's Wild Wild West Comedy Tour at the Palace Station Hotel and Casino. It wasn't located in the strip, but it did make me proud to view my name and picture displayed on the brightly lit sign for all to see. I had enlisted a few good friends to join me on the show.

Marc was sulking in my passenger seat because I hadn't booked him for the show and he was pissed he didn't see his name in lights. I had tried to explain to him that I wasn't slighting him or questioning his ability to be able to deliver, but Cedric the Entertainer's manager was specific about how many acts were to perform before him. Marc was my dude, but I wasn't about to breech a contract just to please him. The fact that I was footing the bill and set him up with a slick hotel room should have been all the proof he needed but that wasn't enough. When the picture of Jemmerio and AJ Johnson popped up in the display, he flipped.

"Man, you booked those two niggas and they ain't even funnier than me."

"Marc, this fight is going to have folks from all over the country looking for something to do and the more diverse I made the bill, the better chance we have at selling some tickets. Jemmerio is hot as fish grease in the south and AJ has been in more movies than Jesus."

"Jesus was never in a movie."

"Exactly and neither have you. So if I didn't book Our Lord and Savior, what the fuck are you complaining about? Look Marc, I know it's not the ideal situation, but you have a room, the city is littered with bitches, and you have money to burn this weekend, so try to have a good time."

It was too fucking hot to be arguing with anyone. The air conditioning on my Range was blowing cool but not cold, and my tolerance for bullshit was at an all-time low.

All I wanted to do was get out of my vehicle, get checked into my room and await my crimson stallion to arrive from Oakland.

Speedy was flying in from LAX with the girls. I thought I would be immune to babysitting anybody's emotions by putting the San Diego Trio on the plane, but I hadn't counted on Marc having his panties in a bunch.

I guess I was taken off guard because Speedy hadn't cracked a word about not performing. He was too busy pushing up on Sabrina and getting money, to be worried about slanging jokes.

It truly surprised me that he was interested in Sabrina out of the three. Speedy dug red bones and Sabrina was far from that. I guess it was her quick wit that intrigued him. What really threw me a curve concerning his pursuit of her was the fact that Sabrina was petite. I had never known Speedy to be interested in a woman that wasn't over two hundred pounds. His motto about chicks was they paid what they weighed. I estimated my friend must have fleeced a few fluffy ladies out of a ton of dollars.

I didn't know why I even drove through the desert. I could have easily booked Marc and me a flight through TMB and rented a fly whip to get around town. I just thought it would be cool to put the Range on the road and hang with my boy, road trip style. I hadn't considered that he would be in such a shit mood about the concert.

"We have a few hours to kill before anyone else gets here; you wanna go to a strip club and throw some dollars on naked bitches?" I asked my disgruntled comrade.

"Yeah, that would be cool. I might as well do something constructive seeing that I'm not going to be able to flex on stage."

We grabbed our bags and checked into our rooms. I told Marc that I needed a few minutes to freshen up and wash the feel of the road off my body. He agreed that it would be proper to be hygienically on deck if we were going to have exotic entertainers rubbing against us.

I never suggested that anyone frequented a strip club during the day shift. I'd heard a lot of cats say they dug having lunch and looking at the ladies while they ate. But having some broad's bare ass over my burger and fries was never a fantasy of mine, but my opinion is just that -- mine.

I didn't know why they named the Crazy Horse, crazy. There was no insanity going on here like Magic City in Atlanta, The Rolex in Miami, or LA's Three Kings. This was sanitized sin.

Marc and I had frequented our share of exotic establishments while we flipped our fraudulent funds. He dug the power the all-mighty dollar had over the entertainers and when we were up in the club, our spending power was virtually limitless.

Marc and I left the hotel and drove to The Crazy Horse.

We were lucky to have the two most attractive dancers to be paying us attention. When I say 'the two best' what I really meant was Marc had the coldest piece in the spot and I had the distant second. All the other dancers looked like they were night shift rejects or headed toward exotic dancer retirement.

I was bored by the blonde who was grinding on my lap. Her lack of ass made it almost painful. I was sure there was someone who would have appreciated her talents. I was too close to being with Jessica to allow myself to be pleased by Candy and her fake double d's.

"You want another drink?" I asked Marc who was totally into the Asian girl bouncing on him. Maybe if she had been grinding on my shit I would allowed myself to get into it.

"Cameron, I got you my, man. I don't even have to ask, I know the drill, double jack, right?" he said, pulling out a wad of cash and peeling off five hundred dollar bills and instructing the waitress to bring us the drinks. He knew that she would bring back change so that he could continue paying for the diversion.

"Hey, man, I'm sorry about the whole you not being on the billboard thing, but when Cedric gets here I'll see if he wouldn't mind you getting in some stage time."

Marc was having so much fun making money and new friends at the Crazy Horse that he wasn't upset about the show anymore.

"Fuck it, if I don't get to perform. Shit, I'm hanging with my folks, I'm getting money, and if I'm lucky, I'll be getting some of this tonight," he responded, tapping Beijing on the ass.

The money had her as intoxicated as the rum-liquored-up Marc. Beijing didn't put up any argument about his objectifying her. I mean really, how could she expect much more from an inebriated man while she paraded around naked?

Marc was throwing around enough money to impress her to take off her shift and come back to the hotel with us. I refused to clown him for tricking. Shit, when you get dough, that's what all men devolve to. My Uncle Snag told me long ago that men only got money, power and position to get pussy, and from my travels I'd have to say his words rang true.

Candy, my dancer, offered to accommodate me as well, but even if Jessica wasn't bound for Vegas I would have rejected her company. I would have rather gone to my room and touched myself off with the complimentary lotion than have her slim body bang against mine. After changing three thousand of the ill-gotten bread, Marc and I went back to the Palace Station with Beijing in tow.

"So, I guess you going to clown me for paying for her time, huh?"

"Hell nah! No man with a bankroll would rather be hunting cooz in this city tonight, man. What happens here, stays here. Now if you were on Figueroa hailing hoes, I might have something to say; but this is fight night in sin city. School teachers from Memphis will be in town peddling gash."

Beijing exited the club as we were discussing the pros and the cons of the world's oldest profession.

I had to admit that Beijing was equally attractive after leaving the dim lit club. What I found most attractive about her was the fact she didn't look like a stripper once she was off work. The diminutive lady came out of the Crazy Horse looking nothing like the gyrating entertainer we had been drinking with. No longer was she standing erect in five inch heels. Beijing had dwarfed down to her natural four-foot-eleven self, rocking earth tone sandals, loose fitting Levi's, and a Wu Tang T-shirt. Sometimes exotic dancers didn't know how to leave it in the dressing room and their appearance screamed -- I'm a dancer -- when they were out in public. I was sure that Marc was happy that his rented escort looked gamed and not bought.

"Cameron, do you mind if we stop by my place so that I can grab my outfit for tonight?" she asked from the backseat.

"Not at all; just point me in the right direction and it would be my pleasure."

Beijing had impressed me again. Here, she had an opportunity to scheme Marc out of a shopping trip, but she let him off the hook by wanting to go grab her own gear.

We drove to her spot on the north side of Vegas. It was a lavish condo she shared with a showgirl named Heather who worked at Bally's. Heather was a caramel skinned sister who had legs for days. She wasn't fine enough to make me forget about Jessica's arrival, but when she inquired if I would like her to join us, I was hesitant to refuse her.

After Beijing retrieved her clothes, we jumped back into the Range Rover and made our way to the hotel.

I was happy to get back to get a nap in. The rest of our party would be in town in two hours. The travel, Jack, and Candy's painful lap dance had taken its toll on me. I wanted to be fresh for the show and energetic enough to welcome Jessica properly.

I didn't even hear my trophy side piece enter the room. What was intended to be a power nap had turned into a full fledge slumber.

"Reesie, are you slobbering?" Jessica chided me.

I arose, wiping my mouth, my hand not finding any moisture, and my eyes beholding the beautiful vision of The Body.

"Oh, I see you have jokes sexy, wassup?"

"From the looks of things you are, handsome," she said looking at the erection that the lap dance from Candy couldn't produce but obviously my subconscious thoughts of her had.

I sat up in the bed and took a full view of Oakland's Finest. Jessica was making her basic black dress look anything but basic. The form fitting outfit hugged her incredible curves in ways I was looking to challenge.

"You like?" she asked, spinning around on patent leather black heels.

"Like isn't a powerful enough response, I love it. You look good enough to eat."

"Oh, really now. Good enough to eat?" she asked, sliding out of her panties, climbing into the bed and mounting my face.

Jessica's sweet musky aroma filled my nostrils and her moist mound was perfectly positioned for my darting tongue to assault her swollen clitoris.

Jessica held onto the headboard to support herself as she allowed my oral talents to work its magic.

"Aw yes, Cameron, that's it, baby. Don't stop, I love the way you love me, baby." She pushed her nether region at me, matching the intensity of my flickering tongue with her gyrating hips.

She closed her eyes and let her head fall back. Jessica moved with fever, then came violently, toppling in a heap next to me.

"Wooooo, I'm going to need a minute to catch my breath. I don't know how you do what you do, but you better not ever stop doing that to me."

Who was I to deny her ecstasy if that's what she wanted? I would oblige.

"I've never known you to cum in such speedy fashion, Carrot. What's up with that?"

"What's up, Reesie, is that mamma has been yearning for you to touch me for too long. There was no need for me to hold out anymore. Now get out of that underwear and give me what else I've been longing for."

I quickly peeled off my drawers and guided myself between her welcoming spread. There, I found a moist home for my stiff rod and I probed her methodically.

"Don't you dare try to make love to this pussy. I've been waiting for weeks, pound her like you missed it," she commanded in my ear.

As instructed, I pushed with vigor, hurling my sword, stabbing her hole.

"Like this? Is that how you want it?" I asked between powerful strokes and hastened breaths.

"Harder! Stop playing, Cameron. Give it to me!"

I slammed myself against her with reckless abandon until I felt the familiar tingle announcing my climax. I tensed up and tried to calm myself.

Jessica wasn't having it; she gripped my ass and locked her legs around me.

"Oh no, the fuck you don't. You're going to give it to me."

I didn't even try to fight anymore. I let my orgasm sweep over me. My hot seed exited my staff and entered my lover's sweetness.

I rolled off Jessica, exhausted and the first thing that I did was apologize.

"What are you sorry for, baby?"

"I didn't mean to get off so fast."

"Cameron, darling, I don't need marathon loving all the time. You've shown me your ability to go the distance. Today I needed you to sprint. We have a whole weekend to do that tantric stuff."

All the experience a man thinks he has is thrown out the window when he deals with a woman. Had I came that fast with Karen, it would have turned into a heated argument.

Jessica had given me another reason to love being in her company. I was about to tell her just that, but she had fallen asleep and wouldn't have heard a word I said.

CHAPTER 32

The concert was packed. TMB was happy with my suggestion that we book Cedric the Entertainer for the engagement. His celebrity had risen. Being on TV twice a day as the host of BET *ComicView* paid dividends at the door. There were other shows and concerts in town competing for patrons who weren't able to attend the sold out Tyson vs. Seldon unification bout.

TMB had balked at the asking price of fifteen thousand, but after I told him the deposit wired to the agent had been them thangs, he was cool as a fan. We had been making money with the comedy concerts and he had been a soldier with the beezles.

The beezles was our nickname for the credit card fraud airline tickets. They came in handy when my crew and I dropped down on the amusement parks and fleeced them. It only seemed fitting that I would include him in on the good thing I had going with Kwan and Jessica. He was a real player in Oaktown and I trusted him not to bend if we were ever to get pinched. Being with Lance taught me to indebt your folks to you and loyalty would prevail. I had already shown myself to be a lucrative asset to TMB and I knew he respected my hustle.

Cedric's manager, Eric Rhone, had made my night easier,

lifting the comic limit and allowing Marc to perform. As expected, Marc went on stage with a vengeance and put up a set that was sure to put heat on the comedians after him. I introduced AJ Johnson to the more-than-warmed up crowd and they responded to his appearance with a rousing ovation.

I was waiting in the wings when I spotted Crystal enjoying the show and the libations provided by the hotel. She was rocking a sparkling gold halter top and some tight black jeans. It was good seeing her relaxed and enjoying herself.

I had them handling business since they touched down in town. The trio had already run a few errands by going to the MGM Grand, purchasing thirty thousand dollars' worth of chips and placing a hefty bet on a first-round knockout.

I made my way over to Crystal, greeted her, then asked, "So, you ladies did like I said and played a few hands of black jack and threw some dice, right?"

"Cameron, since we met you have we yet to *not* follow your lead? You take good care of us and we appreciate it. Ain't nobody trying to fuck around and catch an Anna."

I was slightly humored that the crew had a moniker for being terminated. I wasn't happy that I didn't have another beauty working with us, but when the beauty started acting ugly, beauty had to be dealt with.

"Where's Monica? Have you seen her?"

"Don't you already have your hands full with the red headed girl?"

"Oh, I didn't mean it like that. I was just asking so we would be altogether for the limo ride to the after party."

"The last I saw her she was being pursued by Jemmerio. Between me and you, Cameron I think she's only paying him attention to make you jealous."

I explained to Crystal that we were all business, and mixing the two was the problem I had with Anna.

"I feel you, Cameron but if you have any intentions about Monica, you better speak up now or be prepared for sloppy seconds."

I was glad to see Marc and Beijing come around the corner. Their presence meant the end of this uncomfortable conversation.

Marc was elated that I had got him a spot on the show and he was able to impress his for-hire honey.

"So we cool again?" I asked.

"We ain't never not been cool, dude. I was pissed that I wasn't on the show, but being on that stage and hanging with Beijing changed all that, pimp."

"I never knew rocking the mic and having your mic rocked could have such a mood altering effect. Ah, you did get your mic rocked, right?"

"Man, money takes all the guesswork out of the equation, brother. But on some real shit, she off the clock now and hanging because she wants to hang." He put out his fist for me to bump.

AJ was rounding up his performance and on cue, Jemmerio appeared from his dressing room with a shit-eating grin and Monica trailing him straightening out her ruffled cream dress.

"I hope you didn't over exert yourself before the show, blood," I teased him, keeping it quiet enough so not to embarrass or enrage Monica.

"Nah, Cameron, she said she didn't know nuffin 'bout Jemmerio and you know I couldn't have that."

"I know that's right. Now get your ass out there and put it to this capacity crowd just the same, soldier," I told me him before walking out to relieve AJ of the microphone.

After introducing Jemmerio, I had Jessica make me a double jack and I lit up a celebration cigar. With all of the minor acts already finished and the money already in the box office, my only remaining duties were to introduce the star of the show and call it a day. My gig as a comedian might have been over, but the evening was just about to really get underway with the promise of limo rides, VIP status, and bottle service at The Shark Club. I was riding a high from the cash I stood to gain from the bet placed on the Brownsville Bomber. Bruce Seldon had only survived one minute and forty-nine seconds in the ring with Iron Mike, making me a winner on my one round wager.

As a gambler, I was elated. But as a fan of the fight game, I was utterly disgusted.

One minute and forty-nine seconds!

Shit, that motherfucker didn't even have to train to get that paycheck. I guess he just ran around and sparred in his trunks so he could look good for the bitches. I was disappointed, but I knew I wouldn't have lasted that long against the champ myself. The only other person on the planet capable of putting the hurt on him, besides Buster Douglas, had been that beauty pageant chick in Indianapolis.

"Damn, CB, you gonna kill a brother with your second hand smoke," Speedy complained, feigning like he was choking.

"Nigga, if I don't give a fuck about my lungs, do you think I care about anyone else's?"

"Oh, I know you don't give two shits. I just thought I would fuck with you about it. You motherfuckers cleaned up tonight. I kinda wished that I had bothered you to hit the stage, but it's all good. I was hitting other shit, if you know what I mean."

"Get the fuck outta here. You didn't crack Sabrina's code!"

"CB, you ain't never known me to lie on my dick. If you don't believe me, feel free to smell my fingers."

"Fuck, are you a fifth grader? I believe your nasty ass. I was just returning the favor of giving you the business, brother and don't let me see your ass over at the craft service table until you wash your hands."

Speedy was like Lance in the sense that neither of them put vices into their own bodies but were quick to shove their vice into someone else. He hadn't let his pursuit of Sabrina distract him from getting the work done. We had settled up on all that he owed me and had set up his own thing with my blessing and with Kwan's.

I had been having a good thing with the Monopoly money but knew better than to think of it as a career move. Jessica had seen it coming on and worried that our not hustling together would affect our relationship. But she didn't have to worry; I was too entrenched and invested in her love to even consider breaking it off.

"Hey, Cameron, Korupt invited us to Club 662 for the Row's After Party. You cool with that?" Sabrina asked me.

"Brina, you can go and be a fan if you like but me, I'm going to the spot where I'm VIP, sweetie."

After the show, we all piled into our awaiting limos and headed over to the Shark Bar. My announcement of the after party to the crowd, aided in making our after-set a jam-packed affair.

TMB and Mouton had set it out for us in the roped-off VIP area. There were bottles of high end liquor and champagne for my crew and the celebrities who joined us. Biz

Markie was our special DJ for the affair, and he was bumping sounds of Blackstreet's newly released jam "No Diggity" that had everyone in the place gigging on the dance floor or bopping in their seats, when he interrupted the party to announce that Tupac Shakur had been shot.

Because Pac had been shot before and recovered, it didn't seem to faze the groove. I guess everyone thought like I did -- that he would recover and write a rap about how his assailants had failed to take him off the planet. Unfortunately, we would all be wrong and within a few days he would be with us no more.

The Shark Bar was an upscale two-level establishment. The scantly lit room was only illuminated by the color display at the bar and the dance floor lights. Jessica wanted to get her boogie on. It didn't take much persuasion from her to get me to follow. The dress she wore was more than enough.

Marc and Beijing were already dancing. We took up the space near them.

"I think they make a cute couple. What do you think?" she asked.

"I think he got what he paid for," I replied, stoically.

"Damn, I didn't know."

"I don't think she's a pro. Marc flashed some loot at the strip club and she decided to take the day off. Marc is really just compensating the young lady for her time."

"They say everybody pays for it at some point, " she replied over loud music.

"So at what point do I become the trick?" I questioned.

Jessica responded by turning around and gyrating her round ass into my groin.

"Actually, I've been the one who's been tricking. Remember, I bought you a drink first."

CHAPTER 33

Now that the fight, Tupac being shot, and my big comedy show was all over, it was finally time for my meeting with BET ComicView's Executive Producer, Curtis Gadson, in Burbank.

I entered the building and took the one flight up until I reached the door adorned with the BET logo.

"Good morning, Mr. Bernard, welcome to Black Entertainment Television," said Traci Nelson, the drop-dead gorgeous copper-colored, green-eyed receptionist.

"Look at you being all professional. Mr. Bernard? Really Traci?" I replied.

"Whatever, Cameron, I'm trying to keep this job until another tour comes about," the talented background singer told me.

I assured her she had nothing to fear.

"Curtis likes eye candy in his work environment and you're so sweet to look at, I might need insulin."

"Boy, if you don't sit your flattering ass down. I'll let Mr. Gadson know you're here."

I obediently did as I was told.

Within fifteen minutes, Curtis called Traci.

"Cameron, Mr. Gadson will see you now."

I exited the reception area and took the stairs one flight up. When I reached his office, Curtis was sitting at his massive oak desk with his back to me.

"Good morning, Cameron; please have a seat."

Once I was seated, he spun around and faced me with a cigar clenched in his teeth.

"My lovely wife insisted that it's too early in the day to enjoy a smoke, but I beg to differ. I say smoke them if you got them. Care to join me?"

With the offer of the stogie, Curtis was fattening the calf to be ready for slaughter. I reached into the black finished box and grabbed a Hoya de Hoya. I figured if I was going to be given an offer, I couldn't refuse I might as well be a high-end hoe. As I leaned over to light what *Cigar Aficionado* magazine rated as one of the top cigars, he continued, "So I hear that you are apprehensive about coming to work for me."

"No that's not it at all, brother. It's just that I've been really doing well with this comedy tour and I don't want to sabotage the opportunity by being bogged down in an office."

"Hmmm. So what you're telling me is that you aren't against taking the job?"

"No, not at all. I relish the chance to do business with you and develop my writing skills."

"Tell you what I'll do. I'll make it where you don't have to come into the office. You can do your punch-ups of the scripts via email."

"I'm sure that I can swing that. Thanks for making accommodations so that I can be employable."

The six-foot-three bearded brother rose and walked over to his window.

"I'm willing to bend for you based on two conditions. One, you do a good job on the scripts and two, you and I partner up on your tour. BET would be proud to be a sponsor."

"If the decision was mine alone I would say yes. I have two partners to consider. Let me consult with them and get back with you."

"That's overstood. To sweeten the deal, how about I throw in an hour special? We could film your LA date at Universal."

"Curtis, you do realize the concert isn't TV friendly?"

"Of course I do. It would run on our BET After Dark programming."

The offer was too good to refuse. With BET's branding behind this, the already popular Wild Wild West show would be a smash hit.

There was a wrap on the door. Much to my surprise, it was Sheila Fraser from the black exploitation classic *Superfly*.

"Curtis, I apologize for disturbing you, but those contracts we discussed earlier need your attention."

We were pretty much finished with our meeting. It wasn't like I could make a decision by being there any longer. So I excused myself.

"Give me a couple of days and I'll get back at you with an answer," I told Curtis, rising from my seat and extending my hand.

"Sounds like a plan. Cameron, don't keep me waiting," he replied, ending the meeting with a firm shake.

I left the building feeling proud of myself. I had gone there out of courtesy to reject a job. I exited with a huge deal on the table. All that was left for me to do was to talk with Mouton and TMB.

I was certain they would be delighted with the partnership possibilities, but of course thought comes from not knowing so I dialed them up.

CHAPTER 34

Cameron, I need you to handle my business while I do this bid," TMB said over the phone line.

He had been sentenced to sixteen months for a probation violation and he didn't want to be butt naked on his books.

"Yeah, man, of course I can do that. You just need to show me how and I got you," I replied.

"I will do just that. Can you come to town today?"

I informed TMB that I was free to head up north. Being in the Bay Area had a whole new meaning since meeting Jessica. Telling Karen about another trip to Oakland wasn't going to be easy and I knew there was an argument to be had.

"I'll only be gone for the day and I'll be right back," I promised Karen, even though I knew my promise would be empty if I was having a good time. Hooking up with Carrot almost always guaranteed an extended stay.

Even though I had taken the time and was courteous enough to weave a good lie, Karen gave me hell about it anyway. I packed a light bag and headed over to Burbank airport. Verbally jousting with Karen caused me to almost miss the Southwest airline flight TMB had arranged for me. My hour-long flight was entertaining, the flight crew was hilarious. To me they were wasting their time in the airline industry. They could have easily been peers of mine in the comedy game. Especially the light-skinned short cropped hair wearing, Jodi. Her quick wit and sarcasm was ready-made for a sitcom. I was glad I already had two someone's. If I hadn't, surely I would have made a play at her. When we touched down in Oakland, I waited until the plane emptied so I could walk to the rear and fetch my stowed carry-on luggage.

"I was wondering when you were going to come back here to get your things," Jodi said, holding my computer bag in one hand and her telephone number in the other. "You never know when you might want to reach out and touch me."

I was going to tell her my plate was full, but instead I dishonestly promised to give her Phoenix number a jingle. This was one of those moments when I wished Marc was with me so I could rub it in his face that my celebrity had been my mouthpiece. After my quick conversation with Jodi, I disembarked the plane and made way to the arrival area of the airport.

"Come on outside. I'm waiting for you here," Jessica purred across the cellular connection.

"All right, sweetie, see you in a minute," I replied before pressing end on my StarTac and closing the flip lid.

When I reached outside, I was welcomed by the sight of my crimson curly haired mistress dressed in matching cream pants and blouse leaning against a BMW 850 csi custom painted to match her fiery mane.

Jessica ran into my arms and greeted me with a kiss that didn't care about who might see.

"It is so good to see you, baby. I have missed you so much," she told me as her lips parted mine.

I agreed with her that the two weeks apart had been far too long and I wasn't just saying that to make her happy. I, too, longed for her fiercely.

I was just about to compliment her on the new whip when the Southwest flight crew exited the terminal. I cringed when Jodi started waving.

"It was a pleasure having on the flight, Cameron B," Jodi said, amusing her gay crew mate.

"Oh yeah, you guys were hella fun. Thanks," I responded before hurriedly getting into the car.

"You just are too irresistible, Reesie. Is there not anyone that you don't charm?" Jessica asked.

I was relieved that she wasn't acting all jealous and shit. Had that happened while Karen was scooping me from the airport, there would have been no way I could have convinced her I hadn't become a Mile High Club member with Jodi's help. I wasn't saying this to characterize my baby's mamma as some insecure maniac. I was simply saying Karen was territorial and didn't play that shit.

Instead of replying to Jessica's statement, I just shrugged and smiled.

"This is quite the car, sweetie. Did you trade in the Benz?" I questioned, admiring the cream interior with red piping.

"No, I still have it. We've been so productive I treated myself."

The sleek German coupe powered through the traffic as we headed to Berkley to eat at Picante. TMB said it was the best Mexican food we could get outside Mexico.

I was looking forward to seeing if all his boasting was real or just Bay Area hype.

My friend and business partner, who was soon to be state property, was already there and awaiting our arrival.

"If you want me to hold back while you two talk, I can do that," Jessica said while parking the car.

"What? And leave your pretty ass alone in this bomb ass car? Shit, I'm watching what's mine," I chided, but I was oh so real at the same time.

"Obviously, you didn't read my license plates, Reesie."

I exited the vehicle and smiled when I saw the California vanity plates: TAKEN.

"I didn't want to give anyone the impression that there was even a minute chance," she told me, grasping my hand and leading me toward the two-story brick establishment that had enticing aromas emitting from it.

TMB was sitting in a booth with a bowl of tortilla chips and salsa in front of him.

"Cam Breezie, what's cracking, family? And good afternoon to you, Jessica. Please join me."

Jessica returned TMB's greeting with a smile, then slid in the booth.

"Same shit different day, folks. So you said you had trouble coming your way. How can I be of assistance, my brother?" I asked my soon-to-be imprisoned friend.

"It's not really that deep. It's more of a bump in the road. I don't want to lose my clientele in the interim, ya dig? I see how you move and I know you will be righteous about giving me what's mine."

I assured TMB that he had the right dude. Even when it pained me to do so, I always paid my toll. I was pleased to know he thought of me in such a positive light. But I was curious as to why he hadn't asked our mutual friend to handle his business, so I asked him that.

"You don't trust Cool Mou to do this for you?"

"I figured you would ask that."

"Am I that predictable?" I questioned.

"No, not at all. I figure you would inquire because I would have done the same thing."

Our conversation was interrupted when the waitress came to take our order. Not only did Picante offer authentic Mexican food, their staff looked fresh from the border.

We began by ordering a pitcher of silver margaritas made with Patron. Being the two gentlemen that we were, TMB and I insisted that Jessica order first. She perused the menu and decided on pescado en macum salmon rubbed with achiote layered with tomato, onion & chile dulce, cooked in a banana leaf served with morisqueta rice and plaintain "tostones." I still hadn't decided on my meal so TMB took that as his cue to place his order of chicken served with Mexican red rice, refried beans and four handmade corn tortillas.

I finally decided on beef served with Mexican red rice, black beans and four handmade corn tortillas steak carne asada-style, rubbed with adobo rojo and grilled.

While we awaited our meals, TMB instructed me on how to handle his business.

"Here's my cousin, Joey's number. If this should go south, give him a call," he said, referring to the mountain of credit card profiles he had given me.

I had already seen where a new wrinkle in the game could be applied to simplify the beezles. Instead of calling in to the airlines and being frustrated with their automated phone system. I would book all the flights via the web.

"So how much would you be expecting me to apply to your books?" I questioned.

"Shit, I would be happy to get three g's a month. You'll find that your profit after looking out for me will be well worth your effort. There are platinum, gold and even some black cards in there."

"So we're talking forty stacks in all? Damn, you must be planning on buying a lot of zoom zooms and wow wows! Okay, I can do that," I told him as we shook hands, solidifying the deal.

I reached into my computer bag and pulled out eight stacks of banded hundred dollar bills. I could tell from the look on Jessica's face that she wondered if I had passed him Kwan coinage.

"Nah, it's just that I don't trust my money in no bank."

"What hustler does?"

"None that I know of. Real talk, I can't think of a safer place for my bread than an institution loaded with armed guards."

"I dig that. Look, Curtis is for real about sponsoring the show. Do you have any reservations about partnering up with BET?" I inquired.

"Cameron, if you cool with it, Mou and me are all for it. That will only have me coming home to more money, ya dig?"

"I know Curtis is the real deal Holyfield when it comes to his word. We should be real cool."

As we were concluding our business the waitress came out with our meals. We dined on the delicious entrees and parted ways.

"So where to next, Reesie?" asked my auburn haired lover with her hands on the steering wheel of her Bavarian super car.

"I don't know; I was thinking we could go to your place, lay up and watched some movies. Or maybe go there and get drunk or better yet just go there, strip down and make love," I flirted.

"How about we do all you mentioned," she replied as we zipped off to her Lake Marin lair.

CHAPTER 35

What do you mean you aren't going to take the writing job?" Lisa asked me after swallowing down the food she had in her mouth.

We were dining at one of my favorite little haunts in Glendale enjoying Beef Bowls.

"Exactly what I said. Lisa, I've worked my ass off to get to the point where folks recognize my face and want to see me. I can wait until I'm old to be behind the scenes. If you're worried about your commission, I got that faded."

"So, you are going to pay me fifteen percent for some work I didn't do? Cameron, that has to be the dumbest shit I've ever heard of."

Nothing intrigued and confused me more than white people. You would never find a nigga complaining about free money, not ever. Free might be the African-American collective culture's favorite word in the dictionary. Here I was offering to compensate my manager for some shit she knew she hadn't earned and Lisa was calling me a damn fool. I was dumbfounded, but I saw no reason to flip on her. My reasoning wasn't as simple as me wanting to be in front of cameras and crowds. I was trying to stay in front of the game and from behind bars. My collective of entertainers who didn't frown at making some sitcom cash without actually being on a TV show had been putting in serious work, busting down all that Kwan supplied us with. TMB had been cool enough to secure us flights to destinations that found us breaking down the bad paper at malls, amusement parks and strip clubs. The way we flooded the economy with Kwan's product, I wouldn't have been surprised if we didn't have to do something with all the talk of inflation of the dollar. I could have cared less about that shit; the economy had been dicking around my people since we arrived over here on that boat trip we didn't ask for. As far as I was concerned, it was time for some get back.

There was no way I would have been able to capitalize this opportunity while being bogged down in an office punching up lame gags some non-comedic bastard (who was getting more loot than I was) handed off to me to turn into a gem.

We had already had successful dates in San Diego and Phoenix with the comedy tour; it just seemed to be the chance to seize the moment.

Much to my surprise, Lisa wasn't giving me the blues about the meeting at BET.

"I know what Curtis was intending to offer you. I'm starting to see how you maneuver, so I let you think it was you who sealed the deal," she said.

"Yeah, my business partners agreed to it. Now all that's left is to read the fine print and sign the contract," I replied between bites of my tenderloin beef bowl.

"I'm glad you trusted me to handle that," I said.

"I trusted you to do as you always do."

"And what exactly is that?"

"Handle my job and get me a larger commission than I'm supposed to."

Our afternoon meeting at Yoshinowa Beef Bowl wasn't just about my deal at BET. Lisa had some news to tell me and she wasn't sure how I would react. A good friend of hers, over at CBS Studios, was very interested in buying my script *Barely Standing*. The only problem was that they wanted someone else to star in the role I'd written for myself.

"If they don't want me, they can't have my story," I spat.

"Cameron, if you write and produce it, you'll find it quite profitable," Lisa replied trying to reason with me.

I thought she understood that writing and producing wasn't part of my plan. I wanted and needed to be in front of the camera. "So is CBS our only option?"

"No, not at all. There's ABC, NBC, and if all fails, FOX and UPN are big on sitcoms driven by African-American stars."

"I guess no matter what I do, it's a deal with the devil, huh?"

"I wouldn't call executives the lords of the underworld. Maybe they're more like vampires. They suck the life out of you."

I thought over the comparison that Lisa had made about the industry I was interested in being a part of. "So what do you suggest I do?" I questioned after washing down my food with a gulp of Diet Coke.

"Out of respect to my friend over at CBS, at least hear them out and see what their offer is."

"But I thought you said they were set on using someone else as the lead character?"

"They are, but they haven't sat down with my dynamic client. I'm willing to bet once they see and talk with you, the casting executives will see the double threat they'll have in you."

"Lisa, if I didn't know better, I would swear you just gave me a compliment."

She flashed a smile as she winked at me. "I did and it's not costing you my normal managerial fee."

CHAPTER 36

The aroma of simmering onions greeted me as I entered my home. Karen was in the dining room preparing the twins' meal. Though the scent was pleasant, the knowledge of what was for dinner appalled me.

"Is that fried liver and Brussel sprouts?" I asked, already knowing the answer to my question.

The boys were elated with her choice, but I knew there was a method to Karen's madness.

"Yes!"

The meal from my own personal hell was purposely planned as a prerequisite to a war.

"Damn, Karen, you know good and damn well I don't eat that shit."

"Well, maybe you can get whoever you spend your time with in Oakland to fix you something you like," she spat, causing the boys to grab their plates and take them to their room.

If she had made something we all could have enjoyed I would have done the same and followed them. But she hadn't, so instead, I stood there preparing for her verbal assault.

As she was gearing up for an all-out confrontation, I found myself trying to figure out just how much she knew and how much she was going to try to pry out of me. I knew that Jessica didn't have my address and the fact that there wasn't blood all over the walls meant she hadn't come by.

"Cameron, don't I cook and clean for you? Didn't I bear your children, suck and fuck you whenever you wanted?"

I couldn't answer the barrage of questions. Not because it was complicated, but moreso because no matter what I said, it was going to change the course of the conversation. The most I could muster was a nod of my head.

"Then why the fuck can't you respect me enough to make an effort to hide your infidelity?"

I so wanted to tell her at what great lengths I took to keep my extracurricular activities as far from home as possible. I had always gone to Oakland on legitimate business. The fact I was doing extra shit while on those trips was a whole 'nother something.

Because there wasn't anything I could say, I just stood there with a dumb ass look on my face.

"So what you want me to say?" I finally asked, walking toward her -- though I was mindful of the sharp objects on the dining table.

"I believe your actions and flight destinations says it all, Cameron. You've outgrown us and I can't try to hold on to you any longer," she said smoothly. Her nonchalant delivery frightened me.

I couldn't tell if Karen was giving me a way out or setting me up for something sinister. What I did know was that she was probing and I wasn't about to confess to shit.

I had been in relationships before but this one was different than the others I had ended or forced to come to a halt. Karen had my children and knew the truth of my crimes. At this very moment, I was glad I hadn't confessed to her about my involvement in Gwen's disappearance and Lance's flight. What she could have done with that information caused a chill to race down my spine.

Instead of trying to comfort her by holding her in my arms, I sat down at the dining room table.

There was an uncomfortable quiet that existed between us. I wasn't sure if Karen was considering making our kids fatherless by quitting or killing me, but I knew I didn't have a leg to stand on in any argument that might erupt from her.

"I need you to leave. I need you to leave enough money so that we don't have to involve the authorities about supporting our children and I need you to do that shit now."

It was too late at night for me to hire a moving company or try to get approved at an apartment rental office, so I hoped she didn't expect me to leave and not come back.

"It's too late and I'm too hungry for all this shit, Karen. Be mad with me, hell you can be through with me, but be adult about this," I pleaded with her, already deciding to let Pacino eat that shit she cooked. I was going to grab me something to eat and then, return to retire in our guest room.

"Don't you dare question my maturity, Cameron. If I wasn't mature and of my right motherfucking mind, I would have made your favorite meal tonight instead of the one you hated most."

Her threat registered, but again I cautioned myself on reacting to it. Karen wasn't about to talk me into a DV case just because she didn't know how to leave well enough alone.

I rose up slowly from the chair, grabbed my keys off the table, and headed out the door sparing my kids from witnessing the brutality that could have occurred had I stayed.

Walking out the door, I heard her sobbing, but there was nothing I could do to ease her pain or calm her anger. So I didn't make any attempts to do so.

CHAPTER 37

Two weeks of complete silence from Karen had me on edge. Though I had refused to leave the house and had permanently moved into the guest room, I was sleeping with both eyes opened, one to make sure she didn't stab me in my sleep and the other to make sure she didn't fleece me.

When I received a phone call from an unfamiliar 510 area code I was hesitant to answer.

"You have a collect phone call from Jessica, an inmate in Marin County Jail. To accept this call, press or say one. To block inmate phone calls press zero. Thank you."

I immediately pressed one. "Hey Carrot, is everything okay?" I asked, knowing if all was good I wouldn't be getting a call from jail.

"Reesie, they have me and Kwan on charges of forgery and counterfeiting. Our bail is two hundred and fifty thousand dollars apiece. Can you help us out?"

Of course I had the loot to make the bars before her a memory. Springing my favorite redhead from incarceration was nothing. Helping Kwan was a whole 'nother something. I mean, didn't he have someone he was fucking good enough to bail him out like Jessica had in me?

"Cameron, did you hear me? We need five hundred thousand dollars. Are you going to come get us out?" she questioned again as I was having my inner conversation.

"Yeah, baby, of course I am. I just need to gather up the cash and hop on a flight."

The reality was that I couldn't afford to have either one of them feeling betrayed by me. Nothing made a motherfucker start giving up names like abandonment.

Not only did I have concerns about my own freedom if that happened, Jessica knew my entire crew. If not handled properly, she and Kwan could easily serve us up as part of a conspiracy.

"Thank you, Reesie. Thank you, thank you. I told Kwan we could depend on you."

Her response confirmed what I'd been thinking.

"You're very welcome, sweetie. Like I said, don't worry I got you," I replied as Pacino finally found a spot he deemed suitable for his refuge.

"You have sixty seconds left on this call," prompted the automated operator.

"I love you, Reesie," Jessica said hurriedly before the call was disconnected.

I was caught off guard by her statement of endearment. I probably was only questioning its validity because of the circumstance surrounding its utterance.

"I love you too, " I replied. I wasn't forced to make that response and I was comfortable doing so. I really meant it and not only did I love Jessica, I trusted her as well. Shit, I had to trust her. I was about to part with the equivalent of Michael Jordan's rookie salary to have her and Kwan released. If that ain't love, I didn't know what was.

"Don't worry, I'm on it and will be on my way," I told her not knowing if the call dropped before I could finish my sentence.

When the call ended, I played the good neighbor and picked up Pacino's poop. Doing so was good practice; soon I would be in Oakland cleaning up more shit.

If I was going to be traveling that flush with cash doing so dolo wasn't a good idea. While I was still outside walking Pacino, I called Marc and enlisted him in joining me on the road trip up north. I thought he would have seen it as an opportunity to hangout and have some fun with Ebony. I saw it as a chance for someone whose ass I was saving from the grinder to watch my back.

"Cameron, I have a question for you and you'll probably be pissed with me for asking it."

I braced myself for his inquiry.

"Have you ever thought about how easy your life would be if you just had Karen and the boys?"

"I would probably be so boring you would find it difficult to be my friend. I mean who else would you be able to live your life vicariously through if I was that dude?"

He chuckled at my response.

I told him to get ready and I ended the call.

By now Pacino had tired of sniffing around and was whimpering to go back to the house. I was ready to get home as well seeing there was nothing sexy about walking around with a plastic bag filled with dookie.

Two days later, the look on the clerk's face when I emptied out a half million dollars on her made me smile. The youthful Mexican lady's eyes widened and her hands trembled as she counted the bail money. The quivering of her thin lips told me that she contemplated what her life could be like if she just bolted out of the door and never turned back with that vast amount of cash in her possession.

"It's all here, sir. There are some documents I need you to sign, then there will be about a two-hour wait. Both parties have to clear our nationwide search. After that matter is verified, they will be released," she said.

"You would think that kinda money would speed up the process," Marc stated as we waited by a vending machine that was devoid of any snack I desired.

"If it wasn't being held in trust maybe it would quicken the process. But I'm expecting every red cent of that dough back," I replied, finally settling on a Snickers bar though I actually craved a Milky Way.

Marc looked at me in complete silence.

I knew he had a question and his silence told me he was weighing whether or not to go forward with it.

"Don't just sit there and stare at me. Whatever the fuck is on your mind is better spoken than kept to yourself," I said making the decision for him.

"Are you sure about this, Cameron? I mean are you absolutely sure that Kwan and Jessica are going to see the entire trial process through so you can recoup your cash?"

I took a bite of the candy bar, not so much to satisfy my hunger but to temper my response and to think over the situation in my head. "I'm sure of one thing and that's if I hadn't brought that loot, I was going to lose the woman that I love and I would have been jeopardizing all of our freedom."

The validity of my statement hit Marc dead on.

"Well, instead of sitting here judging you, I guess I should say thank you."

"Man, it ain't shit. I'm sure you would have done the same for me."

"I'm glad you're sure about that. With a half a million at

my disposal I might have dipped off to a country with no extradition laws."

I couldn't even be mad with him for speaking his truth.

Marc hadn't missed my declaration about Jessica.

"So Jessica is the love of your life? What about Karen and the boys?"

It was obvious that no amount of explanation would make my friend understand the spell I was under. Jessica wasn't some minor flirtation. What she and I shared was not an infatuation that had me blind. This was a meeting of two souls who were made for one another.

"My sons will always own my heart and Karen will always be a part of my life because of their existence. What the two of us shared was all about the old me. I was young trying to find my way to the man I am now. To be honest, I'm not sure that Karen cares much for the man I've become. I think she has remained with me only because of how comfortable the money has made things."

"So are you saying you've outgrown Karen, is that it?"

"No, what I'm trying to tell you is the me that needed Karen's love lives no more. The person I've become craves the energy that only Jessica can provide." I finished off the last bit of caramel, peanuts and chocolate I had in my mouth.

Marc digested my long diatribe and for the next hour we sat there in silence.

Maybe he didn't know what to say or maybe it was because my response had left him no room for rebuttal.

I guess the quiet between us made Marc uncomfortable because instead of basking in it like I was, he chose to call Beijing for white noise.

I overheard the two talking about her moving from Las

Vegas to LA and residing with him. Now it made sense to me why he wasn't pressed to get in contact with Ebony as soon as we touched down.

I was bubbling over with the thought of harassing him about the hazards of trying to tame a hoe into being a housewife.

Luckily for our friendship, Jessica and Kwan entered the corridor before I could begin chiding Marc. Two days in lockup had knocked some of the luster off Jessica, but she still radiated as she walked out of confinement from the Marin County jail. Kwan, on the other hand, looked like he had been in a fight for his life.

"You should see the other guy," he said in response to the looks on our faces.

"Reesie, I knew you wouldn't let me down. Those screws and bitches in lock-up tried to convince me otherwise. I kept telling them that you weren't about to let me be locked up," she exclaimed, running into my arms and showering me with kisses.

She was right. There was no way I was going to be without her in my life and since I had no intention on loving her through Plexiglas, this was the only choice to be made. Even if it meant spending a healthy portion of all the illicitly earned money I had. She might not have realized it, though because I hadn't taken the time to discuss my real feelings for her yet. I guess I was hoping that Jessica saw that I not only brought the monies to get her released but this move was also as my promise of commitment.

Marc's disinterest in hooking up with Ebony had put a black eye on my plans to ravage Jessica and robbed me of the opportunity to converse with her of my plans to leave all behind to be hers. Instead, we all piled into a cab and headed to Jessica's swank condo.

I was surprised to find out that the bust occurred there. I was further caught off guard because Kwan had been caught there, too. I had never known him to visit her spot. Being in love with Jessica was fucking me up inside, but instead of allowing irrational jealousy to win, I thought logically.

I figured Kwan must have felt the heat at his crib and brought it to my soul mate's home.

"Cameron, right now all of my accounts have been frozen. Let me sell off a few items and as soon as I'm liquid, I'll slide that bail money back your way," the tech-boy graphic genius told me.

"Don't stress yourself, man. Do what you have to do. Just make sure to secure a top notch lawyer who can get beat the charges. I can wait until after the trial to reclaim the cash," I replied calmly.

I didn't know why I was so relaxed with so much money at stake. Maybe it was to keep Jessica's stress level down. Maybe I was keeping the conversation short for fear that the Feds had the place wired and I didn't want to say shit that would find me up on charges.

More than likely the truth was that I was dumb and in love.

The look on Marc's face told me he felt it was the latter as well.

With as much business that I was comfortable with handling verbally, Kwan wished us safe passage back to LA and bid us farewell.

With Marc in tow and Karen wearing down my battery by blowing up my phone, this had more or less been a fruitless trip to Northern California. Though we were on bad terms, I didn't want to completely piss her off because she was still my babies' mama, plus she knew most of my dirt.

CHAPTER 38

Rushing to get to Oakland, I had made the mistake of forgetting my car charger at home. Karen's insistence on communicating with me while I was gone had doomed any conversation I was to have with my red-haired honey. Whatever Jessica wanted to discuss was going to have to wait until the aftermath of the blowout I was certain awaited me at home. This fight was one I looked forward to because I was sure, it would be our last. When I finally would get to contact Jessica, I would inform her I could be all hers if she would have me.

I made the right turn into our cul de sac, thinking I would find Karen's Land Cruiser in the driveway, but to my surprise it was gone. Normally, it would be blocking me from parking my Jaguar in the garage, but only the Range Rover sat there alongside the house. I took her not being there as a sign that she took my greedy sons for a bite to eat. Karen's absence was welcomed.

I remotely opened the garage door and drove inside.

Before entering my house, I extinguished my half-smoked Punch Maduro cigar. When I opened the door, I was greeted by the sight of total chaos.

Pacino was loose.

Torn paper was thrown all about and piles of shit

decorated the kitchen and living room. Right when I was primed to scold my Rottweiler for escaping from his cage and being a bad boy, I realized that he hadn't gotten out of his cage -- he had been left out.

I grabbed him by the nape of the neck and led him to the fenced-in backyard so I could begin the task of cleaning up his mess.

After finishing with the clean-up, I lit some Nam Chopra incense and cracked a few windows. Pacino was pacing back and forth at my sliding glass door. I couldn't be assured that there wasn't any more shit inside even after picking up what seemed like a ton, but I slid open the door.

"I'm either going to potty train you or teach you to use a litter box."

My words fell on deaf ears. Pacino merely wagged his stub and panted.

I racked my mind trying to remember where the charger to my StarTac might be. When I was cleaning up, I hadn't noticed any chewed wires so I couldn't blame my furry doo doo machine. Then it dawned on me that the last place I remembered it being was in my office or the bedroom Karen and I shared.

I climbed the stairs with Pacino on my heels determined to keep up. The search of my office yielded nothing. It had to be in the bedroom.

When I opened the door to the bedroom I found it in the same condition as the downstairs minus the boo boo.

"Pacino, is this your handy work?"

He responded to me with a low growl. Then he walked over to Karen's open closet.

"You better get away from there. If you fuck up that woman's shoes she'll skin both of us alive," I told him, walking over to close it.

When I stood in front of the closet, I found it devoid of every stitch of clothing and footwear she owned. Instinctively, I ran out of our room to the twin's, only to find it as barren as ours.

There was sweat popping off my brow. I was standing in the middle of the room my sons once slept in when it hit me.

The safe!

I darted back to my bedroom, almost trampling Pacino trying to see if Karen had made off with my dough. I dove into my closet and worked the combination to the safe. Instead of finding the five hundred thousand dollars of the Kwan coinage I had switched out when I left for Oakland, all I found was a handwritten note.

Cameron,

With friends like Anna you don't need enemies. Of course I've known all the time that you weren't faithful to anything except your own desires but foolishly, I told myself you would insulate your family from your fuckery. I've always said that what happens in the dark is sure to come to light. Not only did Anna tell me about your dealings with her, but also about your red headed bitch in Oakland.

So I'm leaving.

This isn't a separation. There won't be any get backs or sequels. That's why I took the money. I figure the liberation of this money you've come to worship will assure you hate me enough to leave me the fuck alone. I haven't stolen this half a million dollars from you. I've earned every penny, if not more.

If it makes you feel better, think of it as all the child support, I won't be suing to get from you. I'll use it to take good care of our children.

The boys begged me to bring along their puppy but I thought it would be cruel of me to have you come home to an emptied safe and home. Take care of yourself. I don't know why I wrote that, of course you will take care of yourself. That's what you do best.

Love, Karen

After reading the letter I realized that Karen's departure had actually only cost me fifty thousand dollars. I couldn't find fault in her on how she left I was just glad that she hadn't deemed all my monies fair game. If that would have happened, I would have been trying to find Lance, this time, for my own 'project'.

I contemplated riding over to Anna's house and kicking that treacherous cunt's ass back to Tijuana. That was what I wanted to do, but of course, I knew better.

I went out to the garage and relit my cigar, then walked back inside. With Karen gone, I no longer had to be worried about her tyrannical rule. I climbed the stairs to find Pacino curled up in front of the boy's old room, snoring like a grown man who just worked a twelve-hour shift. I could tell he missed the twins, hell so did I but there wasn't shit I could do about and sleep definitely wasn't the remedy. I'd fucked around and lost my family, and that thought tore at my heart. But I took a deep breath and reminded myself that I would always be a father to my sons.

With Karen gone, my decision about Jessica and I was on the fast track.

What the fuck am I saying, my decision?

Karen had made my mind up for me when she bolted for Bumfuck, Georgia.

I walked into my office, put on the Motown classic,

"Here my Dear" cd on and poured myself a huge tumbler of my favorite brown liquor.

"Well, I guess it's just you, me, and Marvin," I said, raising my glass, toasting the moment and looking at my slumbering dog.

Pacino halfway stirred as Marvin Gaye's soulful voice filled my empty home.

I was on my third glass when my phone rang. I checked the Caller ID before answering. I was pleased to see the 510 exchange. Had it been anyone else but Jessica, I would have allowed it to go to voicemail.

"Cameron, hey baby. Can you talk now or did I catch you while you were busy?"

I turned down Marvin's musical masterpiece knowing that if she called me by my given name a serious conversation was on the table.

"No not at all. I'm just chilling, what's good, Carrot?" I replied, neglecting to tell her about Karen's flight back south.

"I'm glad you're free because I need to tell you something very important. You know you've been blessed. You have a lot to be thankful for," she started.

"Yeah, things have been good. Even while doing dirt, God has been good to me. I have friends, a house, a condo, a boat, a truck, three cars..."

"Almost two wives, two kids and one on the way," Jessica chimed in.

I had to pause for a moment to let her statement process.

Almost two wives? Well, today's events had changed that truth.

Two kids? Yeah, the twins made two.

One on the way? Oh shit, we were going to have a baby!

"Cameron, did you hear me?"

"Yes, I heard you," I replied, unable to display my excitement because of my other reality and the Jack kicking in.

"Well, I didn't expect you to be ecstatic, but I damn sure would have never imagined you to be so devoid of emotion either. I should have just kept it to myself and had it handled," she replied, disappointed by my lack of enthusiasm.

I took a long slug of my drink and gave Jessica a recap of my day.

After I finished, she was just as upset with Anna as I was and offered to come to town and whup on her ass for me.

"Like you don't have enough trouble already. Don't worry about that Latin cunt. Karma will eat that whore for breakfast. What I need you to be concerned with is getting out of this situation you're in and taking care of our child by taking of yourself."

I was tired of looking over my shoulder when it concerned my criminal enterprise and with Jessica no longer my mistress, I was looking forward to us combining our ill-gotten gains and leaving the life behind.

Karen was right. I loved her, but not enough. Not enough to be faithful and damn sure not enough to keep from falling for the luscious lady I was on the phone with right now.

I knew there was going to be some serious fallout when people found out where my heart was, especially from my mother.

"Baby, why didn't you tell me all this when I was in Oakland?"

"I wanted to, I swear, but I thought my half a million burden was already enough to trouble you with."

To be honest, half of what she said was nothing. The amount spent to help Kwan was a wise business move. What I had done for Jessica was straight from the heart.

"Carrot, as long as we're together, there's nothing you can't ask of me. That's including my complete devotion," I promised. I shocked myself when I uttered my statement. What I felt for Jessica had to be beyond lust. If she were with me at this moment, I would have taken her to Vegas and exchanged vows in front of Elvis. Shit had got real.

I knew that I was truly in love with Jessica. Not since college, when I was engaged to Chandra, had I been willing to forsake all others. The one thing that had stood in my way of already making her mine was speeding down I10 headed east. My boys were going to have a stepmother and a new baby brother or sister. Jessica was relieved to hear me profess my desire to be one with her.

"Reesie, I'm so happy that you feel like that. It was going to break my heart to terminate the pregnancy or raise our child alone."

I assured her that there was no need to be troubled about such things. "What we need to deal with is this case and the charges you have against you," I told her, lighting my cigar until the cherry was red hot and large clouds of smoke filled the room.

There was silence on the other end of the line. I imagined her eyes welling up with tears as her voice trembled.

"Reesie, I can't be locked away from you, baby. I can't even think about having our child behind bars," she blurted out, sobbing.

"Don't worry. You aren't going to jail. Not if I can help it. I'll get you the best legal mouthpiece available," I told Jessica, hoping to ease her troubled mind.

"The prosecution was offering me a deal for seven years."

"Seven years and they call that a deal?"

With the federal charges Jessica and Kwan had pending for counterfeiting, the feds wanted 15 years of their life. To get that pleaded down to half the term, the government was going to ask about accomplices. I had paid my way out of the line of fire, but I feared for the safety of my crew.

"They're going to ask for names."

"I don't know any names to tell them," Jessica replied, letting me know she was a true soldier.

CHAPTER 39

A whole week had expired and there had been no word from Karen or the boys. She hadn't answered or returned any of my calls. I worried about their whereabouts and safety.

"I'm sure when Karen is up to calling you, she will," was all her mother told me when I inquired. At first, I dug the new freedoms I was afforded in my home. Smoking cigars inside was one of them. With the cat out of the bag, I had asked Jessica to come to L.A.

Her smooth, high-priced counsel frowned at just the mention of her leaving Oakland city limits, let alone Marion County. He had been fighting a case in which the prosecution had witnesses and damning video surveillance. He insisted that she cop to the lesser charges in a plea agreement. The prosecution wanted Jessica to roll over on Kwan and anyone else who was associated with them.

Jessica's paranoia was getting the best of her. She was fearful that her line was tapped and she was being followed. Anyone wearing a hat and dark sunglasses must've been the feds. Our conversations had been reduced to whenever she used a burner cell or a pay phone.

While this was going on, I didn't feel like performing nor writing. It was funny how Jessica's legal issues affected my happiness and rendered my creativity to a flaccid state. Here I was all alone, save for Pacino who was missing the boys just as much as me. His sleeping at their bedroom door instead of the foot of my bed attested to that.

"Reesie, if you really love me, you need to be in Oakland and convince me to stay," Jessica stated over the phone.

I didn't understand the urgency in Jessica's tone. I did hear her say, "Convince me to stay." I had two hundred and fifty thousand reasons why she should stay put.

"Jessica, is there any reason to question my love? Have I not been there for you at every turn since we have been together?" I questioned her.

Jessica was frantic and spooked. Her lawyer said there was no way to avoid justice.

"I can't deny that you have. But you don't understand."

"What is there to understand?"

"I can't fathom having our baby behind bars. To have our baby snatched from my arms and not seeing him or her walk, run, and ride a bike."

Yeah, they had her in a pressure cooker. I was torn. Part of me was ready to bolt and hop a flight to Oakland. But another part of me felt a feeling of distrust growing in the pit of my gut. Though Jessica was rambling on about how much she needed me up north, I couldn't help but to play Lance's mantra "Ain't no friends when you are hustling."

I wondered if there were lovers in the pinch.

Ignoring my doubts, I convinced Jessica to hold tight until I got there.

I sat in front of my Macintosh Performa desktop and surfed the net until I pulled up Southwest Airline's website. There were four Oakland flights from Burbank to Oakland that

I could make if my vet could kennel Pacino overnight. It was that, or drop him off with the San Diego Trio in North Hollywood. They adored him, but I was hoping the vet would look out for me.

After entering the illegally obtained credit card information, I printed out my itinerary and jumped my ass in the shower. As I scrubbed off three days of sloth, I laughed to myself, concluding that Pacino had been escaping my funk by not sleeping in my room.

I quickly donned some underwear and blue jeans. Then I applied some deodorant and Lagerfeld cologne before slipping into a blue Cleveland Indians jersey with a Chief Wahoo hat. Pacino was excited. His docked nub of a tail wagged furiously when I put on my red Air Max Trainers. I didn't know if he thought we were headed for a walk or overjoyed that I had washed my ass.

The travel gods had blessed me to be able to kennel my over grown puppy with my vet. After dropping him off, I headed east to catch my flight. Burbank Airport wasn't as large nor as congested as LAX. I was traveling light, so getting my ticket and going through security was a breeze. After a quick pat down, I was headed toward my gate and awaited boarding.

The mildly attractive brunette who took our tickets as we boarded the plane made a snide comment about my Indians gear. I figured her smug ass to be a snooty Dodgers fan and half smiled at her unwarranted remark.

Southwest's policy of choosing your own seat and no class destination found me in the emergency row for comfort. It was an hour long flight and I wasn't trying to be cramped. While the rest of the passengers embarked onto the 737 painted to look like Shamu, I rested my eyelids. I must have dozed off because when I awoke, there was the same brunette gate agent tapping my shoulder, stirring me.

"Yes. May I help you?" I questioned.

"Mr. Bernard, there seems to be a problem with payment. If you will be so kind as to follow me. I'm sure we can clear this up," she told me.

I played it cool getting off the plane. I was surprised to see two security guards waiting to assist me back up the jet way. Their presence didn't alarm me. I was always prepared with my explanation that I was traveling as an entertainer and had enough pocket cash to purchase passage. What I wasn't prepared for was the aircraft's door to be closed and my flight to be departing without me.

"This must be some misunderstanding. When is the next flight to Oakland?" I asked the brunette when she returned to the gate.

"Your method of payment was rejected. We have another flight that departs in thirty minutes and I can only accept cash as a method of payment."

She was lucky that the heat was on the Kwan currency and Karen had taken the last of it in my possession. Had that not been the case, I would have slid her two hundred worth of the fraudulent funds. She took my cash and printed me a ticket. I made a mental note to cross off the credit information that was burned up and awaited my flight. I rested my eyes again and fell into a deep sleep.

When I awoke in the uncomfortable chairs at my gate, I had missed my next flight.

"Motherfucker!" I exclaimed, as I watched my flight pull back from the gate through the large glass window.

"Excuse me, but that plane that just left? Was that the one headed to Oakland?"

"That would be it, yes, Mr. Bernard, we called you several times," said the brunette whom I was beginning to believe was a bad omen.

I explained to her that I was sitting in the chair sleeping. She, in turn, explained to me that waking me wasn't her job as she rebooked me on the next flight.

Not trusting myself to stay awake, I purchased some black coffee from the restaurant by my gate. I was anxious to get to the Bay and it seemed the universe was working against my efforts. Or was the universe working to save me from a fate far worse than losing Jessica and my unborn child, I wondered.

The black liquid coursing through my system was doing its trick. I was wide-awake from the caffeine. When I walked up to board the next plane, I was pleased to see an attractive blonde taking my boarding pass instead of the raven-haired schleprock. When I sat down in my middle seat, I was grateful to be sandwiched in. At least I was securely on the plane and on my way.

"Well, if it isn't Mr. Funny Man." I looked up to see the sassy flight attendant from Phoenix.

"Oh, hey Jodi. How are you?"

"I'm fine, not that you'd care. I have to admit I was sure you would call me. But, nope, you didn't," she said in a manner so dry I could see sand as she headed to the front of the cabin. Now not only was I sitting between two big broads, but they were staring at me like I wasn't shit.

The woman next to me started speaking. "Young man, it ain't my business, but if I was you..."

She was right, my business didn't have shit to do with her. Instead of being rude I acted as if I didn't hear her and played some music over my headphones.

I was thankful that Jodi ignored my presence for the entirety of the flight.

Damned if the big bitch to my right in the window seat didn't have a weak bladder. We couldn't get to Oakland fast enough as far as I was concerned. When we touched down and pulled up at the jet way, I was first to get up and head for the door. Not having any bags kept me from wasting time at the baggage claim. I moved in speedy fashion, as quick as my ex-athletic legs and Air Max Nikes, could carry me through the arrival doors to hail a cab.

I couldn't believe how barren it was outside the terminal. Had I not been sure I was in Oakland, I would have thought I had landed in Tombstone. All that was missing was tumbleweed and Wyatt Earp.

"What's up? Why are there no cars lined up to pick up arriving passengers?" I asked the tall brother in police uniform.

"I heard there was a major accident on the exit. Traffic is backed up for miles. I'm sure as soon as they can clean up the wreckage, everything will be back to normal," he replied.

I called Jessica, even though I knew she wasn't answering her cell anymore.

"We're sorry, but at the subscriber's request this phone is not accepting incoming calls."

Had she already left before I could get here? Was she just not answering calls for fear her line was monitored? These questions played over and over again in my mind while I waited for a taxi.

People from my flight had begun to gather outside. There was grumbling amongst the crowd. Folks had begun making phone calls to their loved ones trying to figure how long they were going to have to wait to be picked up.

"You know everything is hotter in Phoenix, including this pussy I've tried to offer you that you've been ignoring."

Even if she hadn't given me GPS coordinates to her place of pleasure, I would have known it was Jodi behind me.

"I bet it is. I haven't been ignoring you. I've been really busy working on a television project and this tour. Please accept my apology," I replied.

The traffic must have been cleared, because before Jodi could engage me in a conversation I wasn't prepared or interested in having with her, I hailed a cab and her shuttle drove up.

"Keep it hot," I teased as I climbed into my cab.

"You just make sure to reach out and touch me," she quickly quipped back.

I gave the taxi driver the address to Jessica's condo and told him that there was a big tip in it for him if he got me there in a hurry. "If you get me there fast, the whole hundred is yours." I held up the bill with Ben Franklin on it.

My cabbie was properly motivated. He hauled ass getting me to my destination. I hoped and prayed that I wasn't too late.

I hopped out of the cab before it had come to a complete stop. I hurled my driver what I promised, and sped toward the double glass doors. When I entered the building, I pushed the button to call for the elevator.

What seemed like forever for the lift to come back down, made me forsake waiting. I sprinted up six flights of stairs. Sweat had formed on my forehead and I was short of breath. When I finally reached her door, I knocked three times. When there was no answer, I used the key that Jessica had given me and unlocked the door.

There was a stillness in the place that told me a truth I didn't want to believe. She was gone. So was my unborn child. So was the half million dollars in bad money.

I looked around the spacious condo. From the looks of things, Jessica had traveled lightly. Her walk-in closet looked rummaged through, but it still housed the wardrobe that could only fit her fine figure. I guess she figured her shape would soon change and the flashy gear would cause too much attention for someone on the lam.

After relieving myself in her bathroom, I walked into the dining room and sat at the table. Along with a glass, a bottle of Jack, and my favorite cigar, a Monte Cristo II, were the keys to both vehicles and the deed to the condo. There was also the last communication from my soul mate.

My second Dear John letter within a week.

I took the double shot I poured to the head and lit my stogie. I began reading her letter after blowing out a cloud of smoke.

Cameron,

I'm sorry I couldn't wait any longer for you to arrive. Time was of the essence and my window of opportunity was small and closing. I didn't want you to feel fucked over, so I'm leaving you the deed to my home and the titles to both my vehicles. I would have left you the cash, but as you could guess I will be in need of all the untraceable funds I can find.

I don't want you to think I've chosen anyone over you. It was that I couldn't fathom having our child behind bars. I would rather chance raising our baby on the run with Kwan watching over us. I won't tell you not to worry about us because if you love me like I believe you do I know you will. I'll be in touch when the heat has cooled down.

Love You Always,
    Jessica

Jessica's final message to me could have been taken one of two ways. One being a half million-dollar kiss off, but receiving the lovely parting gifts of two whips and a piece of property I didn't want. Or two, her love for me was real enough that running away from the law was her only option to keep both of us free.

I wanted to believe the latter was true.

I put a huge dent in the dark spirits from Kentucky and smoked the cigar down to the nub. My high from the Jack and my low from Jessica's departure paralyzed me. I couldn't get on a plane in that condition. I slept in the comfortable big sized bed that my lover and I would share no more.

I didn't know much about that night, but I was sure I had phoned Karen and Jessica several times. I vaguely remembered talking dirty to someone. I looked at my last outgoing call and it was a 602 number.

"Oh shit. I called Jodi!" I could only imagine the lunacy that my horny, lonely, drunk and depressed ass could have spoken.

I raised my cotton mouthed butt naked body from Jessica's bed and walked barefoot into the kitchen. My head wasn't pounding, but my pipes were hot. I opened the stainless steel door of the refrigerator and drank orange juice from the carton. If Jessica had been here, she would have freaked out. Sadly, she wasn't nor was she going to be, and it had me bugging!

The very thought, coupled with my boiling stomach ruined any appetite I might have had. I had to get my day going. There were decisions that had to be made. One being, what I was going to do with this condo. With Jessica gone and Tasha in a real relationship, having a crash pad in the Bay was senseless. I was either going to sell it or rent it out. My second problem was two-fold. I had two luxury cars at my disposal and only one me to drive them. I decided to drive the BMW back to L.A. and leave the Mercedes Benz to be driven back at a later date.

With my make shift plan in place, I jumped into the shower to wash away last night's gloom.

CHAPTER 40

You know they say a drunk ain't shit. You talked all that shit about what you wanted to do to me, then fell asleep and left me hanging. I waited for you to come to my hotel all night," said Jodi over the phone.

"I apologize for my naughty potty mouth last night. I was feeling some kinda way and that Jack didn't help," I replied as I navigated the Grapevine Highway South in the powerful sleek Bavarian motor car toward my Canoga Park home.

I purposely waited to call her when I was far enough away from Oakland to not be able to back up the talk my drunk dark-side had spewed. Though I was sure my penis was up to the task of rearranging her insides, my heart wouldn't have been in it. My heart was with someone somewhere with no extradition laws.

My heart was taken with Jessica.

"Oh, it's okay. I didn't mind at all your off-color commentary concerning what you wanted to do. I rather enjoyed that. Just know that next time I need to put my soul through the carwash, you owe me a listening ear and a shoulder to lean on."

"Agreed."

Jodi disconnected the phone call when she reached her departure gate. I was happy to get back to concentrating on the road and cranked up Bootsy's Greatest Hits cd. Between the roar of the V12 engine and the thunderous thump of Bootsy's bass, I was in road trip nirvana.

CHAPTER 41

So Karen bounced to Georgia and Jessica is in the wind? Damn, that's some heavy shit, man," Marc said over the phone.

"Yeah. I don't know why I thought the universe was going to ignore all my bad karma and allow me to win," I replied, and sunk in my leather recliner.

"I don't know if it's safe to blame the universe. I mean, you still have your freedom and you just picked up a new piece of property and two nice whips."

"Marc, I never believed I would be saying this, but without the love of that woman, freedom doesn't mean shit," I replied, swirling around the Jack I had in a glass, and contemplating what I had just said while considering drowning my sorrows in brown liquor.

"You just need to get a new girl to take your mind off of your troubles. That Jodi chick sounds like just the medicine to cure your ills."

His suggestion was so typical. Fuck away my troubles, like pussy was the cure-all. In the past, that might have been the case. But I had tapped into something deeper with Jessica...that love and happiness Al Green sang about. My former shallow self was all that my friend could identify with. There was no way I could explain to Marc that Jessica loved me without being square. Marc would have written it off as me being pussy whipped for a week, maybe both.

We continued to talk.

I changed the course of the conversation by asking how he was digging his new housemate.

"Beijing is really liking L.A. She has hung up her six-inch heels and put her skimpy outfit days behind her."

"That's cool, man. You solid on bread? You know if you get in a bind, I'll look out. I might be a half a million short, but I can always look out for my folks," I told him before I had to cut the conversation short. Pacino was sniffing around looking for a spot to handle his business. I hurried to the kitchen and retrieved his black leather leash. We hustled out of the house and began to walk.

"I thought you had to really go badly and here you are smelling every sign post and fire hydrant," I scolded him, though my harsh tone didn't move him any. I'm sure if Pacino could talk, he would have told me to kiss his ass and wait for nature to take its course.

In my haste to make it out the door before Pacino had made my hardwood floors his litter box, I had forgotten to grab a plastic bag to collect his excrements. I also left my phone in the house. I knew better than to do either one. My uppity neighbors had come to my door complaining enough to train me.

While Pacino finally squatted and relieved himself, I looked aver both of my shoulders to see if anyone might have spotted him making his deposit. From what I could see, the coast was clear. We hustled back to my house, much to Pacino's dismay. He tried re-sniffing the whole block.

"If you don't bring your ass on," I spat, pulling him. When we entered the house, I took off his leash and put it back in the kitchen where I kept it.

I sat back in the black leather recliner and fumbled with the remote to my Sony stereo system. I was in the mood for some jazz. After selecting Miles Davis' "Bitches Brew," the music and my mood made the Jack sitting on my coffee table all the more appealing. Before picking up Pacino from the vet's after this last trip, I purchased some Parteguese Series D Robusto sticks from the Cigar Warehouse on Ventura Blvd. If I was going to be without my soul mate and children, Miles Davis, whiskey, and smoke were just going to have to do.

I had contemplated calling Karen again, but my pride couldn't take her ignoring me and feared if Karen had answered the phone, she would have detected my troubled soul. Yeah, it was just me and Pacino, a stiff drank, smoke and Miles. Pacino was sleeping at the door and even he was awake. I was sure there would be no conversation between us. What worried me more would have been if he did begin to speak.

Maybe Marc was right. Maybe I didn't deserve happiness after making the decision to jettison my twin sons to pursue a life with Jessica and my unborn seed. But could it be that simple? I questioned as I knocked back the Jack and poured me another four fingers. My phone rang and the caller ID alerted me to Lisa being on the line.

I dreaded talking to her. As was her custom, she would have told me to tell the boys "hi" and ask how Karen was. I would have had two undesired choices to make. One being to tell her the truth and have her berate me, or two, lie to her, which would have found me beating myself up for not keeping it real. I took the cowardly approach and let her call go to voicemail.

Pacino was preening his ears, the hair on his back stood up, and a low growl was growing in his throat.

When the doorbell rang and Pacino's growl erupted in a full fledge bark. I figured it was one of my neighbors coming to scold me about not scooping poop.

"Hold on...I'm coming, I'm coming," I said lifting myself from the prone position in my Lazy Boy. "Give me a second, I need to put away the dog," I said, grabbing Pacino by the collar and putting him out back.

It didn't dawn on me that Pacino was alerting me to possible danger and putting him out back would leave me vulnerable to what or whoever was at my front door.

I opened the door fully prepared to apologize for my not being a good neighbor. "Hey, I'm sorry about the dog..."

"So you stepped up your security game I see."

I was at a loss for words. The cat at my door wasn't supposed to be at my house. He wasn't supposed to be in Los Angeles. I expected him to be anywhere but at my doorstep. Yet, there Lance was, smiling from ear to ear.

"I know I said we were even. But a brother could use a favor or two," he said, walking in.

Coming Spring 2018….

The Cameron B. saga
continues in…

Barely Standing

Cortney Gee